THE
TWO
OF US

USA TODAY BESTSELLING AUTHOR
KENNEDY FOX

LOVE IN ISOLATION
SERIES READING ORDER

The Two of Us
Elijah & Cameron
A brother's best friend, opposites attract,
forced proximity romance

The Best of Us
Ryan & Kendall
A best friend's brother, opposites attract,
snowed-in together romance

The End of Us
Tristan & Piper
A bodyguard, age gap,
forced proximity romance

The Heart of Us
Easton & Tatum
An older woman/younger man age gap,
close proximity romance

Each book can be read as a standalone, but
they do interconnect. This series also has
special edition paperback and hardback covers.

AUTHOR'S NOTE

Although the romance in this book is fiction, there are some real aspects of the pandemic mentioned throughout. Please go to the cdc.gov and who.int websites for all current information.

Thank you to the heroes who are working in the frontlines during this crisis. Thank you to the essential workers who sacrifice for others. Thank you to our leaders who stand up and fight for our safety.

There's nowhere we need to be, no, no, no
I'ma get to know you better
Kinda hope we're here forever
There's nobody on these streets
If you told me that the world's endin'
Ain't no other way that I can spend it

"Stuck with U"
-Adriana Grande, Justin Bieber

CHAPTER ONE

CAMERON

DAY 1

My heart pounds as I rush around my penthouse, shoving clothes and books into my Louis Vuitton suitcases. It's my senior year at New York University and the campus has shut down indefinitely today. Starting next week, I'll finish the semester online.

No graduation ceremony.

No saying goodbye to my classmates I've seen every day for the past four years.

No final words of wisdom from my professors.

I'm heartbroken.

With a 4.0 grade point average, I can't risk falling behind and losing my spot as valedictorian. Hopefully, this doesn't interfere with graduating on time because I've been accepted into the Master of Business program in the fall.

While I'm upset about no longer attending classes and missing out on the last few months of my final year, I'm more concerned and devastated about what's happening around the country and in the city I was born and raised in.

New York was recently declared a major disaster area. A

dangerous viral outbreak has swept the world, and we're being told to self-isolate to help slow the spread, but the hospitals are already overcrowded.

When the news broke, my parents begged me to come home, but I know my mother. Clara St. James can't function without her housekeepers and personal chefs, and if she continues to let them help, she's directly breaking the basic guidelines of being quarantined. Unless her staff moves in, my parents will still be in contact with people who are carrying germs from the outside world. I love my mom, but she's the classic Upper East Side's cliché of wealth and power who doesn't follow rules because they're below her.

My family owns a billion-dollar fashion empire, so it's all I've ever known. Since I could walk, my mother has groomed me to be involved with the business. As the elite princess of the St. James estate, I'm expected and have agreed to maintain the company when they're ready to retire. I love my family, but behind our socialite status and the media's glamorized portrayal, we're dysfunctional with a capital D.

My brother, Ryan, is four years older than me and graduated from medical school last year. He's doing his residency in one of New York City's top-ranked hospitals and will work directly with patients who have contracted the virus. It's scary as hell to know he'll be there, but he's determined to do whatever it takes to help people and save lives. I'm proud of him, but I worry about his safety.

"Cameron, this is absurd," my mother says on the phone with a long sigh. "Rodrick will pick you up and drive you home."

"I'm staying at the cabin so I can focus on my schoolwork and stay inside." I repeat the same words I said yesterday. I don't tell her my boyfriend, Zane, is meeting me there in a couple of days. She's not his biggest fan because he hasn't proposed yet, but I'm nowhere near ready for marriage. I'm only twenty-two and want to finish school first. This year, we're both graduating, and we plan to move in together this summer as a trial run. So for now, she'll have to get over the idea of planning the wedding of *her* dreams.

I could've driven with him, but I was too anxious and ready to get out of the city to wait. He needed extra time to do his laundry, pack, and buy more supplies. Zane doesn't live on campus, but he slept over at my place a lot, which is why it's better we isolate together.

"Plus, I could've been exposed by someone at school. We really have no idea how many cases there are, so it's best I stay away. That way, I don't risk getting you or Daddy sick."

He has high blood pressure, and my mom smokes. Though she claims she quit, I know she hasn't.

"You two should go somewhere for a few weeks," I suggest. "Your company employees are working remote, so there's no reason to stay in the city. Visit the Hampton lake house or drive to the Tennessee resort."

"And leave all my things?" She gasps. "We'll be fine, dear. Your father and I are usually six feet apart anyway. The housekeepers will wear masks and gloves. You really should just come here so we're together." I roll my eyes as she continues to beg. For the past fifteen years they've pretended to be madly in love in front of the cameras and brush aside any rumors that my dad has a drinking problem. They want the world to think they have a picture-perfect marriage, but it's only an act.

Denying her request again, I explain how labor-intensive my online classes will be, and as nicely as I can, I remind her I'll need this time to focus on finishing my semester and keeping my grades up. She seems to buy it and tells me to check in with her daily. I make her promise to keep her distance from everyone because while she's health-conscious, her smoking puts her at a higher risk, so I worry.

After the call ends, I grab the rest of my essentials and pack my Range Rover. The back is full of enough food and water to last a few weeks. I picked up a large online shopping order today so I wouldn't have to go to the store again for a while. Just the thought of being in public gives me hives, but my mother never believed I had anxiety and didn't allow me to get help or medication. Last year, I secretly saw a therapist and finally got a prescription to help me cope.

Once I have everything, I grab Chanel's carrier and food. She's another reason I prefer not to stay at my parents' house. She's a Sphynx cat, and my mother's Yorkie barks at her nonstop, which means I'd spend the entire time trying to keep *them* six feet apart.

I load her up, take one last look around to make sure I didn't forget anything, then leave. The cabin is in Roxbury, which is three hours away, but with an overwhelming number of people leaving the city, the traffic could make it longer.

I listen to the radio as I drive, watching people rush down the sidewalks. It's complete madness. My mind wanders as I reflect on what's happened over the past few days. Schools and non-essential stores closing. No flights going in or out of the country. National parks and Disney closed. No large gatherings allowed and being told to stay six feet apart from strangers. Not to mention the masks people are wearing.

It's a culture shock and surreal how fast this happened. The sooner I get out of the city, the better.

The past week has been a blur. Between the news reports and social media posts, it's hard to know what to believe and whether our government is really prepared. I'm well aware of my family's legacy and what it's provided me. The media paints me as a privileged white girl who doesn't have to work, who has everything handed to her on a silver platter, and only has an education and future career because of the family business.

I'm an introvert and keep to my small circle of friends I trust. The media's perception is an unfair assessment, but it sells a story and gets clicks online. Reporting the truth wouldn't be as entertaining.

I've worked my ass off in school. I love learning and am passionate about business. I can't deny my closet is full of designer clothes and shoes, but it's to be expected. I wear the family collection and other designer brands my parents personally endorse. I was raised by nannies, housekeepers, and personal drivers and believed this lifestyle was normal until I got a taste of the outside world and reality. Life is different when your family is in the top one-percent richest of the population, which makes me an easy target for ridicule.

It also doesn't get me a lot of *true* friends, and it can be lonely at times.

The scene driving into town is gorgeous. Spring is a few months away. The trees are still bare, and there's a crisp chill in the air, even for mid-February. Once I turn onto our private road and see the cabin, I let out a sigh of relief that I made it. The Roxbury cabin is one of my favorite properties even though my mother hates it. It's not glamorous enough, and she feels too disconnected from her high-society friends here. But that's exactly why I love it so much.

The semi-open layout is rustic yet modern. Large windows and a wraparound deck offer the best views of the sunrise and sunset. It's a three-story cabin that sits on ten acres overlooking two ponds and the mountains. There's no better place to be, and maybe it'll distract me from what feels like the end of the world. And if that doesn't do the job, I have vodka.

"Chanel, we're here!" I sing-song as I park in the three-car garage. "We'll be safe here, baby."

The downside of traveling without Zane is having to unload this shit alone. Fortunately, my mom had the cleaning crew come out two weeks ago, so it should still be decent inside. We rent it out to family and friends once in a while, so we keep the five thousand-square-foot cabin maintained year-round.

I set the cat carrier down and open it so she can explore and get accustomed to the space. She hasn't been here since last year, so it might take her some time to remember it. She immediately sniffs around and flicks her tail, annoyed.

"You'll like it here," I tell her, then lean down to pet her. She purrs, and I smile. "I'll be right back with your litter box and dishes."

After dragging my suitcases inside, I make three more trips until every grocery bag is on the counter. I put the food and drinks in the refrigerator and pantry, then unpack my clothes and hang them in the master bedroom closet. It's the only room on the third floor and has a large window that overlooks the property. The other two bedrooms are on the second floor.

"I'm exhausted." I fall back on the bed with my arms spread out. After a moment, I feel Chanel jump up by my feet.

"What about you, Chanel?" Turning my head, I see she's curled in a ball and falling asleep. "Yeah, a nap sounds good."

I quickly text Zane to let him know I made it and will probably be out for the rest of the night.

Cameron: Chanel and I made it safely. All unpacked and just waiting for you now :) I'm gonna go to bed.
Love you!

Setting my phone on the nightstand, I stand and head to the bathroom. The jet tub looks so damn tempting, but I'll have plenty of time to use it tomorrow.

After I change into my comfy clothes, I brush my teeth and wash my face.

Once I'm tucked into bed, I check my phone and frown when I don't see a response from Zane. Maybe he's on his way here to surprise me and can't text because he's driving. Before I think too much about it, my eyelids grow heavy, and I fall asleep with Chanel snuggled into my side.

Blinking awake, I sit up in bed and recall where I am.

The Roxbury cabin.

Then I remember what woke me. A loud noise.

Chanel is no longer sleeping either, which means she heard it too.

Grabbing my phone, I check the time and for any messages from Zane. It's half past midnight, and I'm exhausted. If Zane decided to come early, he would've called or sent a text to let me know.

Another deafening crash has me jumping.

"Oh my God…" My breathing picks up, and I panic.

Someone's in my house!

Looking around for something, I see one of my mother's marble statues on the dresser. It's heavy and could probably break a skull. I don't have time to think twice before I grab it and tiptoe to my bedroom door. More noise echoes from downstairs, and I know it's probably some dumb kids hoping to steal something they can sell. Joke's on them because my parents never keep any expensive possessions here.

Putting my ear against the wood, I listen for footsteps. When I hear another ear-piercing boom vibrate through the house, my heart drops into my stomach. I could call the cops, but by the time they arrived, the murderer would have me chopped into a thousand pieces and thrown into the pond.

Slowly, I open the door and poke my head out, holding the statue tight in my grip. The hallway light glows, and I check both ways before stepping out. I walk toward the staircase and yelp when Chanel rubs against my leg.

"Chanel, no! Get back here!" I whisper-hiss, hoping she'll actually listen to me. Instead, she runs down the first set of stairs, and I follow as quietly as I can. "Chanel!"

As I chase her, I keep an eye out for a potential killer. If she outs me being up here and gets us both caught, I might strangle her. When I'm on the second level, I notice the kitchen light is on, but I distinctly remember turning it off.

Gripping the marble tighter, I prepare myself to fight for my life as I walk down the final staircase. When I move closer, I see a large duffel bag on the kitchen counter and the fridge is wide open. Did someone break into a multi-million-dollar cabin to steal food?

While I discreetly scan the space, my rapid breathing is the only sound I hear until Chanel loses her shit, and complete chaos ensues.

She hisses, jumping from the floor to the island, then leaps off the countertop as a huge Doberman chases after her. A man is hunched in front of the refrigerator and tries to stand when the dog plows him over. He's unsteady on his feet and tries to catch his fall. The moment he turns toward me, I freak out and throw the statue at his face. It falls to the ground with a deep thud and surprisingly doesn't break.

"Ow, what the fuck?" a deep voice groans as he takes a hit to the cheek. Chanel is having a fit as I try to grab her.

Then to make matters worse, the Doberman barks and growls at me like I'm his next meal. Chanel hisses and runs into the living room, and the dog gives chase at a full sprint.

"Chanel!" I panic and turn toward the criminal. "Get your fucking dog away from my cat!" I beg. "I'll pay you whatever you want, just don't let him kill her!"

"Cami?" His deep voice catches my attention, and my body freezes.

I look over and finally meet his eyes that are squinting at me. Swallowing hard, I narrow my gaze at the man who's broken into my house and called me by a nickname I haven't heard in years.

Releasing a frustrated breath, I'm nearly panting when I ask, "What the hell are you doing here, Eli?"

CHAPTER TWO

ELIJAH

"Cami?" I rub my cheek. She threw a heavy fucking statue at me that could've easily given me a concussion if she had better aim.

She narrows her eyes and exhales a frustrated breath. "What the hell are you doing here, Eli?"

I look at the woman who's haunted my dreams for ten years and notice she's as painfully beautiful as I remember. The tabloid magazines never paint her in a positive light and always snap photos when she's trying to escape or has partied too much, but I knew her before she had the snobby rich-girl reputation.

Cameron St. James is the epitome of perfection—gorgeous, smart, and an heiress.

Unfortunately, she knows it too.

A girl like her would never give a guy like me—lower class, wage-earning real estate agent—the time of the day. Though a decade ago, she looked at me like I hung the moon, and it ended as quickly as it started.

"I was about to ask you the same." Closing the fridge door, I walk over to pick up the statue that miraculously didn't shatter and set it on the island. My attention is quickly brought to Bruno who's chasing the cat. "Bruno! Come."

He immediately stops, rushes over, then sits in front of me and begs for a treat. He's a one hundred pound Doberman who's as tall as I am when he stands.

"Chanel!" Cami runs to her butt ass ugly hairless cat. She grabs her and holds it tightly. My eyes lower to her chest as her tank top slides down, nearly revealing everything.

Swallowing hard, I avert my gaze. "Uh, Cami...you might—"

"You need to leave," she snaps before I can continue. "How'd you get in? The alarm is on and active."

"Ryan said I could stay here," I explain. Her brother is my best friend and gave me the keys and security codes. "Told me to make myself at home, but failed to mention you'd be here too."

"I haven't had the chance to talk to him yet," she says. "But it doesn't matter because you're not staying."

"Yes, I am," I argue. We're in the middle of a goddamn pandemic, and as New York City is the epicenter of it, it's the last place I want to be right now. Not to mention, my three dumbass roommates aren't taking it seriously and will be exposed any day now because they're not abiding by the CDC guidelines and staying the fuck inside. All of them can work from home, but they are still going out like nothing has happened. "The cabin is plenty big enough for the both of us."

"Chanel, stop," she scolds. The hairless rat is trying to wiggle free from her grasp. Bruno just wants to play and keeping him away from Chanel will be difficult.

"Bruno, heel," I command, but he's not always the best listener. I swear he gets way too hyper around other people.

"Big or not, my boyfriend, Zane, is coming tomorrow."

"Alright, so I'll stay in my area, and you stay in yours. Problem solved." I grab my duffel bag, then step around the gigantic kitchen island.

"Like hell it is! You can't. I'm already here and made plans." She pouts, and it's stupidly adorable. Cami is used to getting her way, but she won't this time. I'm not going anywhere.

"Watch me." I flash her a toothy grin on my way toward the staircase. "I'm guessing you took the master?" I ask over my shoulder, then continue before she responds, "I'll take one of the guest rooms on the second floor, so you won't even know I'm here."

"I doubt it," she mutters.

Bruno walks behind me, and she squeals when he gets too close. "Don't worry, he only bites entitled New York princesses."

"Funny."

"It's called having a sense of humor, Cami. Did you lose yours, or is it still up your ass along with that stick that's been stuck there since we were teens?"

"You know, I could call the cops and have them remove you."

"Good luck with that. We're in a national lockdown, and they're only responding to life or death calls, so in this case, they wouldn't come to your rescue." I throw her a wink, then take the steps two at a time with Bruno next to me. Of course, I'm agitating her on purpose, but if I know Cameron St. James as well as I think I do, she's about to have a rich-girl tantrum.

"You better keep that stupid mutt away from my cat!" she screams as I reach the second floor. "Or I'll feed him to the mountain lions!"

I snort, shaking my head at her dramatics. Bruno won't hurt her naked cat, but he'll have fun taunting them both in the process. And so will I.

Once I walk inside the spare room that Ryan typically uses when he stays here, I set my stuff on the bed and look around. It's bigger than my entire apartment, and sadly, I'm not even exaggerating. There's a bathroom down the hall, and the jet tub alone cost more than a year's worth of my rent.

I sit and look around. Without knowing, you'd never suspect Ryan is a St. James. He's two years older than me and an ER doctor in the city. While doing his residency, he's smack-dab in the center of this epidemic, and that scares the shit out of me. Ryan's humble and loyal to a fault and will work as long as he needs to fight this and save his patients.

Being his best friend growing up, I know all about Cameron

and their family's billion-dollar fashion company. I'm from a completely different world, and the only reason we met is because my mother was their housekeeper for years. When the sitter canceled at the last minute, she'd take me and my little sister, Ava, with her, and though we promised to stay hidden and quiet, the moment Ryan saw us, he encouraged us to play with him. I was ten years old when he showed me that money wasn't as important as kindness and compassion. A lesson the rest of his family has yet to learn.

Clara St. James didn't approve of our friendship at first but warmed up to the idea. Her husband, Bradford, was never around to be with his son, and Ryan needed a real friend because he hated his uppity private school classmates. After a while, Clara approved for my mother to bring Ava and me along. Ryan and I developed a strong bond that's lasted for fourteen years.

Cami was eight at the time and wasn't allowed to play with us —Ryan's rules. He couldn't stand his annoying little sister, but for some reason, he didn't mind Ava. Probably because she wasn't a stuck-up sass machine, but I think that's why she never wanted to play with Cami either. They were the same age but had nothing in common. As time went on, Cami grew on me, and the four of us hung out and played. It was the first time I felt included in a group.

But that was ages ago, and I'm not that boy who easily gets his feelings hurt anymore.

My mother saved as much money as she could and made sure we didn't go without even though she had nothing. I never knew my dad but didn't care much about it based on the stories my mother told me about him. When I met Ryan, he opened up and talked about how dysfunctional his family was too, which made me feel not so alone. He was the older brother I always wanted and still is.

I keep Bruno in the bedroom and head back to my rental car to grab the rest of the items I brought. Since I take the subway to the office, owning a car in the city is unnecessary. Parking's a bitch and expensive, but I got my license for random road trips.

After popping the trunk, I grab as many bags as I can. I brought enough perishables, medicine, drinks, cleaning supplies, and toilet paper to last for weeks. Of course, that was before I knew other people were staying at the cabin, so it might not last that long.

My goal is to stay quarantined for at least a month before I have to make a trip to the store. Last weekend, my roommates were out partying and could've infected me. It's why I had to get the hell out of there as fast as I could. Cami's a student at NYU, and it only shut down yesterday, which means she was around dozens of people too. So it's best we steer clear of each other, which shouldn't be an issue. This place is massive.

I have plenty of work and reading to keep me busy. Between that and taking Bruno out for walks and playtime, there's no reason to be around Cami and her tool bag boyfriend.

"What are you doing?"

She's so loud that I nearly jump out of my skin. "Jesus." I groan, shaking my head as I continue to the kitchen and set the bags down. "What's it look like?"

"Looks like you're doing the opposite of leaving."

"Very good. You're *so* observant." Pulling the items out of the bags, I start cleaning them with disinfectant wipes, then look over at her. "Why do you care if I'm here? You've done an incredible job of ignoring me for years. So, it shouldn't be a problem for you now. Right?"

She crosses her arms, tilts her head, and squints at me. "Why do you insist on always being an asshole? Is it ingrained into your DNA or something? Or do you just enjoy pissing people off?"

I hold back a smirk because I'm getting to her as much as she used to get to me. "Nah. Just you, princess."

Cami rolls her eyes, and her arms fall to her side. She's still wearing next to nothing, but I'm sure she doesn't care. She's used to people gawking.

"I already stocked the fridge," she says after I open it and try to make room.

"Yeah, I see that." I move her stuff around and shove mine in. "Except this shit will go bad in just a few days. Unless you plan on growing a garden in the middle of winter, you'll be out of food in a week."

"I have plenty of frozen meals. And I can make a grocery order and have it delivered," she states matter-of-factly.

"Out here? Not likely." I grab the boxed food and put it in the pantry. "Not to mention, they're all booked out two weeks or more with the increased demand."

She wrinkles her nose. "Guess I didn't think about that."

"Do you even know how to cook?" I ask, already knowing the answer. Cameron St. James can't boil water. She may be brilliant in school, but she's not common sense smart. I can't even place the blame on her for it, though, because it's not entirely her fault. Unless Cameron was interested or invested in something, she didn't care to learn more, and her parents never forced her to do anything for herself. It's common knowledge that she'll take over their family business, and she'll have staff who'll do her dirty work while she keeps it afloat.

Cami blinks and nervously shuffles her feet. "Well…not really. But it's not like I was going to bring a chef to isolate with me. We'll figure it out."

"I take it Zaney boy can't cook either?" I chuckle as I finish putting everything up.

"We never have to." She shrugs unapologetically about her privileged life. "It can't be that hard."

I'm unable to hold back my laughter this time, and she scowls. I'm well aware of what Cami's lifestyle includes—gourmet chefs, housekeepers, drivers, family jets, personal shoppers, extravagant *everything*. She'll never know the sick feeling of not being able to pay bills while barely scraping by.

"You're going to either burn the house down, burn yourself, or

14

starve. The virus isn't even your biggest threat. It's your inability to feed yourself."

"Do you always have to be such a dick?" she scolds with her hands on her hips. "Are you capable of being anything other than a condescending ass bag?"

"Well, I don't know. Are you able to determine the difference between sarcasm and country club asshole traits? I'll give you a guess which one your boyfriend is," I say smugly. "And I'm ninety-nine point nine percent positive you're not with him for his *great* personality." Zane Vandenberg is the equivalent of a thirteen-year-old Justin Bieber who was just handed millions of dollars. His maturity level is the same, too.

"Ugh!" She throws up her arms, then stomps away.

"You need to get a sense of humor, Cami!" I shout through my laughter. "You'd think with all your billions, you could at least buy one! Maybe I can order you one and pay for overnight shipping?"

"Go to hell, Elijah!" she screams from the staircase.

"Don't worry, I'm already there!" I yell back. Moments later, her bedroom door slams with a loud bang.

"Well, this is gonna be fun," I mutter to myself.

I have no idea how long this crisis will last, but Cameron St. James may kill me before it's over.

CHAPTER THREE

CAMERON

DAY 2

I WAKE up to the sun streaming through the window and quickly remember I'm at the cabin with Eli.

There's no way I'm spending weeks, possibly *months*, with him. Since we were teenagers, he's lived to torment me. Only God knows why my brother is friends with him, but if I had to guess, it's to piss me off.

I considered Elijah Ross a friend once. When his hormones turned him into the asshole of the century, he became my number-one enemy instead.

The only thing that lifts my spirits is knowing Zane arrives today. I'm not worried about being around him every minute of our isolation because of how we feel about each other. After graduation, he'll propose, and our engagement and wedding will be the event of the decade. The St. James and Vandenberg marriage will make the front page of every paper and magazine.

We're already the perfect power couple, and the media loves sharing photographs of us together.

Zane and I ended up in all the same business classes together and inevitably formed a relationship. When we started dating my second year of college, our parents were over the moon and have hinted about us getting married for years.

Deciding to get out of bed, I head to the bathroom and clean myself up before making my way downstairs. Before going down the second staircase, I stop and listen closely. When I don't hear anything, I tiptoe into the kitchen. Hopefully, that means Eli's still sleeping or is staying in his room away from me.

"C'mon, Chanel. Breakfast time," I say quietly with her following me. She rubs against my leg as she prances along the hardwood floor.

"Why are we whispering?"

Spinning around, I smack right into Eli's broad chest. When I stumble against him, he grabs my arms and steadies me. Once it's obvious I won't fall on my ass, he releases me with a smirk.

"Jesus! Don't sneak up on people!" I scold and playfully slap him. Putting space between us, I then realize he's shirtless. His shaggy, dark hair is pulled back and sweat drips down his neck. Stupidly, I lower my gaze and notice his ripped abs and that sexy V that leads below his workout shorts.

The clearing of his throat brings my eyes back to his. "You always this uptight in the morning?"

"Only when creeps refuse to leave my house," I retort, pissed he caught me staring. I don't want him thinking I was drooling, but it's hard not to when he's half-dressed and looks more muscular than I remember.

Eli pops a brow with an amused grin on his face. "You get that a lot?"

Groaning, I walk to the fridge and grab what I need. I twist the cap off Chanel's water, then pour it into her dish.

"Did you seriously just use a ten-dollar bottle of water for a *cat*?"

Technically speaking, it's more like thirteen dollars, but I don't give him more ammunition to taunt me. He already has enough in his arsenal.

"Cat has expensive taste just like her owner." He cackles.

17

"Why are you still here?" I ask, then get up to grab her cat food. "You need a shower."

"Thanks for noticing. I was about to before I saw you trying to Tom Cruise your way into the kitchen."

Rolling my eyes, I proceed to feed Chanel. If he thinks her water is high maintenance, he'd probably burst a blood vessel at her custom-made organic cat food. She purrs and immediately rushes over.

"Why are you sweating anyway?" It's in the thirties outside, so running shirtless outside isn't an option.

"Wanted to work out before starting this beautiful first day of quarantine with you." He beams, furthering my irritation.

"You're taking the whole *make yourself at home* thing to the next level." I grunt that he used the home gym that my mother insisted on building in the basement. Not sure why she bothered, considering she visits once a year, and it's *never* to work out.

"And for my next trick, I'm going to cook breakfast." He flicks his fingers in the air, mimicking a magician. Then he grabs a pan and sets it on the stovetop. "Or is that off-limits, too?"

"At this rate, I'd expect nothing less." I force a smile, push off the counter, and grab a mug from the cabinet.

"I'm making an omelet. Would you like one?" he asks, digging into the fridge as I mess with the espresso machine.

I raise an eyebrow. "Depends. Will it be poisoned?"

"If by poisoned, you mean it won't be some fake meat bullshit, then yes. But it'll taste heavenly." He whips eggs in a bowl, and considering my options are cereal or a granola bar, I contemplate it. Then on cue, my stomach roars and grumbles loudly.

"Fine, but at least use the low-fat cheese in mine."

He snorts. Fucking *snorts,* then laughs. "Whatever you need to make yourself feel better."

"What the hell does that mean? Do you have to make a comment about everything I say?" I shake my head.

"Only when you say things like *low-fat* cheese. Sounds gross and would ruin my masterpiece." He grabs more ingredients from the fridge. "If you're going to survive being in a house with me for God knows how long, you're gonna have to loosen up."

"Or you could just be a decent human and stop antagonizing me every second?" I push buttons on the espresso maker, and it starts grinding the beans. *Thank goodness.* I can't deal with him much longer without caffeine.

"But bothering you is the only thing on my to-do list today." He flashes a devilish smirk.

Groaning, I open the silverware drawer, grab a spoon, then slam it closed.

"C'mon, Cami. You can't be this wound up all the time. Let your hair down and relax a little."

"Easy for you to say. You don't have paparazzi following you everywhere. If I'm bloated one day, pregnancy rumors are blasted the next week. If I yell for them to stop following me, they say I'm on the verge of having a nervous breakdown."

"Sounds like you can't win either way, so why bother? Just be you, and they'll get bored."

I shoot him a death glare. "Are you inferring that I'm boring?" Turning away, I grab the sugar-free creamer, and when I spin around, Eli's standing in front of me so I can't move.

"That's not what I said," he softly states. I lower my eyes to avoid his, but he tilts up my chin, and our gazes connect. "I meant, the more you give in to what they expect, the more they'll demand it." He drops his arm, and I swallow hard. "They want to sell scandalous tales to magazines by twisting reality. You play into it, and it makes you look bad every time, so if you quit giving a shit, maybe they'll stop targeting you."

I gulp, blinking hard. Eli's split personalities give me whiplash.

"Well, that's easier said than done." I shrug. "The media portrays me in a negative light no matter what I do or say, but I've learned that if I'm presentable and look like I have my shit together, it's harder for them to make up bullshit headlines."

Eli looks around, squinting before meeting my eyes. "You

don't have to worry about being judged here. No paps to follow you around, and I swear I won't take pics of you looking like a hot mess and sell them to the media."

"Do I need to get that in writing?" My shoulders fall as I release a small laugh. "Actually, the idea of being secluded and away from all that was what drew me to the cabin in the first place."

He presses a hand to his bare, sweaty chest. "Was I the second?"

"Hardly," I reply dryly, holding back a smirk, considering I was shocked to see him.

"Well, don't worry…" He steps back and mixes the meat and cheese into the bowl of eggs. "You won't even know I'm here. Bruno and I are very chill."

Furrowing my brows, I shake my head. "Somehow, I doubt that."

Once my espresso is done, I set it on the table and walk back to my room to grab my phone. Zane hasn't responded to my last text, so I send him another one.

Cameron: Babe, are you on your way? There's been a little mix-up. Ryan told his friend he could come here, so he's staying in the guest room. Just a heads-up. Let me know when you leave the city. I miss you!

I go downstairs and am immediately bombarded by Bruno. He gallops into the house after being outside, and he's in my face, sniffing me.

The dog has never heard of personal space. Another reason I love cats more.

"Okay, go away…" I shoo, stepping back, hoping he doesn't follow. Before I can say another word, Chanel charges at him, hissing.

"Chanel, no!" I scold, though she couldn't hurt Bruno even if she tried. She might piss him off, but that's about it. "Elijah, get control of your dog!" I squeal, running around the kitchen table. "Stay! Sit! Stop!"

Of course, the asshole laughs.

"Bruno, heel," Elijah commands. The dog immediately stops, goes to Eli, and sits as though nothing happened.

I'm nearly out of breath from chasing Chanel, who doesn't listen *at all*.

"Your dog…or *horse,* rather…is trying to kill my cat and eat her as a snack. Can't you lock him up or something?"

Bruno licks his chops and pants with his tongue out. I shoot daggers at him as Chanel finally saunters toward me.

"My animal listens. Yours is the prissy bitch," he states, busying himself in the kitchen.

I gasp, ready to murder them both.

"It's not his fault," Eli says, looking over his shoulder at me. "She looks like a meaty, hairless dinner."

Grabbing Chanel, I hold her tightly to my chest. "She does not. She's adorable and better for my allergies." I kiss her head, and she leans against me.

"Do you like ham?" he asks, pouring the egg mixture into a pan.

"What?"

He turns and looks at me. "Ham. Do you like it?"

I shrug. "Yeah, I guess."

"For your omelet," he reiterates. "Otherwise, I can do sausage."

"Um…ham is fine. I'm going to put Chanel in my room." I turn toward the staircase before he can say another word. Between him offering to make breakfast, our pets trying to murder each other, and his sudden subject change, I'm at a loss of what to think about Elijah being here.

When we were kids, Eli would come over to play with Ryan while his mom worked as our housekeeper. Eventually, I started hanging out with them too, and always looked forward to the days he was there. His sister, Ava, would tag along, but we were never close. As time went on, my mother's constant pressure to be classy, elegant, and sophisticated took a toll on me. She wanted me to hang out with the girls she approved of who held a specific social class. It was always about money and power to my parents, and I quickly became too *snobby* to be Elijah's friend. He wrote me off but remained best friends with my brother, who never cared about that sort of thing.

Eli made snide comments about what I wore, how I spoke or acted, and who was in my circle. Nothing I did was good enough for him. He never knew he was the only person I wanted to impress. Being friends with Elijah already pissed off my dad, so there was no way he would've allowed us to date as teenagers.

But that didn't matter anyway because he hated me as much as I hated him. The feud continued through high school, and when he'd hang out with Ryan, I was brought back to those days of him thinking less of me because of my friends.

I wasn't completely innocent, but he escalated the situations. I'm judged by thousands of people who don't know me, but to have someone I cared about have such harsh opinions of me hurt even worse.

I place Chanel on the bed and realize I forgot her bowls. "I'll be back," I tell her before shutting the door.

Once I'm in the kitchen, I grab her food and water. "I'm gonna put these in my room so we can avoid World War Three in the mornings."

"Between you and me or the animals?"

"Ha. You're a comedian now."

"Well, you are scary before your coffee." He squints, then continues, "Or is that how you are all the time?"

"Gonna have to drink mine with alcohol just to deal with your ass."

Elijah releases a deep howl. "Oh, you and me both, *princess*."

I take the stairs to my room, drop off Chanel's dishes, then go back to see Elijah dancing in the kitchen as he flips an omelet. It's amusing to watch a six-foot-something guy who enjoys the great outdoors move around like Channing Tatum. If I didn't know any better, I'd say he was a mountain man stuck in the city. I know he works in real estate, but I'm not sure exactly what that entails.

"If you ever give up on real estate, you should take up stripping. Bet you'd get lots of singles tucked into your G-string."

Eli faces me, popping a brow. "You picturing me in my underwear now? I think we're gonna have to discuss boundaries…" he taunts, and I roll my eyes.

Grabbing my phone, I notice Zane finally messaged me.

Zane: Not gonna make it.

What the fuck? I sit at the table and furiously type a response.

Cameron: What do you mean? Where are you?

Zane: Staying in the city.

Cameron: Why? I thought we were going to be together during this time.

Zane: I don't think this is working out for me anymore.

My blood pressure rises, and I grow more frustrated with each passing second.

Cameron: What the fuck are you talking about, Zane? We had plans!

Zane: I think we should see other people, Cameron. Indefinitely.

Shifting in my chair, I ball my hand into a fist and see red. How fucking *dare* he break up with me over a text message?

Cameron: GO TO HELL, ASSHOLE!

"Okay, one ham and *regular fat* cheese omelet is ready." When Elijah places the plate in front of me, the steam from the food floats toward my face. I wish I could ignore what just happened with Zane, but I'm so fired up that I'm seeing red. "Bon appétit. Do you want orange juice or just your coffee? OJ is full of calcium and vitamin C, which we need at a time like this, so I brought plenty. I'll even share it with a *princess*." He chuckles.

Eli chats as if nothing is wrong while I can't think straight because I'm in shock. I'm not heartbroken over the loss of Zane, but his text definitely blindsided me. I should be upset, considering we've been together for two years, but I'm more outraged than anything. Why are guys such pricks?

As I push back, the chair scrapes along the floor. I stand and grab my mug off the table. "Don't bother."

Instead of giving Eli an explanation, I rush to my bedroom before I have an emotional breakdown.

Zane can kiss my ass.

He made me believe he wanted a future with me, but if he's staying in the city, that means he's not alone. The bastard is probably with another chick, and considering how easy it was for him to break up with me, he's more than likely been cheating the entire time.

Fuck him.

CHAPTER FOUR

ELIJAH

WHAT THE HELL JUST HAPPENED?

I scratch my head at Cameron's sudden mood change and abrupt departure. She can't honestly be *that* upset I teased her about the damn cheese. That'd be a stretch even for Cameron St. James.

"Well, I guess it's just you and me, Bruno." I shrug, setting my plate and juice down on the table. The espresso machine looks complicated, and I had planned to figure it out later, but now I'm contemplating taking a shower and going back to bed to restart this weird as fuck day.

Moments later, Cami stomps down the staircase, and I watch in silence as she marches to the kitchen. I stab a piece of meat with my fork and shove it into my mouth, keeping my eyes on her. When she's not shouting at me or having a tantrum, she's quite breathtaking. Blond hair sweeps along her face and shoulders, her shining blue eyes glance around as her nostrils flare.

"Digging out the alcohol already?" I ask with amusement as she grabs the vodka from the top shelf in the liquor cabinet. Her mood shift has me eager to find out what the hell happened because she obviously has a problem.

She ignores me, opens the bottle, and takes a long swig. My eyebrows pop up, impressed that she swallows it down so easily.

"Did I drive you to drink already?" I grin, waiting to see if she cracks.

She brings the bottle back to her lips, downing another long swig.

"Damn, killer. I made you breakfast, gave you a dance show, and pissed you off all before ten? That's gotta be a new record for me."

"It's not you," she says calmly, gripping the neck and swinging it as she walks to the table. "Zane broke up with me in a text message."

I hadn't expected that. Dropping my fork, I say, "Oh, I'm sorry to hear that."

She sits across from me and gives me a side-eye. "No, you're not."

"Actually, I am. I was hoping he'd bring pot."

Cami laughs, and it's the sweetest, most genuine sound I've heard since we both arrived. "You mean you didn't bring any?"

"Of course, I did. But I figured a rich boy like him would have the good stuff. If you want to wallow, I'll share mine with you." I flash a grin.

"How nice of you," she deadpans. "I don't smoke it with him. He looked like an idiot but did it around his stupid friends to seem cooler than he was."

That's not surprising. Zane's a fucking moron, especially if *he* broke up with *her*.

I inhale half my omelet. "I can teach you. I brought my pipe."

"A pipe? Oh, my God. What are you, eighty?" She crosses her legs on the chair. Right now, in her non-designer tank top and cotton shorts, she looks *normal*. Not at all like she'll inherit billions of dollars before she turns thirty.

"Oh, I'm sorry. Would you prefer to be classier and smoke it rolled in a joint?" I take a sip of my juice and grin.

Cami's frown turns into a full-on smile, and knowing I made her laugh gives me a small sense of pride.

"Vodka and weed. Sounds like the perfect medicine for heartbreak."

"I'll even sweeten the deal…but I'm gonna need something in return."

She waves her hand. "Like what?"

"Since I made you breakfast—a delicious one, might I add—you have to make dinner."

Cami narrows her bright eyes at me. "You're joking."

"No, really. Try it. This omelet is fan-fucking-tastic."

"Not about that," she says. "I can't cook."

That I knew. Cameron St. James has never had to cook a day in her life.

"Well, now's a good time to learn." I flash her a devilish smirk. She shoots a death glare my way, folding her arms. "Okay, okay." I laugh. "I'll *help*. Consider me your personal cooking tutor."

"That's a horrible idea," she states. "I'll probably poison us both."

"I guess that's just a risk I'm willing to take." I tap my knuckles twice on the table, then stand and grab my dirty dishes. "We'll start nice and easy."

"Like what? Boiling a pot of water?"

"Well, that'll be the first step for making pasta." I rinse my plate and mug.

Cami follows with her vodka in hand, and I watch as she takes another gulp.

"You're gonna be drunk before we make it to dinner."

"That's kinda the plan. I'd like to numb as many feelings as I can right now, so you either find more alcohol or you're a part of the problem."

Chuckling, I take the bottle from her tight grip and put the cap back on. "Go take a hot bath and relax. I'll be here to shout curse words at later."

The moment the words fall from my mouth, her shoulders slump, and guilt washes over her face.

"I'm sorry about that," she says softly.

"I know." I flash her a wink, and she groans with an eye roll. "Now, upstairs you go. Take a nap after the tub. Once you're awake, we'll cook a delicious non-poisonous meal, then smoke."

Cami snorts, and I can tell she's already feeling the vodka. "This really must be the twilight zone."

"What do you mean?"

"I'm at the cabin—one I haven't been to in ages—with *you,* and we're talking about weed. I must be dreaming."

"Well, that's very possible, but just in case…we should make sure."

Sauntering toward her, I close the gap between us and grip the back of her neck. She steps forward, and I cover her mouth with mine.

I halfway expect her to push away and slap me, but she leans in and wraps her arms around my waist. Cupping her face, I slide my tongue between her lips and deepen the kiss. Cami moans against me, and her response has my dick reacting. I'm not sure what came over me—especially since she's been single for barely a few hours—but she looked so sad and helpless moments ago, and I wanted to help her forget that asshole.

"Well?" I ask, breaking the kiss after a few moments. We're panting and out of breath.

Cami blinks and brings a finger to her mouth. "Um…" Swallowing hard, she looks up at me. "What the hell was that?"

I shrug as if it didn't affect me, but truth be told, I've imagined kissing her like that since when we were teenagers. "Guess you're not dreaming."

Cami blinks again, licks her lips, then nods. "Apparently not, though I'm unsure if I'm happy about that or not."

"Well, dreaming would almost be better because the current circumstances kinda suck."

"Oh, uh, right. Yeah, that part definitely does."

"Okay, well, I gotta shower and check in with my boss." Walking toward the stairs, I notice she's flustered, which has me grinning, but I tuck it inside. "Don't forget about our dinner plans." I point at her. "Five o'clock sharp."

"Sure. Maybe eat a big lunch in case it's a fail."

"Nah, I have faith in you." I flash her a wink. "But just in case, I have snacks."

Bruno follows me to the stairs, and I take two steps at a time, then go into the bathroom. I'm not sure what the fuck came over me, but I don't regret it. Even though Cameron tormented me for years, I still fantasized about kissing her. And it was everything I thought it'd be—searing hot and passionate, greedy even. Since Zane just broke it off, and she was in a vulnerable state, I shouldn't have taken advantage, but…Cami didn't push me away either.

Once I finish showering and get dressed, I hear the water running upstairs, and smile knowing she's soaking in the tub like I suggested. Cami's so damn uptight; she probably doesn't know how to chill out, but it makes me happy that she's trying.

"Alright, Bruno…work time, buddy." He nudges me with his wet nose, nearly climbing on my lap as I sit at the desk. "Lie down and take a nap. We'll play later," I tell him.

He's used to constant attention because one of my roommates played with him while I was at the office, but he won't be getting that here. I have to complete my tasks remotely through this crisis, which is fucking with my head.

On one hand, I need to figure out new ways to connect with clients and am even hoping to get promoted soon to an appraisal manager. But on the other, I hate pushing people to sign contracts on leases they don't need right now. Nevertheless, I still need a paycheck, and I'm grateful to receive a salary when millions have lost their jobs.

After an hour of responding to emails and following up with a few clients, I take a short break to get a drink. As I'm walking down the hallway, I hear a commotion from above and pause. I wait and then hear Cami scream followed by a loud thump.

Rushing to the third level, I knock on her door and call her name. "Cami? You okay?"

Her feet pad against the floor, and when she opens the door, she's only wearing a towel.

"Uh…" I lower my eyes, not hiding the fact I'm looking. "I heard something. Are you alright?"

"Aside from falling on my ass, I'm fine," she says, breathlessly.

"You fell?" I meet her eyes. "Getting out of the tub or what?"

She bites down on her lower lip and fidgets. "Well, no, not exactly."

Leaning against the doorframe, I wait for her to explain. This is going to be amusing as hell, I can already tell.

"I half-dried off and needed to pee, but then the fucking seat broke, and…" She hesitates, closing her eyes briefly. "I fell off."

Standing straighter, I blink. "You fell *off*?" I hide my smile, trying my hardest not to chuckle at the utter defeat in her eyes.

"Yes. The seat shifted, and I guess I was too wet and slipped."

The expression on her face is pure annoyance and shock that a toilet seat would dare to break while she's using it. Her reaction has me doubling over. I can't help myself and burst out laughing.

"Shut up! I landed on my tailbone, and now it hurts!" She steps closer and smacks me against the chest. "You're such a jerk."

I hold up my hands and grin. "I didn't do it. Why am I a jerk?"

She folds her arms over her half-bare chest and scowls. "You're laughing."

"Well, I'm sorry. But it's hilarious."

"It's not."

"No, trust me. It very much is. Considering you slipped off a toilet seat buck ass naked is the funniest thing I've heard in months. Actually, I'm going to replay it in my head anytime I need a good laugh. This moment might last a lifetime."

"Alright, asshole. Bye." She starts to shut the door, but I stop it with my foot.

"Oh, c'mon. I'm just messin' with you."

"I'm gonna have the biggest bruise." She pouts with a frown.

"It sounds like it needs to be tightened. You have a screwdriver?"

"A what?"

"Oh, God. You don't know what tools are, do you?"

"Can you not mock me right now?"

"Sorry, but you make it a little too easy." I grin. "I'll look in the garage and see if your dad has anything in there. Get dressed, and I'll help you fix the broken seat situation."

"Alright. Thanks."

"And maybe get some ice for your bruised ass," I mumble with a chuckle as I walk toward the stairs.

"I heard that, asshole."

"I know," I mock. "Be right back."

I remember seeing a basic tool set sitting on a shelf in the laundry room, probably from when they installed the appliances. Grabbing it, I notice it's never been opened, which isn't surprising. No one in the St. James family aside from Ryan would know how to use them.

Cami lets me into her room, and I follow her to the bathroom, which is fucking massive. She's dressed in casual black leggings and an off-the-shoulder sweater. With her hair pulled up and face bare, she looks so different from the pictures printed in the magazines. I much prefer this Cameron—casual and not trying to impress anyone.

Kneeling, I discover a screw on the floor. "Just as I thought. The screws were loose. See?" I hold it up. "Now you want to line it back up with the hole and twist the washer while you—"

"Huh?" she asks. "Can't you do it?"

"Yes, but it's time for you to learn, princess."

She folds her arms and narrows her eyes. "I can watch and learn."

"Nope, you've gotta get your hands dirty every once in a while. What would you do if I wasn't here?"

"Use the other bathroom."

I snicker at her immediate answer. "Not happening. C'mon. It's not that hard."

She inhales with annoyance. "Fine." She kneels next to me and takes the screwdriver. "Now what?"

I give her simple instructions, and she grunts with every step. It's quite humorous, considering it's child's play.

"Tighten it up a bit more. That way, it won't happen again."

"I'm trying!" She groans, using all her strength.

"Put a little muscle into it, geez," I tease.

Once she's done, I check and make sure they're secure, then smirk. "Not bad for an amateur."

"Har har." She gets to her feet and brushes off her knees. "I feel like I need another shower now."

"Wait until a light bulb goes out, and I make you change that, too."

"Do you have to mock me about everything?"

I put the screwdriver in my jeans pocket as I stand, then face her adorable pouty face. "Well, it *was* on my agenda for the day, but I could move my mockery to tomorrow if you'd prefer to reschedule?"

"I swear, Eli." She huffs, busying herself by picking up towels around the bathroom. "You wouldn't know how to have a serious conversation if it bit you in the butt."

"Now, that's not true." I cross my arms, ready to play her little game. "How about we talk about why you were such a bitch to me when we were teens?"

"Me?" she snaps, quickly spinning around to scowl at me. "You're the one who teased me every chance you got. Constantly made fun of me for every-fucking-thing, and you're still doing it now." She holds out her arm. "Let's talk about *that*."

"I think you have your memories twisted because you humiliated me anytime your uppity friends were around. If I recall, you started calling me trailer trash because my mom worked for your family."

"Because you called me a Paris Hilton wannabe!"

I take a step forward as both of our tempers heat. "Well, it was true. Hell, it probably still is. You can't even sit on a damn toilet without hurting yourself."

"God!" She comes for me, pushing firmly against my chest with her hands. I barely flinch, which only pisses her off further. "You're such a fucking child. Grow up." She walks around me and storms out of the bathroom.

Well, it wouldn't be a conversation with Cami if we weren't screaming or annoying the fuck out of each other, but I hadn't expected it to be on the same day I finally kissed her.

A kiss I selfishly want to relive.

CHAPTER FIVE

CAMERON

DAY 3

After a day from hell yesterday, I'm ready to start fresh. It's day three of being at the cabin, and I'm already going stir-crazy with Elijah here. Add in my boyfriend breaking up with me, and I'm a ticking time bomb. Last thing I need is to have a full-blown Britney Spears circa 2007 breakdown.

Kendall: Babe, you okay? I heard about Zane and you.

I groan, reading my best friend's text message. Of course, she did. Even during a freaking pandemic, the rumor mill is strong. I hadn't told a soul—besides Eli—which means Zane's already started running his mouth. Who knows what the hell he's telling people because he's known to exaggerate. Kendall Montgomery has been in my life since elementary school, and she's my ride or die. She also loathes my brother, which cracks me up because I believe she's secretly in love with him. While she pretends she can't stand his know-it-all attitude, Ryan makes comments about her being beauty *and* brains. They're a match made in heaven, but both are in denial.

Cameron: I'm fine. He can suck a giant bag of dicks, though.

Kendall: I can't believe he broke up with you! What an asshole. I wish we could go to the club and get shit-faced! I'd make sure you were over that bastard and under a hottie within an hour!

I laugh, knowing she would totally force me to go out and party. Her answer to everything is booze and one-night stands. Chanel startles awake and gets comfortable in a chair by the window. She's not much of a morning cat until she's ready to eat.

Cameron: Well, I started with vodka for breakfast yesterday, but that backfired on me real quick when I kissed Elijah Ross, then snapped at him.

I skip the broken toilet part because it's embarrassing as hell, but also because I overreacted after he helped me. I was frustrated about Zane and confused about Eli kissing me, and all of that mixed with vodka was a dangerous combination. After I pushed him and stormed away, I went to the theater room and fell asleep watching Netflix. When I woke up hours later, it was late, and the house was dark and silent. I ruined our dinner plans and ended up eating cereal before going to bed.

Kendall: Wait, what?! You're at the cabin with Eli? How'd that happen?

Cameron: Ryan told him he could stay without telling me, and we both showed up! Now we're stuck here since neither of us wants to be in the city. I told Eli to leave because having Zane here would be weird, but now that he's out of the picture, I kinda don't mind him here. Though he's still a jerk, and he brought his freaking dog!

Kendall: I'm laughing so hard right now. You and Eli have fought for as long as I've known you. I can't picture the two of you being stuck together. It's like a reality TV show.

Cameron: Trust me, it wasn't a pretty picture when he arrived. I threw a marble statue at his face.

Kendall: I don't know why you don't just bang it out already. Clearly, you have some animosity to work out. Now would be a PERFECT time ;)

Having her encourage me to cross that line with Eli makes me shake my head. Kendall comes from a wealthy family too, but her life wasn't thrust into the limelight like mine. The Montgomerys are old money, and she inherited so much after her grandparents died five years ago.

Cameron: Kinda ironic since I've told you the same thing.

Kendall: What are you talking about?

Cameron: You and Ryan.

Kendall: Why'd you have to ruin my day by mentioning him? If he wasn't dealing with some serious shit right now in the hospitals, I'd say some not-so-nice things.

Cameron: Your hostility toward each other is comical. Just fuck already—like you said—and work out whatever tension you have.

Kendall: That's a hard fucking pass. He probably recites medical journals in bed to stay hard.

Oh my God. That's not an image I ever wanted to have of my brother. It's hilarious she pretends she hates him when I know she's crushed on him forever.

Cameron: Ew, I just cringed. What the hell is wrong with you?

Kendall: SAME.

I laugh, and it feels good to talk to her after having a crappy couple of days.

Cameron: We should FaceTime and drink together since we can't in person. Though I need to get started on my schoolwork. So, maybe not tonight.

Kendall: Yes, definitely soon! Then you can give me all the juicy details about Eli :)

Cameron: Literally nothing to tell.

Kendall: From his Instagram pictures, he's gotten pretty buff. How does he look in person?

I roll my eyes, though it's true. I hadn't seen Eli in over a year before this unexpected reunion. He's had shaggy hair for as long as I can remember, but graduating college and getting a job has agreed with him. Eli's really taken care of himself, and it shows.

Cameron: OMG. Don't go there.

Kendall: So, are you gonna tell me about this kiss, or are you determined to make me beg?

Cameron: NO! It was a total fluke.

Kendall: Fluke or not, get some quarantine action! And you're no fun. I bet his lips were super soft and warm. Did he use tongue?

Cameron: Go away.

Kendall: That's a yes. But fine. I need to take a shower anyway, so go climb Elijah like a tree so you can give me some gossip to share that'll "accidentally" spread to Zane.

Cameron: I'm not gonna hook up with Eli just to piss off Zane.

Kendall: No, you're going to because you know you want to ;)

Cameron: Bye. Xo

Kendall: Love you!

My mood instantly lifts, and I'm determined to have a better day, which starts with apologizing to Eli. Even though he gets a kick out of teasing me, there's no excuse for how I reacted when he brought up the past after helping me. He tried to teach me something new, but I was a brat. I can't take my frustrations out on him because we're stuck here for weeks. Given the circumstances, I need to make the most of it.

I decide to message Ryan and check on him.

Cameron: Hey, big bro. You doing okay?

I watched the news last night before I cleansed my thoughts with Netflix. It was heartbreaking and depressing to see what was happening in the world and terrifying that New York City is the epicenter of the virus outbreak in the US. It scares me even more that Ryan's in the middle of it.

Ryan: I'm about to leave for a 36-hour shift. It's been pretty rough.

Cameron: The news says things haven't peaked yet and that hospitals are running out of protective gear. That true?

Ryan: Unfortunately, yes. Don't watch that, though. It'll make you more anxious.

Cameron: I'm already there.

Ryan: Exactly. How are things going at Mom and Dad's?

His abrupt subject change doesn't go unnoticed, but that's how Ryan is. Blunt and to the point.

Cameron: I didn't go home. Decided to stay at the Roxbury cabin so I can focus on my classes. But then an unexpected visitor arrived...

Ryan: Hahaha.

Cameron: I hate you.

Ryan: You love me.

Cameron: Yeah, yeah. Well anyway, he brought his big ass dog and scared the shit out of me and Chanel.

Ryan: So, where did Eli go then?

Cameron: What do you mean?

Ryan: I assume you sent him packing...

Cameron: Well, I tried. But he refused and said we could "share" the cabin. So we are.

Ryan: I'm glad you let him stay because he had nowhere safe to go. Though, I'm not sure being quarantined with you is much safer.

Cameron: Okay, jerk. I'm getting enough shitty remarks from Eli. I don't need it from you, too.

Ryan: Oh, come on. As your older brother, it's my job to pick on you. He just does it to get a rise and response from you.

Cameron: I've noticed the last ten years.

Ryan: Well, I gotta go. Glad you two are isolating together. Be nice!

Cameron: Tell that to him!

Ryan: I'll get right on that ;)

Cameron: Ha, I'm sure! Please be careful. I love you.

Ryan: Love you too, sis. Stay there so I don't have to worry about you.

Cameron: I will.

I laugh, knowing Ryan is purposely keeping things light so I don't freak out even more. Losing a sense of control as a perfectionist only fuels my uneasiness. I managed to get a refill of my anxiety medication before I left, but I'm trying to save it for when I really need it.

Once I've showered and dressed for the day, I go downstairs.

"Good morning," I sing-song when I find Eli in the kitchen and head to the fridge for the OJ. "How'd you sleep last night?"

He turns toward me, one eyebrow arched as if I've grown a second head. Fortunately, he's wearing a shirt this morning, so there's zero temptation to ogle him.

Walking around him, I reach inside the cabinet and grab a glass, then pour myself some juice. Silently, Eli closes the gap between us, and my breath hitches as he leans in closer. He places his palm on my forehead and squints.

"What're you doing?" I ask, confused.

"Checking to see if you have a fever." He steps back, dropping his hand as he examines my face.

"Why?"

"Because I'm concerned that you're sick."

I immediately touch my cheeks. Then I slide my palm down my neck to see if my glands are swollen. "I don't think so." I feel fine, anyway.

"Hmm…then perhaps you were possessed by a friendly ghost while you slept because you skipped down here way too cheerfully." He smirks, and then I realize what he's doing.

Grinding my teeth, I narrow my eyes and bump him with my hip so he's forced to take a step back. "You're such an ass. For a second, I thought I was dying."

"Yeah, I hear Jekyll and Hyde is a symptom. Better be careful."

I take a sip of juice, then scowl. "And to think I was going to apologize to you. Never mind."

Eli dramatically puts a palm on his chest over his heart and widens his eyes. "Oh, God. Don't do that. I might stroke out."

"At the thought of me saying sorry?" I ask as he moves around the space, grabbing a pan and items from the fridge.

"At you admitting you were wrong about something," he confirms, cracking an egg into a bowl.

"I never said that."

He shakes his head and smirks. "Alright. I'm all ears."

Sucking in a deep breath, I lean against the counter and mentally prepare myself for his sarcastic remarks.

"Okay, well first…" I lick my lips and watch as he continues to prepare breakfast. "I'm sorry for how I reacted after you helped me with the toilet seat. I should've said thank you and that I appreciated you checking on me when you heard me fall. I was angry with Zane and took it out on you, and it wasn't right. It won't happen again."

"Apology accepted." He grins. "You hungry? I'm making scrambled eggs and hash browns."

Blinking, I stare at him. "That's it?"

"What do you mean?"

"You're not gonna give me some smart-ass comment? Make a joke about how I'm a spoiled rich girl who uses her money to right my wrongs or some shit like that."

"Were you offering me money?"

I sigh. "Well, no, but that hasn't stopped you before."

"See, you're not the only one who can turn over a new leaf."

"So, no more snide comments?" I wait as he mixes cheese and milk in the bowl, then pours it into the pan.

"Now, I never said *that*."

Chuckling, I move to the espresso maker. "Figures."

We easily move around the kitchen, him making breakfast and me brewing coffee. Bruno even lies close and doesn't attack me, but his head perks up when he smells the eggs.

"Would you like some toast?" Eli asks.

"Sure, did you bring any bread?" I haven't had any in months.

He laughs. "Yes. But it's not the healthy no-carb shit. It's the good stuff."

"That's fine. I'll have a fruit smoothie for lunch to even it out."

Eli smirks, shaking his head as he pulls a loaf from the cabinet.

"A protein smoothie would be better for you. It's more nutritious than blended fruit and is balanced."

"Is that so?"

"Yep. I drink one after my workouts as a meal replacement."

"When did you start going to the gym so much?" I ask after he sits across from me at the table and hands me two slices of buttered toast. "Thank you."

"Welcome." He stabs his fork into his hash browns. "It became a habit for me after college."

"Any particular reason?" I say before taking a bite.

"Needed a distraction."

"From what?"

"A girl."

"Oh." I swallow. "Were you together long?"

"Not really. About six months."

This is probably one of the most personal conversations Elijah and I have ever had, and it's oddly normal. I had no idea he'd dated someone, but that's not surprising since we hardly crossed paths after high school.

"What happened?"

"Found her mouth wrapped around my roommate's cock." He says it so casually as he continues stuffing his face.

I nearly choke on my eggs. "You're kidding."

"Nope." He shakes his head. "The icing on the cake is we still live together, and they started dating after we broke up."

"Oh my God, no way!" My eyes widen in horror. This chick is a straight-up bitch.

"Yep. So, it was either be in the same apartment with them after work or go to the gym."

"Wow…" I take a sip of my coffee. "Are they still together?"

"Engaged, actually."

This keeps getting worse. "Please tell me he didn't ask you to be in their wedding."

"Fuck no. They invited me, though."

"What a douche. Both of them. Seriously. I can't believe some people."

"Don't worry, karma came to play."

"What do you mean?"

"The ceremony was supposed to be in two weeks, but with the restrictions on social gatherings, they had to cancel it. They're losing their asses in the money they spent."

I laugh, smiling wide at his victory. "Good. I mean, the circumstances are awful, but at least they got what they deserved."

"I'm over it now. We weren't right for each other, but I would've preferred she break it off before sucking off one of my friends."

"No kidding." I finish my eggs that seemed to melt in my mouth. "I'm pretty sure Zane cheated on me."

"Zane's a fucking moron. For several reasons, but especially for taking you for granted."

"Yeah, he really is. I guess I was fixated on the *idea* of us, not really him. I should be more upset than I am. It's not our relationship I'm grieving, but rather the fact that he made a fool out of me."

Bruno gets up and walks over to me, setting his head down on my lap. I'm a little stunned and don't know what to do.

I grin down at him. "What do you want?"

"He knows you're sad," Eli explains, standing and grabbing our empty plates. "He's offering you himself to pet so you'll feel better."

I snicker at the way Eli talks about Bruno as if he can read the dog's mind. "Is that so? You want to be my comfort animal?"

"He's a good boy, aren't you?" Eli saunters over after placing our dishes in the sink. "I'm gonna take him out for some exercise for a bit. Wanna join us?"

I look at my phone and notice the time. "I would, but I have to start my schoolwork so I can stay ahead. Need to make sure that ho Francine Withers doesn't steal my valedictorian spot."

Eli raises his brows, amused.

"She flirts with all the professors, so trust me, the label is accurate. I'm pretty sure she slept with the dean just to get into the program."

"Wow, desperate times call for desperate measures. Well, if you change your mind, you'll know where to find me." He grins, then finishes his coffee. "My offer to help you make me dinner still stands, by the way."

Laughing, I get up from the table and grab my mug. "How sweet of you."

"I'm a nice guy, babe." He winks, then calls Bruno, and the two of them head to the front door.

I grab Chanel's food and water dishes from my room, then refill them in the kitchen. As I walk back to the staircase, I peek through the window and see Eli throwing a stick for Bruno in the backyard. He's smiling wide as he grabs it from Bruno's mouth and stretches his arm back, tossing it as far as he can. Bruno gallops like a small horse and happily fetches it.

As I watch them, a strong sensation ripples through me. I'm relieved and glad Eli's here, so I'm not alone, but he's also great company. It doesn't hurt that he cooks, too. However, he's helped keep me distracted from what's happening right now. My anxiety spikes just thinking about it, and if I were here by myself, I'd drive myself crazy watching the news. I'm not being ignorant about the extreme situation we're in, but it doesn't help to overly obsess either.

If there's anyone I have to self-isolate with during times of uncertainty, I'm glad it's Elijah.

CHAPTER SIX

ELIJAH

CAMI HAS GIVEN me whiplash the past couple of days, but I'm managing the best I can.

One second, she's blazing hot, and the next, she's ice cold.

Then she's apologizing.

I must be living in the twilight zone because Cameron *rarely* admits she's wrong, so I certainly appreciate her apology. Though she may not believe it, I'm actually glad she's here and keeping me company. It beats being in this big cabin alone, and if we can get along, even better.

I throw sticks for Bruno until my arm nearly gives out, then we head back into the house. I grab some bottles of water, go upstairs and take a shower, then log in to my laptop. I have a video conference with some clients and my supervisor for two hours, which is as boring as it sounds. The only bonus is the view of the snow-capped mountains in the distance and clear blue skies. Though it's a little chilly outside, it's common for Upstate this time of year.

Once I'm off the call, I return dozens of emails and decide to turn on the news.

Bad fucking idea.

Reporters show footage of doctors working in the ER in New

York City under extreme distress, and it has me on edge thinking about Ryan. Though he might not be able to text me back, I message him anyway so he knows he's on my mind.

> **Elijah: Hope you're doing okay. Shit is looking scary on TV.**

I'm shocked when his reply comes minutes later.

> **Ryan: It's fucking bad. Never in my life have I ever seen anything like this before.**

> **Elijah: I can't believe it. It doesn't seem real.**

> **Ryan: I heard you're stuck with my sister. Sorry, I didn't know she'd be there, but I'm glad you guys are together and safe. Gives me one less thing to worry about.**

> **Elijah: Did she chew your ass out?**

> **Ryan: Not really. She said she was worried about me so I tried to downplay things so she wouldn't have an anxiety attack.**

> **Elijah: Does she still get them?**

I knew she did in high school but wasn't sure if she still did. Since the media is constantly in her business and making up stories, she's overly private about her personal life.

> **Ryan: Yeah, sometimes. She doesn't always tell me, so it could be happening more than I know.**

> **Elijah: I'll keep an eye on her. Did she tell you Zane broke up with her?**

Ryan: What? No. That fucker. I'm gonna punch his pretty boy face.

I laugh, knowing he totally would too.

Elijah: Don't worry, she's taking her anger out on me.

Ryan: I believe that. Don't let her near the vodka…

I snort.

Elijah: You're a day late and a dollar short on that tip.

Ryan: Fuck. Sorry.

Elijah: Don't be. We'll be fine. She's coming around. We'll be married in no time ;)

Ryan: I'm not sure if I should worry about the virus killing you or my sister, but good luck either way!

Elijah: Be safe, bro! Keep me updated with how things are going. I'll make sure Cami is safe.

Ryan: Appreciate it, man. I gotta run. Talk to you later!

I'm not a religious guy, but I whisper a little prayer to keep my best friend safe and healthy along with his coworkers and patients.

By three thirty, I'm tired of glaring at my computer screen and want some fresh air, so I take Bruno outside. I chase him around the yard, throw the stick a dozen times, and am nearly out of breath after thirty minutes.

"Alright, let's get some water, bud." I pet his head, and we go into the house. As I reach the fridge, I spot Cami at the kitchen table with her cat lying next to her computer.

"Hey," I say as she pounds her fingers on the keyboard. Grabbing a bottle of water, I offer her one, too.

"No, thanks." She doesn't take her eyes off the screen.

I chug half of it before taking a deep breath, trying to get as much air as possible. Bruno drinks every drop in his entire water dish, and I fill it up for him. When I turn around, I notice Cami's cat is moving around the table, taking notice of the dog. To avoid another war between them, I put Bruno in my room.

"You okay?" I ask Cami when I return downstairs. "I don't think you've blinked in five minutes."

"Just working on a paper."

"You look like you're about to fire someone." I chuckle. She finally drifts her gaze toward me and shoots me a death glare. "What? You seem tense. That paper piss you off or something?"

"It's called focusing."

"Why are you down here anyway?"

"I got tired of looking at the same thing upstairs," she explains. "Plus, I needed more caffeine."

"Speaking of which, can you teach me how to use that machine? I mean, unless your plan is to make it for me every morning. And if that's the case, I'd prefer it be delivered to my bedroom." I smirk, sitting on the edge of the table.

"You have a better chance of a meteor hitting us than me bringing you coffee in bed."

"Ouch." I chuckle, placing my hand over my heart. "Why don't you take a break? Have you eaten yet?"

"Not since breakfast."

I check the time and see it's already after four. "That was hours ago. C'mon, shut down the laptop and make me dinner."

Her fingers finally stop moving, and her shoulders shake as she laughs. "You're not as slick as you think."

"Really?" I stand. "Because I think I just got you to finally smile."

She rolls her eyes with a groan. "Fine, but after we eat, I have to get back to it. This professor is a hard-ass, and instead of taking it easy on us during this time, she's *added* assignments."

"Sounds like a bitch move," I say. "But you're a genius, so I'm sure it's cake for you."

Cami flashes me a look of uncertainty. "I can't tell if you're being sarcastic or not."

I hold up two fingers. "I swear, totally genuine." Her expression softens. "You're obviously smart, Cami. You got into NYU on your own merits. You're just not...fix a toilet seat smart."

She leans back in the chair, and her arms fall to her sides. "And you're clearly not make coffee smart."

Laughing, I nod and shrug. "Right. So it's perfect. I'll be in charge of the hard labor, and you're in charge of making sure I'm caffeinated enough to do it."

Her gaze lowers to my mouth, and I wonder if she's thinking about our kiss like I am. When she licks her lips, the temptation to lean in is strong, but I refrain. The last thing I want is for things to be more complicated between us. It's only the two of us, and it's too easy to blur the lines. If we're going to stay here and get through this together, we have to be civil and respectful of each other

"Okay, deal. But don't expect room service," she teases, closing her laptop.

"Oh..." I say slowly. "So then I guess it's a no for personal lap dances?"

"Are you always this obnoxious?"

"Only when I know it gets on your nerves." I beam, staring into her crystal blue eyes. They're brighter than yesterday.

"I'm gonna need way more vodka to deal with you." She stands and pushes in her chair, then moves to the kitchen.

"Actually, I was informed to hide that."

She looks over her shoulder and glares at me. "If you know what's good for you, you won't."

I follow her, then rummage through the fridge for the meat I brought. It'll go bad if we don't eat it soon. "Do you like chicken fettuccini Alfredo?"

"Is that pasta?" she asks, leaning against the island.

Turning to look at her, I furrow my brows. "Are you serious?"

"What?" She shrugs. "I don't eat a lot of pasta." I tilt my head at her. "Okay, fine. I *never* eat pasta."

"Guess that means you're about to have the best meal of your life," I tell her, gloating. "Wash your hands."

"Why?"

"Because I'm not making this alone. Time for you to learn how to cook, woman."

She sighs and goes to the sink, then suds up her hands. "Don't get your hopes up."

I chuckle at how she exaggerates her inability to cook and grab all the ingredients for dinner. After I place the box of pasta and chicken breasts on the counter, I grab a knife and cutting board.

"Alright, you're in charge of the chicken. Cut off the fat, then slice it into long pieces. Think you can manage that?"

"I guess we'll see." She steps closer to the counter and opens the package. I hold back a smile when she grabs the chicken breast and cringes. Carefully, she places it on the cutting board as if it's going to jump out of her hands. "This is really gross."

"Dry it with a paper towel first," I tell her.

Cami does what I say, and I'm amused by how helpless she looks. You'd think she was dealing with a live animal by the way she's holding it. With her back to my chest, I lean into her ear. "Don't worry, it won't bite ya."

"Not funny," she deadpans.

I place my hands on her shoulders, and she shivers. "I have faith in you."

She inhales sharply, and I release her so I can prepare the sauce. "Wanna learn how to make homemade Alfredo sauce?"

Cami looks over at me, unamused. "Sure, why not?"

Chuckling, I grab the butter, heavy cream, garlic cloves, parmesan cheese, and parsley. Then I tell her what I'm doing as I do it. After I melt the butter in the saucepan, I add the cream, then let it simmer.

"You wanna whisk it?" I ask after I check the sauce, not wanting it to burn.

She looks over her shoulder. "Do what?" Before I can respond, she drops the knife. "Fuck!"

When I rush to her side, she's holding her finger that's bleeding. "Did you cut yourself?"

"Yes, and it hurts like a bitch."

"Let me see it." I grab her arm, turn her toward me, then grab a paper towel before holding her hand in mine. "Oh man. I think I'm gonna have to amputate."

"Stop!" she whines. "That stupid knife is really sharp."

"I think this was caused by the operator's error," I say, laughing. "It's just a small cut. But I'll grab some supplies and bandage you right up. You'll be as good as new in no time."

"You distracted me with your sauce." She pouts, looking down at her finger as I race to the staircase. I'm full-on laughing as I grab the first-aid kit I packed from my bag and bring it back to her, cradling her hand.

"Raise your arm over your head to slow the bleed." I stand in front of her and open the kit, finding the items I need to play doctor.

After a moment, I grab her hand and inspect her finger again. "Let's rinse it under some warm water for a second, and then I'll clean it with an alcohol pad before putting some Neosporin and a Band-Aid on it."

She nods, and I lead her to the sink, carefully placing her hand under the stream. She winces for a moment, then relaxes. It's a baby cut, but I think it freaked her out more than anything.

Once it's clean, I dry off her finger, then continue to help her. "There," I say, meeting her eyes and pressing a soft kiss over the wound. "All better."

She sucks in her lower lip, and I admire the way her freckles sprinkle over her face. Cami's barely wearing any makeup, but she doesn't need any because she's a natural beauty.

"Thank you," she says softly.

"You're welcome." I pat her hand before releasing it. "Perhaps I should take over this part, and you can stir the sauce."

"You still want my help?"

"Of course I do. A deal is a deal, and it's pretty hard to fuck up pasta."

"Don't underestimate me." She snickers. "We just started, and I'm already injured."

"Well, good thing battle wounds are sexy." I flash her a wink, and I swear I catch her blushing. Cami would never admit it, but I think I'm getting to her the way she's always got to me.

She continues to stir, and I show her how to make the pasta with my salt and oil trick so the water doesn't boil over and the fettuccini doesn't stick together. I bake some garlic bread, and soon, our meal is complete.

"Wow, this smells delicious," she says as I set our plates on the table. "Even the bread."

"Don't hate on bread."

"I'm not, but I don't typically eat this stuff. It'll probably put me in a carb coma."

"Maybe it'll force you to relax for a change." I smirk, sitting across from her.

"What's that mean?"

My smirk deepens. "Means you're uptight."

She narrows her eyes as she lifts her fork and stabs a piece of chicken. "I'm not uptight."

I smile when her deadpan expression breaks, and she laughs at her own statement.

"If I get anything out of this situation, it's gonna be to hear more of that sound come out of you."

"You act as if I don't know how to laugh."

"Do you? All I heard from you growing up was 'Go away,

Elijah!' followed by a door slamming in my face." I cock my head, challenging her to deny it.

"Well, I'm not slamming doors now," she says, the tension in her body nearly melting away.

"No, just throwing expensive statues."

Cami playfully rolls her eyes, grinning. "I thought you were a burglar!"

"One who knows the security code and brings food…"

"Keep being a jerk. I just might change the code, and you'll be out on your ass." She points at me with her fork, trying to act all serious.

"I'm willing to risk it." I shrug, knowing she wouldn't know how to do that. You have to call and verify a bunch of shit with the security company. I know because Ryan tried to change it so we could sneak up here one weekend, but his parents busted him after they got an alert.

"So how's your sister doing?" She changes the subject abruptly, but I don't mind. My sister was one of my best friends growing up and still is.

"Ava's great." That reminds me I have to text her and make sure she's self-isolating, too. "Not exactly your biggest fan…" I mock, finding it ironic she's asking about her. "She's going to freak out when I mention the two of us are here."

Cami groans, sucking in a deep breath. "Another person I need to make amends with, I suppose."

I shrug, twirling the pasta with my fork. "Wouldn't hurt."

"If we ever get to leave and go back to civilization, I'll make sure I do. I'd rather apologize in person."

"I'm sure she'd appreciate that. I know I would."

CHAPTER SEVEN

CAMERON

Day 4

AFTER DINNER LAST NIGHT, we talked casually as we cleaned the kitchen and put our leftovers in the fridge. Yet again, I was reminded of how being a selfish teenager affected Eli's sister, Ava. She'd come over with him, and I could tell she was desperate for a friendship, but I had this false idea in my head of who was allowed in my life. Knowing I hurt a lot of people is something I live with and regret every day. I don't want to be that person anymore, and I'll do whatever it takes to make things right with those I treated poorly.

We said good night and went our separate ways. I still had some homework to finish but could feel my anxiety spiking. When Eli and I are hanging out, even for like five minutes, I forget that we're in the midst of a global pandemic. It's when I'm left alone that reality smacks me in the face. Uncontrollable fear resurfaces and reminds me that this isn't some nightmare I'm stuck in.

It's reality.

Chanel wakes me up earlier than usual, nudging me with her nose to feed her. It's chilly, so I wrap myself in a throw blanket and slide my slippers on before grabbing her dishes and going to the kitchen.

"Alright, alright. Calm down," I tell her as she meows louder, following me downstairs.

Bruno's asleep on the couch, and I look around for Eli but don't see him. Thankfully, Chanel is more concerned about eating than antagonizing the dog this morning.

Once her bowls are full, she follows me back upstairs to my room. That same uneasy feeling that visited last night returns, and I know a panic attack is coming. I've gotten them periodically since high school, but I haven't experienced one in months. Things are starting to get to me, and it hasn't even been a week.

Crawling back on the bed, I curl into a ball and wrap my arms around my legs, holding them tight to my body. I close my eyes and slowly count. My heart races even though I'm not moving, and my head is heavy.

After ten minutes, I stand and pace the room, unable to calm down. It agitates me more. My chest tightens, and I know the worst is still to come.

Sitting on the edge of the bed, I take deep breaths and try to picture what life was like before all of this happened. Somehow, weeks seem like so long ago.

A knock sounds on the door, and I look up, trying to stabilize my breathing.

"Come in," I say.

Eli peeks his head inside before opening the door wider. "You okay? I could hear you pacing up here."

I blow out an unsteady breath and nod. "Just working through a panic attack." Placing my hands on my knees, I slouch over and close my eyes.

"Jesus, Cami. Let me help," he says, stepping inside.

"You can't." I inhale, then slowly release it. "It'll eventually pass."

"Did something trigger it?" he asks, sitting next to me on the bed.

"I don't really know. Just…everything. All the unknowns are a lot to handle right now," I explain. "I guess it started to really hit me that this is happening. I was watching some news footage on my phone last night and read a few articles, which didn't help my anxiety. Then I started thinking about Ryan and how scared I was for him. I tried to sleep through it, but it came back in full force this morning."

Eli stands, then leans down and lifts me until my arms wrap around his neck. "What are you doing?" I squeal.

"Just hold on," he instructs as he walks us to one of the oversized chairs by the window. I'm still wrapped in a blanket, but my temperature always rises when my anxiety is high. I'll start sweating soon, but I don't care.

Eli sits and cradles me against his chest. It settles me, and when I rest my head on his shoulder, he holds me a little tighter.

"This okay?" he whispers softly.

I nod, closing my eyes and snuggling deeper into his chest.

"Remember when Ryan invited me to the Hamptons with you guys the summer before my junior year?" he asks after we sit in silence for a while.

"Yeah," I say. "Why?"

"It was the first time I saw you in a bikini," he replies, chuckling. "I was a hormonal teenage boy, thinking very dirty things about my best friend's little sister. You were only thirteen or fourteen, so I kept telling myself not to stare at you. But it was nearly impossible." He rubs a soothing hand over my arm, caressing lightly. "You had basically written me off at that point, but I was determined to get your attention any way I could. Even if it was having you tell me off."

"Is that why you were flirting with Cherise the whole time?" I quip. I brought my best friend with me that week too, and she thought Eli was cute, which I hated. I didn't want him to like her, so I kept telling her bad things about him, hoping she'd stop. It didn't work.

"She flirted with me first!" he defends. "I was innocent."

That has me grinning. "I was ready to tell her you were gay so she'd leave you alone, but then you kept spewing out sexual innuendos, and I knew she'd never believe me."

"Wow…thanks."

Looking up, I peer into his gorgeous green eyes. "I didn't want her to know I was crushing on you. She would've sabotaged me and told everyone, especially *you*."

"And why would that have been so bad?" he asks, studying the sincerity on my face.

"At the time, it would've been. Now? Not so much," I tell him honestly. "I thought you'd think I was a dumb kid, especially after all the fighting we did."

Eli licks his lips before responding. "Perhaps you weren't aware of or I hadn't made it obvious enough, but I had the biggest crush on you in high school." The corner of his lips sweep up. "I still do."

Instead of feeling nauseated like I typically would during one of these attacks, butterflies surface in my stomach and a shiver runs down my back. Our eyes connect as we sit silently, staring at each other. My heart hammers as he leans down, and I tilt my chin upward.

Before our lips can connect, Bruno barges into my room, and Chanel immediately loses her mind. She hisses at him, and he starts chasing her around the bed.

"Bruno, heel!" Eli orders, standing and carefully setting me on my feet.

Chanel runs under the bed, and Bruno has a barking fit. He loudly howls and tries to wedge himself underneath, but he's too damn big.

"Out, Bruno. Let's go…" Eli grabs his collar, pulling hard and forcing him into the hallway. A moment later, he returns, closing the door behind him. "I'm sorry about that. He needs to go outside and burn off some energy."

The whole scene has me laughing. "It's alright. He likes your attention. I can relate."

Eli pushes off the wood and saunters toward me. "You feeling okay now?"

Nodding, I flash him a small smile. "Yeah, I think so. Thanks for talking to me and helping me think about something else."

He brushes a hand through his hair and fixes it. I love when he casually throws it up like this. Eli's the exact opposite of every guy I've ever dated, but it's why I've never been able to get over my feelings for him. I've fought them every chance I've had, allowing statuses and other's opinions to affect my choices, but I don't want to live that way anymore.

"You're very welcome." He winks. "I'm gonna take the beast out. Wanna join us?"

"Uh, sure. Let me get dressed, and I'll meet you out there."

After he leaves, Chanel slowly comes out from underneath the bed and jumps on my lap. I pet her and try to calm her down because she's as on edge as I was earlier. "Bruno just wants to be your friend," I tell her, jokingly.

Once she's chilled out a bit, I move her off me and find some warm clothes. With leggings, boots, and a sweater under my jacket, I put on a hat and gloves, then go out the back door. Eli is throwing a rubber toy to Bruno who is happily fetching it. Eli has him dressed in a bright-colored coat.

"Oh, look at Bruno all fancied up." I giggle.

"Yeah, Dobies can't be in low temperatures because of their body fat percentage and short hair. He'll start shaking without it, and I can't let my boy get cold." Eli looks me over and smirks.

"Wow, I had no idea. Chanel won't move an inch when I dress her and acts like she's being smothered or something. Bruno's totally in his element." I laugh, watching him run around as though it's no big deal, and place my hands in my pockets.

He lowers his eyes down my body. "You look like you're going to the North Pole," he teases. I notice he's wearing gym shorts and a sweatshirt.

"Not all of us are natural ovens," I retort, wrapping my arms around my body. "I'm always cold, even in summer."

"So when I felt you shiver upstairs, it wasn't because of me?"

I blush, my cheeks heating at his bluntness. "You're quite full of yourself, aren't you?"

"Only when I know I'm right."

Rolling my eyes, I ignore his stare and refuse to admit it. Bruno returns, and as Eli praises him, I lean down and roll snow between my palms. After Eli throws the toy again, he turns toward me, and I throw the snowball directly at his face. He's so caught off guard, he doesn't move, and I burst out laughing at his expression.

Brushing off his face, he narrows his eyes at me. "You're *so* dead."

The moment he comes for me, I start running. Something hits my back, and when I look over my shoulder, I see he's leaning down for more snow. Bruno barks at us, chasing us both, and I keep running even though my lungs burn.

"Get her, Bruno!" Eli shouts.

"No!" I yell, laughing so hard I can barely catch my breath. "Go away!"

Of course, Bruno quickly catches up to me and is all up in my shit, giving Eli the opportunity to tackle me to the ground. He's on top of me, holding me hostage and grinning like he's won the Super Bowl.

"Payback, princess." He cups a handful of snow and holds it over my head.

"No, please, no," I beg, squinting my eyes. "I'll do anything!"

"Anything, huh?" He stops and cocks his head, amused.

"Yes! Just don't get me in the face," I plead.

Strands of his hair fall over his perfect face as he releases the ball. The scruff over his jawline reaches up to his hairline, and he keeps it nicely trimmed. It's probably a good thing he has longer hair, considering a haircut is impossible to get right now.

"Alright, I'll bite." He flashes an evil grin, and I know whatever he's gonna make me do will be torturous.

He stands and helps me up, brushing the snow off my jacket. "Tonight."

"Tonight, what?"

"You will see…"

"I don't like the sound of that," I say as we walk back to the house.

Bruno is still energized as hell as he gallops into the kitchen, bringing a trail of snow with him. Eli follows me, smirking as I remove my coat.

He walks around me, removing his boots, and looks at me. "I'll clean up my mess, don't worry."

"I wasn't." I swallow.

He snorts. "Yeah, right. I can tell when you're lying."

Furrowing my brows, I ask, "How?"

"I've known you for over ten years, Cami. And for most of that time, when you were around, I watched everything you did. Being observant allowed me to learn a few things about you."

"You're starting to sound like a creep," I tease, taking off my boots.

"Which is exactly why I didn't tell you." He grins, then continues, "Your nostrils flare."

"What?"

"When you're lying."

Immediately, I cover my nose with my hand. "They do not."

"I bet you hate that I know so much about you," he says. "But you know a lot about me, too."

He's right, I do, but I hadn't thought about it in a while. "Like how you haven't cut your hair in seven years."

"Aside from trims, that's right."

"I'm jealous it's thicker than mine." I chuckle.

"Gotta use the right products," he says, smirking. "If you're nice, I'll share them with you."

I place a hand over my chest, faking excitement. "You're *so* sweet!"

"It's not your three-hundred-dollar shampoos, but it does the job."

Crossing my arms, I scoff. "I don't spend that much."

"Go clean up and do what you gotta do. You owe me, and I want payment tonight," he says, walking backward toward the staircase and pointing at me. "After dinner."

"Well, I should be relieved you aren't going to make me cook again, but somehow, this sounds more terrifying."

He grins, waggling his brows, then turns and walks up the staircase with Bruno following.

When he's out of sight, I let out a sigh and go to the kitchen. As I make a smoothie and think about how much has changed in only a few days, I can't contain my smile. He admitted he had a crush on me—and still does—and I realized those feelings I had for him have never faded. They've always been bubbling under the surface, and I've constantly fought to keep them under control, but not anymore.

Eli made me feel comfortable and not at all like a burden when I was at my most vulnerable. It's hard for me to admit I suffer from anxiety and panic attacks, but instead of judging me, he stepped right into action. I should've known Eli would want to help, and I'm so thankful he did. My thoughts drifted away from our reality as he held me, and I feel a hundred times better now. Though the circumstances suck, I'm so damn grateful he's here with me.

Whatever he has planned for us, I'm in. If it means spending more time with him, I'd agree to just about anything.

CHAPTER EIGHT

ELIJAH

INHALING THE MOUNTAIN AIR, I close my eyes and smile. Bruno runs around, and I laugh at his playful antics.

Four days ago, my world turned upside down, and I thought I'd go stir-crazy being here alone. Having Cami here too has changed everything.

And for once, it's changed it for the better.

Away from her high-profile life and the pressures of status, Cami's the same girl I first met before any of that shit mattered. Before she let the idea of who she was allowed to date get into her head. I resented her for a long time, even while crushing on her, but those hurt feelings are long gone. Before now, it'd been months since I'd last seen her, and being around her has only cemented the way I've always felt.

Yes, she did just get out of a long-term relationship, but I know he wasn't right for her. She was arm candy for their public appearances and played along to appease her parents. Cami might've thought they had the picture-perfect relationship, but her eyes always gave away her true feelings regardless if she smiled wide. I know her well enough to see the sparkle was missing, proof she didn't love him like everyone thought she did.

Every photo printed and posted was forced and had no real meaning behind it.

Given that we're here together and we have this second chance, I'm not taking it for granted. I'll get Cami to admit she hid her feelings for me and find out if she still has them.

"What'd you make? It woke me up from my nap." She laughs.

I arch a brow. "Nap, huh? Thought you had lots of schoolwork to do."

She groans while taking a seat at the table. "I do, but I get fatigued after a panic attack."

"You feeling better now?"

"Yes, very much so. I took a hot bath and fell asleep to an audiobook."

"Couldn't have been that interesting then if it made you pass out."

"It's one I've listened to a hundred times. The narrator's voice is soothing," she explains, which I find adorable. I never thought to do that.

"Well, I made pork chops slathered in cream of mushroom soup with a side of angel hair pasta."

"More pasta." She releases a dramatic sigh. "I'm going to leave here fifty pounds heavier."

"I doubt that." I set the plate in front of her. "But even if you did, you'd still be gorgeous."

"Thank you," she says, but I'm not sure if it's for the food or compliment. Either way, I meant it. Cameron St. James is a beautiful woman, always has been.

"Wow…this is really good," she admits after she tries the meat.

I grab my plate and sit across from her. "You sound surprised."

"Well, kinda. It sounds so simple, but it's really flavorful." She shoves another bite into her mouth, making me smile.

"I'm genuinely curious how you planned on surviving here

without knowing how to cook," I add with amusement. "Once the Lean Cuisines were gone…you were gonna do what exactly?"

"I hadn't really thought that far ahead. My focus was getting out of the city as fast as possible, and the shelves at the grocery store were already bare."

"Lucky for you, I brought a lot of frozen meat."

"And double lucky that you know how to cook it," she adds, grinning.

"I'm determined to turn you into a chef before we leave." I cut into my pork. "This recipe is so easy, it'd take a miracle to fuck it up."

"Don't underestimate my ability to do just that."

We chat as we eat, and the conversation's never forced or awkward. The fact that it flows so easy should be weird, but I'm soaking up every second. Once we finish, I take our plates and rinse them in the sink.

"I'd help you, but you're gonna have to roll me and my food baby off this chair," she says, leaning back and patting her flat stomach.

I chuckle. "Don't worry about it. Gonna put them in the dishwasher anyway."

"So you gonna tell me what your payback plan is?" she asks once I finish wiping the counters. "I'm getting nervous, so just tell me."

"Well…" I move around the kitchen, grabbing a bottle of Jack and two shot glasses. "It includes these things and a TV."

She squints her eyes, looking confused as hell. "Hmm…you're going to get me drunk and make me watch porn?"

I raise a brow. "Is that an option?"

Cami scowls, shaking her head.

"Alright, well then onto plan B. C'mon." I wave my hand, and she huffs.

Begrudgingly, Cami stands and follows me to the couch. I grab the remote, turn on the TV, and click to A&E.

"What are you gonna make me watch?" she asks, curling her feet underneath her butt.

"You ever seen *Live PD*?" I ask, setting the bottle and shot glasses down on the coffee table.

"No…" she answers hesitantly.

"Oh man…" I beam. "You're in for a treat."

"Why do I have a feeling I'm about to regret this?"

"Depends what kinda night they have." I chuckle. "Now, there are rules to this drinking game. You ready?"

"I suppose." She shrugs.

"We take a shot every time there's a police car chase, someone gets tased, or the cops find drugs in the car and the person says it's not theirs."

"Dear lord, we'll be tanked before the end."

"That's the point."

She laughs, and her eyes go wide as soon as the show begins. I pour the whiskey into the glasses and sit back, knowing it won't be long before this game starts.

On the very first traffic stop, an officer pulls someone over and smells marijuana as soon as the window comes down. Of course, she asks him when he last smoked it, and he denies using it. The smell gives her probable cause to search the vehicle, and then…he tells her it's his buddy's car and that the drugs aren't his.

"Oh, here we go!" I cheer. "Shot time."

"I feel like that's such an obvious lie…" She scowls. "What an idiot."

I hand her one of the glasses, and we clink them together. "Cheers."

We choke down the burn in one swallow.

"This is a horrible idea," she slurs after the third shot. "How long is this show?"

"An hour," I reply. It's only been twenty minutes. "Be glad I only listed three. There could've been a lot more."

"Did he seriously think he could drive off and get away with it?" Cami holds out her arm, getting pissed at the screen when

66

another police chase starts. "This is why we can't have nice things." She shakes her head, takes the glass, then tilts her head back.

Cami's blinking obsessively, and I start cracking up. "You gonna be okay?"

"Oh, sure. I'm starting to see stars, but I'm totally fine."

"Perhaps we should turn this off…" I chuckle.

She stands, wobbling on her feet. "No, no. I'm fine. Totally got this." She swings out her arm and attempts to touch her nose.

"What are you trying to do?"

"A sobriety test." She lifts one foot and steps it in front of her other, tripping over the coffee table.

Quickly, I catch her arm to stop her from falling, then get to my feet. "You're gonna hurt yourself. Maybe you should stay sitting."

She turns and scowls. "I think you got me drunk on purpose."

Taking her hand, I guide her back to the couch and sit next to her. "I didn't realize you were such a lightweight."

"I'm not!" She hiccups, then narrows her eyes at me when I try to hide my smile. "Shut up."

I snort and chuckle because she's adorable. "I'll get you some water."

"Wait." She grabs my arm, then within seconds, her legs are around mine, and she's straddling my lap.

"Cami, what are you doing?" I securely hold her waist as all the blood rushes to my dick.

"Well, if I have to explain it to you, then perhaps I shouldn't be on top of you."

"I think you're drunk and—"

"Are you saying you don't want me?" She leans in closer, and the strong smell of whiskey on her breath reminds me how inebriated she is.

"I do, but not like this."

"Maybe this is the only way I can be brave enough to make a move…" she states clearly. "You're the one who said I'm uptight, so this is me being…" She pauses, thinking. "*Un*-uptight."

My face splits into a grin at her hesitation and response.

Cami sinks down harder against me, and I groan at how good it feels. She's making this too fucking difficult.

"I appreciate that, but the next time I kiss you, you'll be sober." Bringing my hand up to her cheek, I brush away her hair and cup her chin. "That way, it'll be a moment you won't forget or regret."

"Okay." She nods, contemplating my words. I can tell she's thinking about something before she moves off me. The silence draws on for a second, and I wonder if she's embarrassed. "Any chance we can pretend this didn't happen?"

I smirk. "Not a chance in hell."

She crosses her arms over her chest, but she's smirking.

Cameron St. James throwing herself at me is a moment I'll never forget. Intoxicated or not, it's something I'll always find humor in.

After helping her upstairs and into her room, I tuck her into bed and kiss her forehead. "Night."

She's snoring by the time I shut the bedroom door.

I take Bruno outside, then get ready for bed and text my sister before passing out. Ava and I were super close growing up, but as we got older and focused on school and work, we didn't spend as much time together. I miss her a lot. The same age as Cameron, she's finishing her last semester of college online since the stay-at-home order was issued. I know she's bummed about it, but everyone's suffering one way or another.

Elijah: Hey, sis. How's it going?

Ava: Fine, I guess. Bored as hell already. How's the cabin?

Elijah: You'll never believe who's here with me.

Ava: Barack Obama?

I snort. She's obsessed with the Obama family. He's why she decided to study politics in college.

Elijah: Cameron St. James. I didn't know she was coming, and she didn't know I was either. We both just showed up.

Ava: Oh my God. Did she freak out? I bet she did.

Elijah: You could say that. Demanded I leave. Haha.

Ava: Of course. I'd expect nothing less from her.

She sends an eye-roll emoji, and I laugh.

Elijah: We're getting along if you can picture that.

Ava: That's because you're in love with her.

Elijah: I can't even deny it.

I send her a shrugging emoji. My feelings for Cami have always been more than just infatuation. Being here with her has made me truly realize how much she means to me. There's no hiding that.

Ava: Well, I hope you survive the quarantine with the fashion princess. Looks like we'll be locked inside for a while.

Elijah: There goes your dating life. HAHA!

Ava: Don't be a dick! I didn't have a dating life before this.

Elijah: Good. Guys are idiots. Stay away from them.

Ava: Says the idiot.

Elijah: Yeah, yeah. I'm going to bed. Good luck with your online classes. Stay safe!

After tossing and turning for two hours, I give up trying to sleep and decide to work out in the basement. I want to stay positive during this whole situation, especially since Ryan's on the front lines, and I need to be strong for Cami, knowing she's worried about him. But the truth is, it's been keeping me up at night. Everything is so surreal that I can hardly wrap my mind around it.

There are so many people who I love and want to stay safe, which only adds to my stress. I worry about my grandparents who are both in nursing homes. My mother is still cleaning houses to pay the bills. Then my sister staying with friends in the city. And of course, for my best friend. Without him, I'd be stuck in Brooklyn with three dumbass roommates who think this is a hoax. I'm not sure how long this lockdown will be, but I know I don't want to go back there.

Being with Cami is the only thing keeping me sane, even when she's the one driving me crazy. Crushing on her from afar was one thing, but having her here, literally on top of me, is testing my willpower. I don't want to be her "quarantine hookup" or a rebound if that's all she's looking for.

I'd give her forever if she'd let me.

CHAPTER NINE

CAMERON

DAY 5

BEFORE I OPEN MY EYES, I know it's going to be a miserable day.

Between my head pounding and my stomach rumbling, I'm not sure I can even get out of bed.

I pull the blankets over my head and groan. Last night, I tried to make a move on Eli, and he shot me down.

Rejected.

In retrospect, it was one of the most humiliating things I've done in a long time. Not to mention, it involves the one person who already thinks I'm an uptight royal princess.

He'll never let me live this down.

Sinking further under the sheets, I want the mattress to swallow me whole. Knowing Eli, he's shirtless in the kitchen wearing a smug smirk and waiting for me to grace him with my presence. One part of me wants to get this over with, but the other part hopes I can hide in here and he'll forget my existence.

After a few minutes, the throbbing in my head worsens. I debate whether to suffer through it or search for some medicine. Then an annoying beeping starts.

God. I'm already at this stage of the hangover.

The beeping continues.

Sitting up in bed with my hair in disarray, I look around and notice Chanel's staring at me.

"Do you hear that, too?" I ask, but she blinks at me, then starts licking her paws.

The annoying sound grows louder.

"What the fuck is that?" I grumble, deciding to get out of bed. Wrapping a blanket around my shoulders, I walk across the room and listen for it again.

Opening my bedroom door, I'm convinced it's coming from downstairs.

The fuck?

Dragging my sorry ass to the staircase, I brace myself for Eli's inevitable gloating. He's going to have a field day teasing the shit outta me.

Sure enough, Elijah's in the kitchen with his hair looking sexy and perfectly messy. I imagine running my finger through his dark strands, then remember the embarrassment I felt just moments ago.

"Good morning, sunshine." His deep voice echoes against the walls, causing a shiver to run down my body.

"Please tell me you hear that noise…" I plop down on the stool behind the breakfast bar.

He spins around and looks at me—the smirk I knew was coming planted firmly on his chiseled face. "What noise?" He furrows his brows, studying my face. "Feeling okay?"

"Not really." I rest my arms on the counter and lower my head. "I swear, something is beeping in this house."

"Here…" I hear him walk closer. "Drink this."

I blink, and a glass of orange juice is in front of me. "I can't. I might puke."

"Nah, it'll help. Go slow. I'll make you some waffles to soak up the alcohol."

He shuffles around, and I try to focus on not throwing up, but the high-pitched squeal is driving me insane. I get up to walk around the dining area and living room, searching for where it's coming from.

"Are you sure you don't hear it?" I drag my blanket with me. I know I'm not imagining it.

Moving back to the kitchen, I see his shoulders shake, and soon, he's full-on laughing.

"What's so funny?"

He smirks. "You."

"Are you enjoying my pain?"

Eli arches a brow. "What pain?"

Pinching the bridge of my nose, I inhale sharply. "Can we pretend last night didn't happen? *Pretty please*, for the love of God, don't gloat about what I did either. It's embarrassing, and this fucking beeping in my head is going to make me lose it! Not to mention, I have a headache."

"You mean, the part where you crawled into my lap and begged me to fuck you?"

"Okay, I know I didn't do that…you've lost your damn mind. I tried to kiss you, not bang you."

"I remember it differently…" He beams. "You were grinding against me, trying to get my dick all excited."

I hang my head, knowing my cheeks are burning bright red. "I hate you. Shut up. Go away. I'm leaving now."

"Wait, wait, wait…" He grabs my arm and pulls me back, tightening the blanket around me.

"What?" I snap.

"You're somehow even more adorable hungover as hell, but don't be embarrassed. I wanted to kiss you last night, but I didn't want you to regret it this morning. So, if you still have the urge to straddle my lap and rub against my cock, do it when you're sober so I know it's what you actually want."

I swallow down the lump in my throat, my heart hammering relentlessly in my chest, and nod. "Okay," is the only word I can muster.

The noise returns.

"Are you sure you don't hear that?" I tilt my head.

Eli retreats slightly, dropping his arms. "Yeah, it's the smoke detector. The backup battery is going out."

I step toward him and swat his chest. "You asshole! You heard it all along!"

He chuckles, moving back to avoid my wrath, but I quickly give up. Eli shrugs with a motherfucking grin. "Sober up so I can teach you how to change it."

Narrowing my eyes, I follow him to the table. He brings me my glass of juice and then busies himself with the waffle maker.

"Why does it sound like it's in my room and down here at the same time?"

"Because the ceilings are so high, and the sound echoes off the walls."

"There are a few up there, so how do you know which one it is?"

"You're supposed to change them all at the same time. But I'm not sure how many batteries you have, so we'll have to check."

"I'm part relieved it's not just in my head, but the other part wishes it were so it'd stop when my headache disappears."

"Speaking of which, take these." He hands me a couple of white pills. "Waffles are almost done."

"Thank you," I softly say, then swallow them down with my juice. "How are you not hungover this morning?"

He shrugs. "I'm twice your size. I can tolerate more."

"Next time we play your stupid game, I'm drinking vodka."

"You'll be puking for sure. Ryan told me it doesn't agree with you."

"Ryan is a fucking tattletale." I roll my eyes. "And he shouldn't talk."

"That's true. Ryan doesn't drink enough to be able to handle more than a few beers at a time."

I slap a hand against the table. "Exactly, thank you!"

Eli brings our plates over along with the butter, syrup, a can of Reddi-wip, and silverware.

"You ready for the best breakfast of your life?" he gloats.

"What's in these?" I ask, poking at one.

"Chocolate chips."

"That's a lot of carbs in the morning."

"You won't be worried about that once you take a bite." I watch as he slathers his toppings on. "Don't forget the whipped cream."

"I'm literally going to go into a sugar coma," I say as I add everything on top of mine.

The timer on the oven goes off, and he returns to the kitchen. Moments later, he returns with a plate full of bacon.

"You made enough for an army, geez."

"I made extra for BLTs later."

Good thing I packed leggings and yoga pants because there's no way my skinny jeans will fit after eating Eli's delicious meals.

"So? Thoughts?"

"I like it! I can't remember the last time I had waffles."

"Seriously?"

I shrug. "I live off smoothies and salads. Paparazzi, remember?"

"Fuck the paps. For real. Who cares?"

"I'm starting to wonder why I did so much," I state honestly. "But when I'm unable to fit into my clothes, you have to stop cooking this junk."

Eli snorts, shaking his head and stuffing more food into his mouth. "You have a home gym, so I wouldn't worry too much. I used it this morning. We could work out together," he suggests.

"What time were you down there?"

"I couldn't sleep, so I went around one."

"Oh damn." I blink. "Why couldn't you sleep?"

"Too much on my mind, I guess. Couldn't turn it off."

I nod. "I know how that feels. Especially now. My anxiety is the highest it's ever been, which is crazy, considering my life."

"I hear pot helps with that." He smirks. "Just sayin'."

"You know…" I bite down on my lower lip. "One day, I might take you up on that. Especially if I can't get it under control."

"I only do it when I need it."

"I wasn't judging you," I whisper. "I'm always worried about—"

"The media," he finishes for me. "I know."

Nodding, I take another forkful and swallow it down. "This really is delicious. Thanks for an amazing breakfast again."

"My pleasure. It's nice cooking for more than just me for a change."

"Maybe I'll try making something for you, but don't have high hopes. It'll be something easy."

"Like what? Cereal?"

I scoff, shaking my head at him. "Nothing with that attitude."

He laughs, shoving two pieces of bacon into his mouth.

"I have been craving grilled cheese and soup. Is that weird?"

"That sounds fucking amazing actually." He pats his bare stomach. "Think you can do that for lunch?" Eli pops a brow.

"No!" I chuckle. "Don't expect anything from me today."

"Okay, fair enough." He snaps his fingers with a wicked grin. "Tomorrow then."

I groan as he stands and takes his plate to the sink. "I'm gonna see if I can find a ladder and some batteries for that detector."

"Okay, good luck. I have no idea where either would be."

Eli smiles. "That's why I didn't ask."

He takes off as I continue eating. Bruno stares at me from the floor, giving me puppy eyes. "What?"

Bruno sits up and edges closer.

"I'm not giving you anything."

He blinks, licks his chops, then nudges his nose against my hand. Groaning, I pet his adorable head. "Fine, but don't tell your daddy. He'd probably yell at me. It'll be our little secret."

I take a piece of bacon and give it to him. He gobbles it up in one bite, then begs for more.

"No more!" I stand with my plate and bring it into the kitchen.

Looking around at the mess, I decide to help the best I can and rinse off all the dirty dishes. I even manage to load everything into the dishwasher and find the detergent under the sink. There are a dozen buttons, so I press a couple and hope it's right.

At least ten minutes have passed, and I'm growing concerned that Eli hasn't returned yet. I decide to look for him, and Bruno accompanies me. There's probably a ladder in the garage, so I head there first. I open the door and glance around, then see Eli on his knees with his hands to his chest. He's wheezing like he can't breathe, and his lips are blue.

"Oh my God, Eli." I panic and rush to him. "What's happening?"

He pats his chest, then bows down, sucking in air. If I didn't know any better, I'd say he's having an anxiety attack, but then he leans back, and mouths, "Inhaler."

"Inhaler?"

He nods, and my eyes widen in shock. "You have asthma?"

He nods again, and I can't believe I didn't know this about him.

"Okay, inhaler. In your room?"

He confirms, and I quickly run out of the garage, then jump up the stairs. Rushing into his room, I realize I have no idea where to look. I start in the bathroom, rummaging through the drawers and cabinets. When I come up empty, I go to his nightstand. Scattering his shit everywhere, I frantically look for it.

Spinning around, I panic as I try to figure out where he keeps it. I go to his desk and finally find it next to his laptop.

"Thank God," I mutter, then rush back to the garage.

He's in the same spot I left him, and he's bent over, taking in shallow breaths. Bruno's lying next to him as if he knows how to comfort Elijah during his attacks.

"Sorry, it took me forever to find it." I hand it over, and he quickly presses the top and sucks in the medicine. I watch eagerly for him to recover. He takes a few more puffs, and after a moment, he starts breathing regularly.

"Are you okay?"

He nods, blowing out a breath. "That was a bad one."

"How did I not realize you had asthma?"

"It's not something I've broadcasted." He gets to his feet. "Don't feel bad."

"What triggers them?"

He winces, and I step back. "What is it?"

"It's a little painful. My chest and lungs feel sore afterward, but I'll be okay. It'll pass."

I fidget with my shirt, feeling helpless and wishing I could do something to make him better.

"I think it was the dust," he states after a moment. "I found the batteries and came in here to get the ladder."

"Well, let me change them out. I'm sure I can figure it out."

He flashes me a wary look.

"What? I can. Just talk me through what to do."

"Okay, well. You gotta carry that ladder inside the house. Think you can do that?"

I look up at the wall where it's hanging. It's at least eight feet, and there's no way I'm gonna be able to lift it on my own. "Oh, definitely."

Eli chuckles and backs away. "I'll put on a mask and get it. Don't worry."

"Hey." I grab his arm and move him toward the door. "I can totally do it."

His eyes lower to my hand, and he smirks. "Alright, be my guest."

CHAPTER TEN

ELIJAH

WATCHING Cami struggle to carry the ladder is comical. She's about to take out the dining room chandelier, and no matter how many times I offer to help, she insists she's got it.

I direct her to a spot in the living room where we should check first, but honestly, it could be any one of the smoke detectors. It's too high to actually know until you're closer to it.

"Alright, here is good." I grab one side of the ladder and set it on the floor. "You climbing up or am I?"

"Nope, you stay right there. I'm doing this."

Digging into my pocket, I grab a battery and hand it to her. "Okay, here you go."

Once the ladder is secure, I hold the other side and watch as she carefully climbs it. Her face pales the higher she goes. "You're not afraid of heights, are you?" I ask.

"No. Well, maybe a little."

I snort, chuckling. "Don't worry. I won't let you fall."

"That's very reassuring when I can hear you laughing." She makes it to the second to the top step and reaches the smoke detector. I instruct her on how to remove the old battery.

"Now make sure the positive and negative are lined up correctly."

"Okay, I'm not that stupid," she retorts.

"I'm just trying to be helpful," I say, moving to the other side so I can get a better look. "But if it's wrong, you'll have to go back up and fix it."

She sighs loudly. "Fine. I'll double-check."

Once she snaps it in and secures the cover, I tell her to hold the test button until it beeps. "You did it."

"You doubted me?" she taunts, slowly climbing down. I hold the sides of the ladder even as her ass brushes against me.

"I'd never," I tease, but it's hard to concentrate with her this close.

"I think you can let go now. I can't hurt myself falling from one foot off the ground," she states as my chest presses against her back.

Releasing my grip, I step away, giving her space. "Good job," I tell her when she spins around and faces me. "Only ten more to go."

Her proud expression drops. "Are you serious?"

I grin. "Nah, you got the right one."

She smacks me, and when I cough, her eyes go wide, and she covers her mouth. "Oh, shit. I'm sorry. I forgot already."

My chest still feels a little tight, and not getting enough oxygen exhausts me, but she's been a good distraction.

I haven't had an attack of that magnitude in months, and it's a good thing we never did smoke since there's always a chance that can trigger an attack. I was caught off guard, but I should've known better. The garage hasn't been used in who knows how long, other than Cami parking her Range Rover in there, and there was dust everywhere. As soon as I moved shit around, it triggered my asthma. I typically only need my inhaler when I work out too hard or during allergy season, but I'm thankful she was here to get it for me. Her springing to action and being so concerned made me realize she cares about me more than she lets on.

"You're fine, but maybe don't beat me up right after I can breathe again."

She rolls her eyes and shakes her head. "Now you're just trying to make me feel bad."

"I'd never." I retreat, putting space between us.

"Mm-hmm. Well, it's not gonna work anyway." She takes a step toward me.

Folding my arms over my chest, I step forward. "Don't want your pity anyway, *never have.*"

"Do you have to argue with me on everything?" She closes the gap between us until our bodies press together.

Leaning down, I retort, "Do you have to argue with *me* on everything?"

She narrows her eyes. "Just for that, you can haul that ladder back into the garage on your own."

Smirking, I laugh as she walks around me, and Bruno follows her. Damn dog has already abandoned me for her. Not that I can blame him. She's feisty and somehow even more pretty when she's annoyed. It's probably why I've always enjoyed pressing her buttons so much. Not to mention, it's so easy to get a rise out of her.

Once I get the ladder back in the garage, I head to the kitchen to clean the mess from breakfast and realize she already did it. I see she even figured out the dishwasher.

Well, that's progress.

I head to my room and take a shower, needing to check in with the office. My supervisor has been blowing up my phone all morning, but I've been ignoring him. Not that I ever thought it was possible, but he's somehow been more annoying than usual. I've told him as such, too, which of course he didn't appreciate, but he seriously needs to chill. People aren't spending money unless it's essential, so sales are down company-wide.

By the afternoon, I'm exhausted from staring at my laptop screen, and my stomach is grumbling from hunger, so I get up to go find something to eat. When I get downstairs, I see Bruno has betrayed me and is on the couch with Cami. I'm surprised she's down here, considering how she was feeling this morning. I figured she'd be sleeping or attempting schoolwork.

She continues messing with her phone, so she either doesn't hear me or she's ignoring me. Tiptoeing closer, I look over the sofa and notice she's on TikTok.

Leaning down until I'm in the camera frame, I smirk. "Whatcha doing?"

"Jesus, Eli!" She jumps and quickly spins around. "Stop doing that!"

"Are you making a video?" I ask with amusement. "Can I see it?"

"No, you can't. Go away."

"Oh, come on. I wanna see."

"No!"

Reaching over, I try to grab it from her hand, but she moves away.

"Stop!" She laughs when I climb over the couch and land on top of her. She holds it up above her head, trying to keep it out of my reach.

"What're you hiding? Why can't I watch it?"

"Because it's just a dumb skit, and you'll laugh at me."

"Now I definitely wanna see it." I grin. She shuffles underneath me, and I hold myself up with one hand so I don't crush her.

"Never gonna happen!"

I bring my fingers under her arm and tickle her side. "Oh my God!" She wiggles long enough for me to grab the phone from her grip, and she screams. "No!"

Laughing, I pull back until I get a better view of her screen. With one arm, I hold her back as she struggles to fight against me.

Cami sucker punches me in the gut, causing me to lean forward. She tries swiping it, but I'm faster and move it out of reach.

"Nice try," I say. "You can't hurt steel."

She rolls her eyes at the reference to my abs. "So I should aim lower?"

"God, no. Don't do that." Especially since she's underneath me and my mind is going fucking wild with ideas.

"Give it back and no one gets hurt."

"Just let me see it. How bad can it be?"

She pushes herself up, trying once again to take it, but I pull back just far enough so she can't. With my other hand, I grab her wrist and hold it above her head. Towering over her, I bring my face close to hers.

"The more you fight it, the more I want it." My cock throbs in agreement.

There's a fire behind her eyes as we stare at each other. She brings a hand around my neck and pulls me closer until our mouths connect. My body stiffens for a moment, but when she slides her tongue between my lips, I instantly relax. Cami's legs wrap around my waist, and she arches her back, grinding her body against mine.

I drop the phone, sliding one hand to her face and squeezing her hip with the other.

"Fuck," I growl when she pushes into me harder.

Her hand roams down my body, and I kiss down her jawline until my lips find her ear. "If you think this gets you out of showing me that video, you're sadly mistaken."

Trying to be sneaky, she stretches her arm and searches around the floor for it. Grabbing her elbow, I suck on her neck and stop her. "Nice try, princess."

Pinning her to the couch, I squeeze my hand around her wrists. She attempts to shuffle out of my grip, but I'm too strong.

"You can't distract me with your mouth."

"Is that so?" She licks her lips and lowers her eyes to my noticeable erection. It doesn't help that I'm wearing gym shorts.

I study her and notice the way her body reacts to me. With flushed cheeks, she gasps for air as her chest rapidly rises and falls. She might've used kissing me to get her phone, but she wants this as much as I do. Cami's just as affected as I am but doesn't want to admit it.

Instead of giving in, I grip her hips and flip her over until she's on her stomach so she can't wiggle loose. She squeals as I take her wrists again then put her arms around her back, making sure I'm being careful with her. "What are you doing?" She rests her cheek on the couch and doesn't try to get away.

"Tell me what you want me to do…" I lean down and whisper in her ear. "Did you make a move because you only wanted something or because you want *me*?"

She swallows hard and licks her swollen lips, staying silent.

"You want to use me? Then use me," I challenge.

Blinking, she clears her throat and furrows her brows, trying to look at me. "I'd never do that to you, Eli."

"Good," I say with a smirk. I release my grip, giving her room to leave, but instead, she sucks in her bottom lip and stays put.

Shifting my body, I roam my hands down her back, then slowly lift her shirt. I press my lips to the little dimple above her ass, and she lets out a bated breath. Kissing up her spine, I remove her clothes in the process. Cami releases a moan, and I nearly embarrass myself with the way my cock responds.

She puts her arms between the couch and her body, slightly lifting herself so I can bring a hand around her and cup her bare breast. The softness of her skin almost has me tearing everything off and giving in to what we both want. Pressing my head into the crook of her neck, I groan at how good she feels pressed against me. She shifts and turns slightly until her gaze meets mine. Without a word, I capture her lips with mine, and when she moans, I grab her jaw and deepen the kiss. I taste the sweetness of the syrup she ate with breakfast this morning, and we both fight for more.

My other hand slides up, and I wrap my fist in her hair, slightly tugging. The heat burning between us is so hot, I wouldn't be surprised if that annoying smoke detector started beeping again.

Then the doorbell rings.

What the fuck?

We pull apart, both gasping for air as we look at each other confused.

"Did you hear that?" she asks.

"I did." I furrow my brows. "Are you expecting someone?"

"No. Are you?"

"No." I lift off her, then straighten my shirt and shorts. Holding out my hand, I help Cami to her feet, and she adjusts herself as we stand awkwardly in front of each other. "I'll go check it out."

"I'll come with you."

She follows me as I walk to the front door. I look through the peephole, but don't see anyone. Relief floods through me until I swing it open and see a bouquet of at least two dozen roses on the welcome mat.

I step to the side and watch Cami's reaction.

"I'm gonna take a wild guess and say those are for you."

She releases a heavy sigh and grabs them. The crystal vase alone looks like it easily cost a grand, and I know I can't compete with that. They're obviously from Zane, and no matter what, he'll always have an advantage over me.

Cami takes them into the kitchen, and I shut the door, then follow her. The flame that ignited our hot make-out session has extinguished, and she notices when I walk past her and grab a bottle of water from the fridge.

"So, who are they from?" I ask bitterly, unable to look at her. Chugging the water, I keep my back to her and wait for the inevitable.

"Zane," she responds. "And he left a note."

I finish the bottle, twist the cap back on, then toss it into the trash. "Congrats."

Heading for the staircase, I call Bruno and demand he come upstairs with me.

"Wait," she blurts out.

"What?" I ask over my shoulder.

"Why are you congratulating me?"

I know I'm being a dick, but I'm so goddamn tired of trying to win her over and failing. We take two steps forward, then something like this happens—a reminder that I'll never be good enough for Cameron St. James—and we move five steps backward.

Turning around and facing her, I flash a smirk and shrug. "For getting back what you wanted."

CHAPTER ELEVEN

CAMERON

DAY 6

Staring at the vase of roses on the dresser, I wait to feel something. *Anything.*

I was tempted to throw them out yesterday, but the flowers are beautiful, and I would have felt bad for tossing them. Not because of who sent them, but because it seemed like a waste of a perfect bouquet. I didn't want to upset Eli further, so I brought them to my room

Zane has always showered me with gifts, and I was too blind to see the reason behind them. They'd make me so happy, knowing he thought of me enough to send something so pretty, and I'd forget whatever problems we were having. Then another issue would come up, he'd buy me something else, and the cycle would repeat.

I'm an idiot for not realizing this sooner and allowing this nonsense to happen for as long as it did.

But now, I look at this bouquet and feel nothing. Well, except indifference. I couldn't care less about him or that he's trying to win me back.

To my dearest Cameron:
I was stupid for breaking your heart. Please forgive me and let me make
things right again.
I love you.
-Zane

If I had to guess, Kendall started a rumor about Eli and me, and it got back to him. She was never his biggest fan, and him breaking up with me pissed her off even more. I'd bet my trust fund she had something to do with his miraculous change of heart.

But honestly, fuck him.

Nothing could make me take him back nor do I want to.

In the past week, I've seen a new perspective in life, and it's nothing like the one I had during the two years we dated. For all I care, Zane can jump off a bridge and forget that I exist. The only man I *do* care about isn't talking to me and avoided me last night. I plan to do whatever I can to help push his insecurities away. I nearly melted against him yesterday, after finally giving in to my inhibitions, and he left me high and dry because a bouquet of roses that I don't even want arrived.

As I undress and get into the shower, I think back to our younger years before we fought all the time. We were close until I ruined it by picking my snobby rich friends over him. I don't even know why I did it aside from wanting to be liked by the popular girls. My mother's constant pressure to fit in didn't help either. There was no excuse for treating him the way I did, and I will make it up to him. The last thing he deserves is to feel less than because of our past because right now, I don't feel good enough for him.

Remembering the way he touched and kissed me has my body temperature rising all over again. The warm water melts across my skin as I slide my hand between my legs. I rub circles over my clit, and my eyes roll into the back of my head. Imagining Eli's fingers on me along with his bedroom eyes have me moaning until the buildup is too much. I bite down on my lower lip to keep from screaming his name. It was so intense, I stand under the stream until I catch my breath.

I dry off, get dressed, then fix my hair. For the first time in ages, I feel brave enough to finally go after who *I* truly want. Deciding to take advantage of this newfound courage, I leave my room and go to the second level.

My heart hammers in my chest as I knock on his door. Waiting for him to answer has me sweating with the anticipation of what I'm about to do, but he doesn't answer. I take the stairs and check in the kitchen, but he's not there either. There are two plates on the table and a covered dish. He made breakfast, but he's not here.

Where the hell could he have gone?

The gym.

Taking the stairs to the basement, I hear the clanking of the weights as he works out. Peering around the corner, I spot him on the bench press in a sleeveless T-shirt and black gym shorts. His hair is pulled up, and sweat's dripping down his neck.

Weirdly enough, it's fucking hot.

I'm in my leggings and NYU shirt, looking like a hot mess, but I don't care because it's comfortable as hell.

I walk in, waiting for him to finish his reps so I don't scare him. He's wearing earbuds and is breathing hard, so I know he can't hear me, but it doesn't stop me from watching. I'm completely mesmerized by his focus and strength.

Eli sits up and finally looks in the mirror across from him. His eyes shoot to mine, and he arches a brow as he reaches for his phone and pauses the music.

"Enjoying the show?"

Leaning against the doorframe, I cross my arms over my chest and grin. "Actually, I was."

He turns and faces me, then grabs his bottle of water from the floor. Our eyes stay locked as he inhales his drink, and the intensity of our gaze has me second-guessing my plan, but I'm determined to do this.

No more being a coward.

"Did you make breakfast, then bail?" I ask.

He stands and saunters toward me. "I've been waiting for you."

"Why didn't you tell me? I thought you didn't want me around after yesterday," I say shyly.

"I've been waiting for you," he repeats, closing the gap between us. "For a *long* fucking time."

I blink, swallowing down the lump in my throat. "It's only ten," I counter.

He chuckles softly, the corner of his lips turn up into a panty-dropping smirk. "Years, Cami. I've been waiting for you to finally see me, and as soon as you did, reality smacked me in the face, and I remembered you're not mine. Never have been." He brushes his arm over his forehead. "You just got out of a relationship, and I shouldn't have crossed the line, but the temptation was too hard to resist."

"I wasn't saying no," I tell him. "I kissed you first yesterday."

"I know, but—"

"But *nothing*," I interrupt, tilting my head at him. "Stop trying to convince yourself that you're not good enough for me because that couldn't be further from the truth. I'm not worthy of *you*." Licking my lips, I bring a hand to his chest and fist his shirt, yanking his face lower. "If that doorbell hadn't interrupted us, we would've ended up naked on that couch, and my only regret would've been that it didn't happen sooner."

His intense stare burns through me, and I anxiously await his reaction.

"I don't want to be your rebound, Cami. Or your quarantine fling. So unless you can say with one hundred percent certainty it's not, then I can't. Don't give me false hope. Please," he begs.

"I swear it's not like that at all," I whisper, panic building inside me. "I want you, Eli. I've always wanted you."

He clenches his jaw, not saying a word, but he continues to stare. After a moment, he blinks. "Say it again."

Butterflies invade my stomach at the roughness of his voice, demanding and sultry. "Kiss me. I want *you*, Elijah Ross."

One second, my feet are on the floor, and the next, they're wrapped around his waist. My back presses against the wall as our lips collide. My arms grip his shoulders, holding him tightly as he effortlessly supports me with one palm under my ass. Our tongues tangle together, and we're barely breathing as we desperately taste each other.

I moan against his mouth as he pushes into me, and I feel how hard he is for me. He was turned on yesterday too, and my mind went wild, imagining how it'd feel to touch.

"Fuck, Cami," Eli whispers my name with painful exaggeration before moving his lips over my jaw.

My head falls back as he sucks on my neck. It sends heat straight between my legs. I want his tongue and fingers there, but honestly, I want all of him, everywhere. *Now.*

"I need you inside me," I plead as he presses himself into me again.

"Christ," he hisses. "I want to, Cami. I really do…"

"But?" I meet his hardened gaze. "What's the problem?"

"I don't have any condoms," he responds.

Furrowing my brows, I ask, "You don't? Seriously?"

He sucks in his lower lip and shrugs. "I was coming up here to isolate, *alone*. Didn't know I'd need them."

Shit. He's right. I don't have any either because Zane was bringing his stash.

"Any chance you think Amazon would deem them essential and overnight them?"

Eli laughs. "Maybe it's a good thing. It'll force us to go slow."

"That sounds like the opposite of fun, though." I stick out my lower lip and pretend to pout.

"Ohh, Cami. How wrong you are." He releases me until my feet touch the floor, then he kneels in front of me, grabbing the hem of my leggings and pulling them down to my ankles.

"Did you forget something?" He arches a brow as I step out of them.

"No, I shaved this morning, thank you."

He tilts his head and licks his lips. "I can see that."

"Oh, no panties. That's because I came down here to seduce you," I tell him matter-of-factly and am almost embarrassed by how quickly I blurted that out.

"Jesus," he chokes out. "You're making it hard to say no."

"Then don't," I say. "I'm on the pill and always get my annual screening." If he doesn't touch me soon, I won't be able to stop rambling.

He groans, wrapping his fingers around my thighs. "Spread your legs."

I part my feet, my heart beating faster with every eager second. Eli moves a hand up and slowly brings a finger to my pussy, then slides it across my slit. "You're already wet."

"Mm-hmm," I hum, my eyes rolling. He's torturing me. "I wasn't lying when I said I wanted you."

"I guess not," he says, chuckling softly.

If I admired his facial hair before, it's nothing compared to how it feels when it rubs against my skin. It's rough and tickles, and I crave more of him. His tongue slides to my clit, and he squeezes it between his lips.

"Oh my God." My fingers curl in his hair as the sensations ripple through me. "Don't stop. Please, for the love of all that's holy, do not stop."

"Don't worry, *princess*." He emphasizes the nickname he's called me for years, except this time it sounds sweet and hungry. "I could please you for fucking hours."

My back arches as he pushes two digits inside me. The pressure feels incredible as he fucks me with his fingers and flicks his tongue against my sensitive spot. The buildup comes fast, and soon, I'm falling over the edge as he increases his pace, driving as deep as he can.

I clench my teeth, then moan out his name, breathing rapidly as I come down from the highest high I've ever had. Eli doesn't stop like I expected and continues his sweet torture.

"You thought I was done?" He flashes a cocky grin. "I'm just getting started with you." He stands and takes my hand, guiding me to one of the equipment benches. "Lie down."

My brows rise in hesitation. Eli nods his head toward it, encouraging me to oblige. Before I do, I grab the bottom of my shirt and take it off. If being naked doesn't drive him as insane as he's making me, then I don't know what will.

"Jesus fuck," he grunts. "What are you trying to do to me?" He kneels with me spread in front of him. Bending my knees, he pulls my ass closer and places his mouth back between my thighs.

Feeling his fingers and mouth on me is so damn intense that everything goes white, and stars invade my vision. I fist my hands in my hair, trying to breathe through the best orgasm I've ever experienced.

"I need you," I whimper, begging him to fuck me. "Inside me."

"Cami," he growls, wiping his mouth as he stands. "Don't tempt me."

"Don't deny me."

"I just gave you like five orgasms. There was no denying."

Laughing, I sit up and am eye level with his crotch. He's so hard; I can't stop myself from touching him outside his shorts. Thick and big. He steps back, and my hand drops.

"No."

"No? You don't want me to return the favor?" I arch a brow.

"I do. I *really, really* do, but the moment your mouth is on me, my willpower will snap."

I smirk, knowing he's struggling as much as I am. "Well, you either let me take care of that or you get to jerk off in the shower like I did earlier."

He swallows hard, groaning. "You didn't."

"I swear! The real thing, though? One thousand percent better, so let me."

"I'm walking away now. Put your clothes on and meet me upstairs for breakfast." He steps toward the doorway.

My arms drop to my sides, and my jaw nearly hits the floor. "Are you serious?"

"Cami," he pleads. "Trust me. I'm going to rub my dick raw later thinking about you, but we can't just jump into sex."

Rejected. *Again.*

CHAPTER TWELVE

ELIJAH

CAMI IS the sexiest woman I've ever laid eyes on, but damn, when she's annoyed, she's somehow even sexier.

It's quite fucking adorable too how hard she's trying not to be mad when I know she is. With her shoulders squared and her nose in the air, she walks to the table and silently sits.

"Good morning," I say, holding back a smile. "I warmed this up, so it's nice and hot."

"Great," she grits out. "What is it?"

"French toast with berries."

"Sounds *delicious*," she blurts out, flashing me a fake grin. It's hard to keep a straight face when she's worked up like this. But if there's one thing I've learned about Cami, it's that she's used to getting her way.

Not this time, though, and it's killing her.

I might be getting a bit too much enjoyment out of this, but it's best for both of us that I not cave. It doesn't erase how much I desperately want her. I've always used a condom, but *when* Cami and I cross that bridge, I don't want anything between us anyway. I could tell her that, but watching her squirm is far too entertaining.

I place the syrup and butter on the table, and after she puts them on her food, I hold out a small bowl. "Powdered sugar?" I ask.

She narrows her eyes, grabbing her fork. "Sure. Why not?"

"It's tasty. Especially with the cinnamon in the mixture."

"Load me up then." She moves her plate closer.

I snort, shaking my head at her fierce determination to be bitter. "My pleasure."

We eat in silence, casually stealing glances across the table. She keeps a pissed-off expression as she chews even though she's obviously enjoying each bite by the way she scarfs it down. Once our plates are nearly cleaned, I stretch my leg underneath the table until it touches hers. At first, she flinches, but I continue until my foot reaches between her thighs.

"What do you think you're doing?" She gives me an incredulous look.

"Checking if you're still wet for me."

With the corner of her mouth tilted up slightly, she pushes her chair back until my foot falls. I watch her closely and am confused as hell when she slides down to the floor and crawls between my legs.

"Uh…" I pull back, but she grips the hem of my shorts and yanks them down. "Cami…" I lower my voice, pushing the chair out from under the table. "You better not."

Her delicate fingers wrap around my shaft, and my entire body succumbs to her touch.

Fuck. Me.

She rises up on her knees just enough to place her lips around the tip of my cock, and I scramble to move away because she's testing my control. However, she digs her nails into my thigh with one hand while gripping my length with the other and halts me in place. The moment I feel her hot breath brush over my sensitive skin, I know I don't have a fighting chance to resist her.

I've wanted her for so long and can't deny how incredible it feels to have her mouth on me. Tilting my head, I watch as she devours every inch of me. I fist her hair and admire how gorgeous she looks on her knees.

"You suck me so fucking good, Cami." My eyes roll back. She twists her wrists, stroking me faster and harder while twirling her tongue like a goddamn goddess. "*Shit.*"

My arms fall, unable to concentrate on anything other than how good she's making me feel. I'm already close and about to explode. With a loud pop, Cami leans back and wipes her mouth. She flashes a wide, perfect smile, then gets to her feet.

Confused, I glare at her. "Uh…" I clear my throat, unsure of what I'm supposed to say.

"You finish inside me, or you don't finish at all."

"You know I can just get myself off, right?" I challenge, shifting uncomfortably in the chair.

"Sure, but you'll have to live with the fact that you chose your hand over my pussy."

"Cami," I growl. "Quit being a sadist and get your sexy mouth over here."

"Mmm…nah. Good luck with that." She points at my painful erection and winks, then walks away.

I'm not about to let her get her way and win, so I quickly pull up my shorts and follow her. She sees me coming and runs.

"No! Go away!" she scream-laughs, rushing up the stairs as fast as she can. Before she gets to the third floor, I grab her wrist and yank her to my chest.

We're both panting and smiling as she tries to escape my grip. "Where do you think you're going?"

"To my room. *Alone.*"

"Wouldn't you rather have some company?" I arch a brow, pushing her into the wall with my hips so she can feel my cock rub against her. If she wants to play games with me, I'll make the next move and show her who's gonna win this battle.

She glares at me, looking like pure temptation, and shrugs. "I got off. You're the one with blue balls."

Burying my face in her neck, I chuckle against her ear as I slide my hands over her body. "I have plenty of bikini images of you in my spank bank to finish what you started, but you wanna know the best part? You're not talking in any of them. I'll blow my load in less than ten seconds flat."

Cami gasps, pushing hard against my chest, and I release her. She sneers and takes off to her room, slamming the door behind her.

I can't help laughing as I make my way to the kitchen to clean up the mess. She has no idea what she's in for if she thinks I'm just another person who'll give in to her demands with the snap of her fingers. Granted, I want to fuck her senseless until we're both panting, but I'm not giving in that easily. If she wants me, she's going to have to work for it.

After everything is cleaned, I take Bruno outside for his daily exercise, then jump in the shower. I can't wipe the grin off my dopey face when I relive Cami's lips on me. That image will forever be ingrained in my mind no matter what. It's a fantasy I've had since I was a teenager, and as soon as it became a reality, it was programmed into my eternal memory.

I reply to emails and take a couple of video calls to appease my boss, but it's a waste of time, considering nothing's changed in the past few days. I'm keeping in contact with my clients and trying to prove myself, but I refuse to be annoying and pushy when so many jobs have been furloughed, and people have been laid off. I'm fortunate I can do some of my work from home and still earn a paycheck, so I'm not taking that for granted, but I'm also empathic.

I can put people first and be good at my job, regardless of what my supervisor thinks.

Checking my phone, I notice a missed call from Ryan and immediately worry. I return it, but he doesn't answer, so I text him instead.

Elijah: Sorry I missed your call. I was on a conference call. Everything okay?

Ten minutes later, he finally responds.

Ryan: As much as it can be, I suppose. Shit is freaking crazy here. Just checking on you guys. Cameron said you had an asthma attack yesterday. Are you alright?

I'm surprised Cami told him or that she's talking about me to him period. I'm tempted to ask if she mentioned the panic attack she had the other day, but I won't air her business in case she doesn't want him to know.

Elijah: I'm fine. Freaked her out, though. She nearly nose-dived the concrete running to get my inhaler.

Ryan: She would've had a royal meltdown if that had happened.

Elijah: Trust me, I saw a glimpse of that while she changed the smoke detector battery.

Ryan: You mean you got her to actually help? What kind of spell did you cast on my sister?

I'm tempted to fuck with him and tell him what else I got her to do, but I don't need him thinking I'm using her because I'm not. I also don't want a brotherly speech from him about not hurting her. He knew how much I crushed on her in high school, but he has no idea it never stopped.

Elijah: It's the quarantine, man. She even loaded the dishwasher this morning.

Ryan: Shit. I think she's cracked.

Elijah: Haha…wouldn't surprise me. She's gonna have a hard lesson in doing laundry soon.

I chuckle to myself because I'm almost certain she's gonna need to wash her clothes in a few days.

Ryan: Just don't let her near the stove. She'll burn down the cabin, and then you'll both be homeless or recovering in the burn unit.

Elijah: Considering she doesn't know how to turn it on, I'm not too worried. I've been cooking to prevent any hazards.

I feel guilty talking shit about Cami to her brother, but if I start throwing out compliments, he'll grow suspicious.

Ryan: Good. I wouldn't be surprised if this shit lasts for months, so get comfortable.

I'm torn on how I feel about that. Honestly, I don't mind being away from the city, especially with Cami here, but the consequences of an epidemic are terrifying. What long-term effects will it have on the people and our economy? Only time will tell.

Elijah: Please be safe. I worry about you.

Ryan: I'm doing my best with what we've got. Taking all the precautions I can.

Ryan: I gotta run. Love you, man. Take care over there, okay?

Elijah: Will do! Stay safe!

I set my phone down and say a quick prayer for my best friend and all the frontline workers. I've always looked up to him, but now even more. Ryan's my hero.

Though I read the news every morning before I get out of bed, I only allow myself ten minutes because the government's handling of this is a mess. No one can agree on anything, and it's like watching toddlers fighting over toys. Watching the press conferences or reading the briefings only spike my anxiety and nerves, and if there's anything I can control during this time, it's how much outside noise I allow in while keeping my ass at home.

Deciding I need a break and to leave this room, I head downstairs with Bruno, plop on the couch, and click on Netflix. I'm in the mood for something that'll keep me interested for a few hours, so I end up clicking on an original documentary about a guy who owns a tiger zoo and needs a different hairdresser. Within thirty minutes, I've asked myself *what the fuck* at least a dozen times.

"This guy is bat-shit crazy," I mutter after finishing the second episode. It's a train wreck, but I can't look away and end up clicking on the third episode.

"Who's bat-shit crazy?"

I look over my shoulder and see Cami holding her cat as she walks toward me.

"This redneck with a bleached mullet," I explain. She's quieter than usual and looks nervous. "What are you doing down here?" I assumed she'd stay in her room the rest of the night, doing homework and staying pissed at me.

She shrugs, biting down on her plump lower lip. "I got hungry, and I need to refill Chanel's water."

"I could make something," I offer. "I'm hungry too."

"Okay, thanks." She rounds the corner and sits in the recliner. "Wanna watch the first episode while I cook? Or I can give you a recap and catch you up?"

"Sure, I'll start it, and you can fill me in on the rest when you're back," she says sweetly. The tension in the room is so thick, I nearly choke on it, but we're not bickering, so I won't set her off on purpose.

I restart the first episode and smirk. "Get ready for the best shitshow of your life."

Cami shivers and reaches for a throw blanket.

"Are you cold?" I ask. "I can make a fire." One of the best things about this cabin is the wood-burning fireplace. None of that propane, press a button crap.

Yesterday, I noticed there wasn't much wood left, but maybe enough to last tonight. There might be more in the shed, but if not, I'll have to chop some so we have it for the next few weeks.

"Yeah, that'd be nice," she answers.

I get it started, and her face contorts when the first episode begins. It makes me laugh.

"This is what you've been watching?" She looks just as confused as I was.

"Hey, I'm blaming it on the quarantine. Plus, the memes I've seen for this are fucking hilarious, so I had to see it for myself. So far, it hasn't disappointed in the entertainment department."

"But why does he look like that?" She cringes, curling her legs underneath her and settling into the seat. She's more invested than she's willing to admit.

I dig through the fridge and pantry, trying to figure out what to make us. I'm in the mood for some comfort food, and when I see the can of tomato soup, I remember how she said she was craving a grilled cheese sandwich yesterday.

Grabbing all the ingredients, I put together four sandwiches and two bowls of soup, then grab a few napkins. It looks so damn good, I'm ready to dive in before I deliver it to her.

"Oh my God. That smells heavenly," she says, moaning when I set it all on the coffee table. She perks up, her mouth opening in surprise. "You remembered. Thought you said I had to make this for you?" She raises her brows.

"Sounded too good to risk you screwing it up," I tease.

She stares at me for a moment, her eyes softening as I meet her gaze. "Thank you for this."

"You're welcome." I take a seat on the couch and reach for one of the plates and bowls. "I wasn't sure if you liked extra cheese in your tomato soup, but I sprinkled some in anyway." I grin, remembering how dead set she was on eating low-fat cheese when we arrived.

"Mmm." She hums around a spoonful. "So good."

"You better calm down over there. You're getting my dick excited with all that moaning."

Cami quickly covers her mouth as she spurts hot liquid from her lips. Her shoulders bounce up and down as she laughs, trying to swallow down the soup. "Don't say shit like that when I'm eating." She wipes her mouth on a napkin.

Chuckling, I shrug. "Sorry. Don't moan like that then." Though I *really* like hearing it come from her. Especially when she's underneath me.

"I was moaning about the *food*," she emphasizes. "Quit being a perv."

I flash a smirk when she glares at me. "Don't make noises that remind me what it felt like having your mouth on me."

She blushes, and instead of throwing a retort at me, she focuses on the TV and tries to ignore me. It's cute, but this is just foreplay for me.

Driving Cami insane the same way she drove me wild is just the beginning of what I know is to come.

CHAPTER THIRTEEN

CAMERON

DAY 7

I'VE BEEN at the Roxbury cabin for a week, and somehow, it feels like a month has passed. Though it hasn't been horrible, it's been a drastic change from my normal routine.

My daily schedule used to consist of two to four classes, meeting up with friends for lunch or a quick shopping trip, and then studying for a bit before Zane and I went out for dinner. On the days I only had a couple of classes, I'd work out or go to a yoga class with Kendall. We'd also do spa days every week that consisted of pedis, manis, and body waxes. Massages were a bi-weekly adventure, and my hair would get cut or colored every four weeks. If the paparazzi are going to take pictures of me, the least I could do was try to look put together to avoid their criticism, but that didn't always work. They'd catch me off guard, then blast rumors. Oftentimes, I wouldn't feel good enough based on what they wrote, and my self-esteem would take a hit. Regardless of their opinions, I took so much for granted and kinda miss my old lifestyle. I don't know if things will ever be like it was before. In a few months, I'll be graduating with my undergrad degree, then I'll start my postgraduate classes. Eventually, I'll take over more responsibility in the company while I finish my master's, and then I will shift to a higher position. I shouldn't complain, but I'm grieving everything I was accustomed to.

But it could definitely be worse, so I'm counting my blessings. I remind myself this isn't forever. It's temporary, and if Ryan and all the other essential workers can risk their lives and work on the front lines, then I can suck it up and stay here for as long as it takes.

After my embarrassing tantrum in front of Eli yesterday, I know I'm slowly losing it. Being trapped here should be fucking easy. I'm safe. I have everything I need and more, but I'm going stir-crazy without being able to see my classmates, professors, friends, brother, and parents.

I didn't anticipate the emotional aspect. I'm pretty stable, considering all the shit I've had to deal with in my life, and I just wish people knew the *real* me.

The media never highlights the positive things I do. They never talk about how I donate my time to help charities, attend fundraisers, rally for women's rights and equality for all, and I even proposed grants for underprivileged students so they could afford to attend NYU. Unfortunately, the tabloids have created a persona that's not me, and I'm not sure if I'll ever have an identity of my own. The biggest disappointment is knowing Elijah grew up thinking those things about me too. Though I haven't always presented myself in the best way, I'm still human and make mistakes. And I can admit when I'm wrong or I've overreacted.

I felt awful for the way I treated Eli yesterday, so that's why I went into the living room. Besides being hungry, I wanted to see if he was downstairs so I could apologize. Instead of ignoring me like I deserved, he brushed it off and made me the best damn grilled cheese I've ever had. As we watched his weird but equally entertaining documentary and ate our dinner, the fire crackled. It was the most relaxed I'd been in days. The setting felt romantic, but after the way things ended earlier in the day with me on my knees under the table, I was too embarrassed to sit on the couch next to him.

Eli's the most forgiving person I've ever met. He didn't force me to admit my wrongdoings, so I want to thank him and return the favor.

It won't be much, but I'm going to try to make breakfast this morning and hopefully smooth things over with him. If we're going to get through this together, we can't argue like we have the past seven days.

Chanel rolls to her back, waiting for me to give her tummy scratches. The sunlight beams through the drapes, and I know if I'm going to beat Eli to the kitchen, I need to get moving.

"C'mon, girl. We can't stay in bed all day." I pet her for a moment, then push off the covers.

As soon as I stand, I hear a weird noise. A loud, continuous thumping echoes and when I peek out the window, I see Eli by the shed chopping wood. He's in dark blue jeans, a college sweatshirt, and wearing a beanie with his hair down. Simple but somehow, so damn sexy. Bruno runs around barking, happier than ever, and buries his nose in the snow as he eats it.

I'm mesmerized as I watch Eli pull his arms back and strike the log, splitting it in half. He makes it look so effortless. Without him here, I'd be fucking doomed. Even if Zane hadn't broken up with me, we might've lasted forty-eight hours without calling our parents to rescue us. I appreciate Ryan sending Eli here more than he'll ever know. Otherwise, I'm not sure what I would've done.

I head to the kitchen and am relieved when I don't see breakfast already made. He probably doesn't expect me up this early, which is perfect. I can ace college exams and outsmart professors who've been teaching for decades but ask me how to make an omelet, and I become a freaking moron. But hell, I'm determined to learn.

Digging out the egg carton, shredded cheese, and ham, I set

everything on the counter, then grab my phone to search for a YouTube tutorial. Undoubtedly, someone's made an instructional video on how to properly do this.

I'm relieved to find a decent one by an actual chef and get started. I dice the ham steak first, then crack three eggs into a bowl and whip them with a fork. The instructor says to use an eight-inch pan, and when I dig around the cupboard, there's at least three different sizes. Shamelessly, I picture Eli's cock and figure out which one is eight inches by how big he is.

Next, I turn on the stove and add the vegetable oil and butter to the pan like I'm told. "That's a lot of freaking butter," I murmur when I see how much coats the bottom.

Once it's hot, I add in the whipped eggs. It sizzles and the oil flicks up and burns my finger.

"Fuck," I hiss, grabbing a towel, then rewind the video, knowing I missed a step.

I'm confused as hell and quickly dig around in the drawers in search of the same utensil used by the instructor. Realizing we don't have one, I grab the next best thing, which looks like some kind of flipper device.

Good enough.

As I move the eggs around like he is, it splatters and burns me again.

"Ouch! Goddammit," I growl, stepping as far away from the stove as possible while still somehow reaching the pan. I keep listening to the video and try to do what he says, but honestly, this is a mini-disaster waiting to happen.

"Next, you're going to carefully flip the omelet, and while sometimes it breaks, just roll with it and flatten it out," the instructor continues.

"Yeah, easy for you to say…" I mutter, stepping closer and trying my best to flip the damn thing. It goes as expected—half flipped, half smooshed. I try to even it out so it's level and the other side can cook.

While that happens, I add in the ham and cheese, then allow it to cook for a few more minutes.

Once it looks done, I grab a plate and try to slide it on there without dropping it.

"Well, that looks horrendous." I set the pan to the side and stare at the saddest omelet I've ever seen. I add more ham pieces and cheese on top so he won't notice how badly I botched it.

Grabbing the loaf of bread, I slip two pieces into the toaster. Once it's ready, I slather on butter and set them next to the heaping mess on the plate.

Bruno comes charging in just as I place the dish on the table. Eli follows, and we lock eyes. The intensity behind them has my entire body burning with desire.

"Morning," he greets, carrying a stack of wood in his arms. "Did you...cook?" He sniffs, then grins.

"Yes." I quickly clear my dry throat. "Well, I *tried*."

He blinks, then chuckles. "Smells good."

"Hopefully, it's edible. I wanted to make breakfast to repay you."

Eli walks in farther and goes to the living room, then drops the wood by the fireplace. He pulls off his gloves and sets them on the island, noticing the huge mess I've made.

"You didn't have to do that," he says softly. "But I'm starving, so I appreciate it."

"It's on the table," I tell him. "Do you want some coffee?"

"Sure, I'd love some."

He sits down and dives in, moaning as he chews. I make him a cup of black coffee, and when I bring it to him, half of the omelet is already gone.

"This is really good, Cami," he mumbles around a mouthful. "You really made this?"

"I have the oil burns to prove it." I chuckle. "Admittedly, I had to watch an instructional video. Don't judge me."

Eli licks his lips, holding back his laughter, but there's

amusement in his eyes. The whole thing is pretty hilarious. Poor rich girl who's twenty-two can't cook to save her life and has to research the simplest recipes. Regardless, I'm determined as hell to take advantage of this situation and learn some useful basic skills.

"No judging." He holds up his fork, taking another large bite. "It's delicious. In fact, now that I know you can cook, I'll be expecting this every morning."

My head falls back with laughter, but his encouragement warms my heart. It's nice to hear that it wasn't a complete epic fail.

"Baby steps," I mock. "There are one-minute how-to-cook videos on TikTok, so I might be able to learn a second dish before this is all over."

"I have a super easy one called toad in a hole. It'd be really hard to screw that up."

I furrow my brows. "Toad in a hole? Where you fry the eggs in the middle of a piece of bread?"

He confirms with a nod.

"Then you mean egg in a basket." I fold my arms, challenging his weird name. I've never made it, but our chef did when Ryan and I were kids.

He scrunches his nose and shakes his head. "Toad. In. A. Hole," he emphasizes slowly. "Is the correct term. Fight me." He smirks.

"That doesn't even make sense. If you're going with an animal, wouldn't it be chick in a hole?"

He snickers, shrugging. "Aren't you going to eat anything?" he asks once he realizes I don't have a plate.

I cock my head, pursing my lips. "It was hard enough making one omelet. I'm not pressing my luck again."

"Cami."

"Stop, I'm fine. I wanted a smoothie anyway." I slide the chair back and stand.

"Let me make you something as a thank you for breakfast," he urges. "Please."

"No way!" I scold, walking to the kitchen island to clean up. "I made you that as a thank you. You can't thank me for thanking you."

He squints, grabs his plate, then walks toward me. "Wait, what?"

I sigh. "You've cooked since we got here, so I wanted to repay you for that. You can't in return thank me for it when I was already thanking you."

"Says who?" he challenges, setting his empty dish in the sink.

"Me," I remark. "If it'll make you feel better, I'll eat a big lunch."

"Hmm." He thinks it over, brushing his fingers over his scruffy jawline. "Alright, fine. But lunch is in an hour then."

"Oh my God." I shake my head, laughing at his persistence. I open the dishwasher and load it, add in the detergent, then hit start.

Eli silently watches me with an amused expression as he leans against the counter, crossing his ankles.

"What?" I ask. "Why are you staring at me like that?"

"Just thinking how sexy you look right now." I was certain he was going to make some smart-ass comment about me using the dishwasher properly, but I hadn't expected *that*.

I look down at my outfit, which consists of the same clothes I wore to bed. Normally, I'd never be caught wearing loungewear around anyone other than my family, but I'm comfortable around Eli. Plus, he doesn't care about any of that.

"You mean, greasy hair and an unwashed face are your kink?" I release a dramatic gasp. "Who knew?"

"Actually, I was thinking you being all domestic and shit makes me horny as fuck."

I set my hands on my hips and narrow my eyes at him. "Let me guess, you want your woman barefoot and pregnant, am I right? A traditional housewife, dinner on the table at six every night, sex on Saturday nights after *SNL*."

"Oh, there'd be sex *every* night," he retorts. "Especially if I want to keep you knocked up."

"Well, sorry to burst your 1950s era bubble, but I plan to have a career," I state matter-of-factly.

His shoulders rise and fall. "So? Have a career. You can be a mom and wife at the same time. Millions of women do."

"And what will you do? Chop wood and fix light bulbs while I raise the kids and bring home the bacon?"

He smirks. "I'll pick up the kids from school, take them to the park to play, then bring them home. I'll give them a bath, then read them a bedtime story. Once they're asleep, I'll pleasure my wife and make sure she goes to bed completely satisfied."

"Wow. Sounds like you have it all figured out."

He bobs his head back and forth, pushing off the counter. "Except for a few minor details."

"Like what? Pussy or anal?"

His cocky smirk returns as he takes a step toward me. "Is everything about sex for you?"

I roll my eyes, leaning against the island. "What then?"

"I'd prefer to marry a woman who wants me as much as I want her. I don't mind the chase, the challenges even, but I don't want to constantly second-guess her feelings for me."

A lump forms in my throat, and butterflies swarm in my stomach. His reference is about me, and the way I've been hot and cold. It's no wonder he's confused.

Hell, I was confused by the way I acted just days ago.

"So what could she say or do to help alleviate those fears?" Our eyes lock on each other, and my rapid breathing echoes between us.

"She could be honest," he states, closing the gap until he's standing in front of me.

Swallowing hard, I suck in my lower lip and feel the heat from his gaze burn into my skin. He wants a real answer—not based on just the physical aspects but the emotional too—and I've never been good at that. I've struggled with who to trust and how much of myself to give to keep from getting hurt. Growing up, I had numerous friends who I thought would be my ride or dies, but they'd use me, then toss me out like trash. That emotional wall was built to help protect myself. But if anyone's capable and worthy of protecting my heart, it's Eli.

"I want *you*," I admit. "Even through the constant arguing and teasing, I've wanted you. I convinced myself it'd never happen, so I pushed you away instead, but don't think for a moment I didn't care about you or wasn't attracted to you. I was and still am."

I inhale sharply as he palms my face and brings his mouth close. Not quite touching, but just enough to feel his hot breath against my lips.

"I never want us to stop arguing or teasing each other because that means the fire is still there. We're both a little hotheaded but at the same time, down to earth and easygoing. We share a lot of common traits but have a lot of opposite interests. I'm someone who enjoys cooking, and you're someone who enjoys eating."

"So, what you mean is we're a match made in heaven?" I smile.

He plucks the pad of his thumb over my bottom lip. "Precisely."

I gulp. "Are you going to kiss me yet?"

"I was thinking about it." His deep voice rumbles low in his throat, sending vibrations between my legs.

"What are you waiting for?" I challenge, feeling more anxious with each passing second.

"To see if you're going to change your mind."

Without hesitation, I fist his sweatshirt and pull him toward me until our mouths collide.

He tilts my head back as he deepens the kiss. My arms wrap around his shoulders, and he quickly slides his hands down until he grabs my ass and lifts me off my feet. My legs go around his waist as he sets me on the island counter and settles between my thighs.

The last time we had a heated moment was on the couch, and the damn doorbell rang, interrupting what I had hoped would turn into more, but knowing he doesn't have a condom has me wondering how far we'll go.

"I still don't—"

"I know," I say, breathing heavily. "It doesn't matter. I want you."

Eli releases a deep moan, moving his mouth lower to my neck. "I agree, but not yet."

My arms drop to my sides, and I groan in frustration. "We've waited long enough," I argue. "If you add in all the years we pined over each other, it's overdue at this point."

He pulls back slightly with a mischievous grin. "When I imagined being inside you for the first time, it's not like this. Not when I've been sweating and chopping wood all morning. I want to wine and dine you first."

"Seriously? You're worried about *that*?"

"It should be romantic," he states. "And I'll try my best, considering..."

"Okay, so how much time do you need? I can be shaved and showered in an hour."

He snickers, shaking his head. "Gimme a few days."

My eyes widen in horror. "*Days*?"

"Anything worth having is worth waiting for."

"Don't get poetic on me."

He leans in and softly brushes his lips against mine. "You're even more adorable when you're sexually frustrated."

"Imagine when I'm sexually satisfied," I counter.

His whole body shakes with laughter. "The longer we wait, the better it'll be. I promise."

"I'm willing to prove that theory wrong."

"Don't challenge me, Cami. Resisting you is something I've

perfected over the years. You're at level one while I'm at level fifty. You really wanna play this game?"

"Sure, let's gamble," I say confidently. "You have to resist me while I seduce the shit out of you. If you crack, and we end up in bed together, I win."

"Technically, if I give in, we both win."

I bite my lip, grinning. "But I'll have bragging rights for life."

CHAPTER FOURTEEN

ELIJAH

I'M EITHER a genius or the biggest fucking idiot in the world for telling Cami I wanted to wait a little while longer.

Now, it's a game to her. She wants me as badly as I want her, and she's ready to do whatever it takes to make me crack.

As much as I want to give in to what I've fantasized about since we were teenagers, I'm determined to resist her.

Cami saunters around the kitchen and prepares her smoothie. I watch carefully as she puts fruit, yogurt, and milk into a blender, and when she looks over her shoulder and winks, I know it's game on. She's not gonna make this easy, no matter what I do or say.

I help clean up the counters and wipe everything down while she pours her drink into a glass. Walking into the kitchen to find her cooking for me was a nice surprise, but I actually enjoy making her food. It's the one thing I can offer that isn't about money or status.

"You have a lot of schoolwork to do today?" I ask casually with her back to me.

"Nope. Planned to take the day off, but now it looks like I'll have nothing to do." She shrugs, then takes a sip of her drink. "Any ideas what I could do?"

Fuck, she's cute when she wants something. Who knew someday it'd be *me*?

Walking up behind her, I wrap my arms around her waist and bury my head in the crook of her neck. She instantly freezes at my touch, then melts her body against mine. "You could relax for a change and watch a movie with me," I whisper. "Cuddle, you know, that sorta thing."

"Cuddle? You cuddle, huh?" She turns and faces me, and I quickly give her a peck. She sinks into me, but I stop it before things get too heated. I'm determined to keep the willpower I've controlled around her for years.

"I'm a great cuddler. You should see for yourself," I offer with a smirk. "I'll start the fire, and we can watch something together."

"Is this your way of forcing me into another weird as fuck train wreck about gay throples and tigers?"

I push back slightly until I'm leaning against the opposite corner. "Nope. I'll even let you pick. Lady's choice."

She gives me a skeptical look, sliding her straw between her plump lips, then eyes me curiously. "Anything?"

I wave out a hand. "Anything."

She ponders and then her mouth sweeps up into an evil grin. "Alright, deal. Bring the vodka and meet me in the living room."

"Vodka?" I raise my brows. "It's not even noon."

"It's time to play *my* game. You scared?" she challenges with a cheeky grin.

I chuckle. "Very."

She saunters past me, fluttering light on her feet with a booty shake, which drives me insane. My eyes lower as I take in her curves, knowing I'm only making it worse for myself.

Once I grab the bottle and shot glasses, I find her on the couch and set everything on the coffee table. Lighting the fireplace, I create the perfect atmosphere. She turns on the TV when I settle next to her.

"Well, what'd you pick?" I ask, putting my arm around her. I'm close enough to smell the sweetness of her hair.

"I'm *so* glad you asked." She smirks, and I see a bunch of twentysomethings in swimsuits. Then the trailer begins.

"What the fuck is this?" I ask at least three times within the first thirty seconds.

"Netflix's new reality dating show about personal growth and resisting temptation. Thought you'd especially be interested in it."

"Am I really supposed to believe they don't give in? This feels like a trap…"

"Oh, Eli. I'm going to enjoy this." She chuckles as the narrator begins explaining the "experiment" and how they have to abstain from kissing, sex of any kind, and masturbation, or money will be deducted from the hundred-grand prize.

"You're withholding and not even being rewarded with any money…" she taunts, resting her hand on my leg.

"Which means, I should've gone on that island because I would've won!" I gloat.

Cami shakes her head. "You just wait."

"Wow…" I say after all the participants are introduced. "So they picked the absolute most shallow people they could find on the planet, grouped them together at a beach house with nothing else to do besides sunbathe and work out, and they have to try not to jump each other's bones?"

"The goal is to form a connection that isn't based on sex."

"Precisely what I suggested we do…" I counter.

"Yes, but they all literally just met. We've known each other for a long ass time," she argues. "So…"

"But we only kissed days ago. You can't go from hating each other's guts to getting naked in a matter of days."

She turns and faces me. "You really hated my guts?"

I look at her, frowning. "Well, I've always had underlying feelings for you, but when you called me out for being poor and made me feel like I wasn't good enough for you, it was hard to like you as a person. Yet for some reason, I couldn't get you outta my head. Or my heart, apparently."

"I was an awful teenager, I know." She lowers her gaze.

I tilt her head up until her eyes meet mine again. "We fed off each other's hostility. I don't blame you. I provoked you just as much as you provoked me. There was tension because *something* was bubbling between us that neither of us understood. But I do now. The chemistry and connection, it's real. It always has been, and I'm glad we can use this time to get to know each other better."

"Yes, I agree. But we can also have some fun while doing so."

I sigh with a small chuckle. "Okay, so what are the guidelines for your drinking game?"

"Every time a couple breaks a rule, we take a shot and mimic their offense."

"You mean, do what they did?"

"Right!"

"Cami," I warn, easily seeing right through her.

"Don't worry. We don't actually see them having sex or doing anything more than touching and kissing."

"Baby, listen…I like your intentions, but I don't trust you with this one."

Her hand slides up my thigh. "Did you just call me baby?"

"Don't interpret that as me giving you the green light to jump me," I tease.

"Fine, but you can't stop me from wanting you to whisper that in my ear while you're inside me. I'm definitely gonna be imagining that very thing while I'm in the shower later."

I grab her hand and stop her from going higher. My dick is well aware of her presence and doesn't need further temptation. "You can fantasize all you want, *baby*…" I bring my mouth close to her ear. "But that's all it's gonna be for now." Pulling away, I smirk at her pouty expression.

"You won't even kiss me?"

"I'll kiss you," I tell her. "But you can't get handsy."

"We'll see. I played your stupid drinking game, so now, you gotta play mine."

"Did that girl really just admit she's ditzy?"

"She's actually one of my favorites," Cami replies. The longer this show goes on, the more I know it's going to be painful to watch.

"The rules should be to take a shot every time one of the girls flips their hair." I snort after we meet the sorority chick who flipped hers six times in thirty seconds.

"I didn't think you'd want to be hammered by the end." She chuckles.

Taking her hand from my leg, I interlock our fingers.

"David is my reality husband, by the way. He's my number one."

"Really? So he'd be your celebrity free pass?"

"Can you blame me?"

"I mean, if rock hard abs and a chiseled jawline are your thing…" I snicker.

Cami looks over at me. "You're quite comparable."

"Am I? Would I still be in the running to win your heart then?"

"Yeah. I mean…" She shrugs casually. "Probably."

"Probably?" I remark, bringing my hands to her sides and tickling her.

"Stop!" She laughs, collapsing on the couch. I tower over her, digging my fingers under her arms.

Bringing my mouth to hers, I brush it softly without quite kissing her. "That's what you get for making me watch this ridiculous show."

She pushes me until we're both sitting again. "It's payback, so deal with it."

I smirk, knowing she enjoyed that crazy documentary even if she's denying it.

"I love how everyone's in their bathing suits, showing off ninety-five percent of their bodies, and this guy waltzes in looking like Jesus."

"Just wait till he takes off the hat…"

He finally does, and I nearly choke when he reveals his bun and starts taking it down. "So that's me? I'm Jesus."

Cami laughs. "Well, I imagine there's a lot of *Oh my Gods* in bed with you."

I nearly blush, but I don't tell her that. "I might actually like that guy." Then the scene continues. "Okay, then. Never mind…" I say when Jesus claims he doesn't believe in monogamy and wants to spread his seed to as many women as possible.

"He's Jesus on the outside, but the devil on the inside." Cami chuckles.

"Okay, this show is making us dumb, and it's only been ten minutes." I groan.

"It's about the journey. You're supposed to see their growth throughout, so of course they all look like morons in the beginning."

"The best part of this is the narrator's jokes. Even she knows it's ridiculous."

"She's actually a comedian and is pretty funny. No one is there to explain to them what's going on—that we see anyway—so they'll meet their virtual host soon," she explains.

"So how long until one of them breaks the rules?"

"Keep watching…"

More time passes, and my brain cells start to dissolve. There's a dressing room where they get ready and do their hair and of course, gossip.

"What are they supposed to do all day? What are they preparing for?"

Cami glares at me, and I shrug. I thought those were valid questions…

"Did he really just say four weeks was considered a long-term relationship? Oh my God, I can't." My head falls back in agony, groaning as we continue watching. "Wait. She climbed on his lap after just meeting him. Oh shit, now they're kissing!"

"It's technically not breaking the rules because the ban hasn't started yet," Cami explains.

"Because they just arrived!" I hold out my hand. "This is absurd."

"Have you never watched a reality show before? They go from zero to sixty in an hour. That's the whole premise, and why there's so much entertainment value in trash TV."

"During this quarantine, I'm going to introduce you to *quality* entertainment. I'll do this one little game with you, but afterward, we're onto better shit."

"We'll see, we'll see…" She grins. "You might be a fan after the eighth episode."

"*Eight*?" I raise my brows. "Seriously?"

"That's how many there are total. They're only like forty-five minutes long. We can binge the whole series by dark."

Blowing out a slow breath, I brush my fingers over my jawline.

"That dude just said, 'there are plenty more days left for her to choose the right guy,' and if that wasn't my teenage brain every time I saw you with some idiot, I don't know what was." I laugh as she blushes, and soon, we're cracking up.

"So you're saying you're the one for me? The *right* one?"

"I've known forever. Just been waiting for you to catch up."

"Am I allowed to kiss you yet?" She looks at me and bites her lip.

"Not until the contestants start breaking the rules…"

She rolls her eyes, trying her hardest to be mad.

"Okay, I think I know why that girl's your favorite," I tease after a twist in the show is announced. She immediately elbows me in the rib cage, and I choke out a laugh. "If she's challenged to wash or cook, she knows she's fucked and won't win the prize money."

"Excuse you, I *did* cook this morning! For you, might I add."

I take her hand and kiss her knuckles. "And it was delicious."

The first episode finally ends, and as we get previews of the next, I know we're gonna be taking several shots.

"Should I start pouring the vodka now?"

As expected, the first rule break comes ten minutes into the show.

"Ready?" I grab the bottle, pour the liquid, then hand her one of the glasses. We clink them together before shooting it down.

Next, I grab Cami's face and capture her lips with mine. She sinks into my chest, moaning as our tongues collide. Heat builds between us as our hands slide over each other, and I feel goose bumps cover her soft skin. Cami keeps our tongues fused as she climbs over my legs and straddles me, then wraps her arms around my neck. She rocks her hips and grinds against my cock, making me harder and desperate for more.

"Cami…" I warn, pulling back slightly. "This is a bit more than what they were doing."

"Trust me, they will be soon," she quickly retorts.

I chuckle against her mouth and somehow garner enough strength to move her off me and place her back on the couch.

"You get off on telling me no, don't you?"

I eye my crotch, and her gaze follows to the noticeable erection. "That's not the case. If my dick was capable, it'd cuss me out right now."

"Whoa…that guy totally threw his chick under the bus after initiating the kiss and even saying fuck the money. What a douche."

"Those two…" She blows out an exaggerated breath. "Drive me crazy."

"The two chicks are now making out…" I shake my head. "Another rule break." We each take another shot.

"Saddle up for kiss number two."

I grab one of the pillows and put it over my crotch before she can grind against me again.

Cami chuckles as her eyes lower. "Trying to resist temptation?"

"Trying to keep myself from blowing my damn load. These people are gonna get me drunk with blue balls."

She cups my face and kisses me, sliding her tongue between my lips. Moaning at how amazing she tastes, I deepen our connection as her head falls back. My fingers thread through her hair as I pull her closer, but before things go too far, I create space as we gasp for air.

"I think I need a cold shower."

"Nope! No self-gratification per the rules."

"You're going to be the death of me, aren't you?" I inhale sharply, then exhale. I'm really trying to take things slow with Cami so I don't fuck it up, but damn, she's making me second-guess my decision.

With the episode nearly over, the show takes a turn, and I can't stop laughing at how dramatic everyone is.

For the next few hours, we continue watching, taking shots, and making out. Honestly, it's a goddamn miracle I don't tear off her clothes.

By the final episode, there were eight rule breaks, three of which were more than just kissing. One couple had sex and another almost did, but none of that is shown, other than glimpses of a blow job.

At that point, I was eight shots deep and couldn't say no as Cami kneeled between my thighs and took me in her mouth.

And as every member of the cast who broke a rule said—it was *totally* worth it.

CHAPTER FIFTEEN

CAMERON

DAY 10

IT'S BEEN three grueling days of seducing Eli and him denying me before we get too far. We watched my show and played my drinking game. There was some action in between, but since then, he's insisted on an "above the waist only" rule.

He'll kiss me and lay with me on the couch no problem, but anything more and he resists.

Eli's encouraged me to watch the "classics" with him, including *Ferris Bueller's Day Off* and *Groundhog Day*—which ironically feels like what we're living in—and I had him watch a few of my favorites like *Pretty in Pink*, *Breakfast Club*, and *Sixteen Candles*. It's been nice hanging out with him and using this time to talk. I definitely feel like we've grown closer and have created a tighter bond, but now I'm ready to jump his damn bones.

Cameron: No matter what I do, Eli still says no! Even when I basically straddle his lap and grind on his cock. And trust me, he's hard!

Kendall: Did you try just walking around naked? As

someone who's seen your boobs before, there's no way he'd be able to resist them.

I chuckle, knowing she has a good point. I do have awesome tits.

Cameron: I don't know. That seems too obvious. And a little chilly, honestly.

It's been in the thirties and windy.

Kendall: There's a trend on TikTok where you walk in on your man naked and record his reaction. Most don't deny the opportunity and chase after their women. It's worth a shot!

Cameron: You're right…I'm playing to win here!

Kendall: Yes, you are! Take off your clothes and go get your man!

Cameron: I'll report back!

After I get out of bed and take a shower, I slather myself with lotion and spritz body spray. I towel dry my hair and put moisturizer on my face. Wrapping myself in only a robe, I head downstairs to find him. He's probably making breakfast, and he can stare at my naked ass while I prepare his espresso.

The moment I get downstairs, I untie my robe and prepare to take it off. I'm not going to film his reaction because then he'll know something's up, but I will seduce him until he cracks.

Eli's facing the stove, and my eyes trail down his bare back and stop at his gray sweatpants that hang low on his hips.

This asshole is testing me.

There's no way he's wearing anything underneath them either. I want to tear them off with my teeth.

"Morning," he calls out, and as soon as he looks over his shoulder, I slide the robe down my arms, and it falls to my feet. He quickly does a double take and blinks.

"Good morning," I sing-song, walking closer. "What's for breakfast today?"

Staring, Eli licks his lips and studies me as I open the fridge and grab my creamer.

"Uh…thought I'd make you my famous toad in a hole dish," he answers, then blinks. "Isn't it a little…nippy to be walking around naked?"

Fuck yes, it is. "No, I'm pretty hot actually." I go to the espresso machine and make him a cup of coffee. *"Eggs in a basket* sounds great."

I feel his eyes on me as I move around, neither of us speaking as we work. He grabs two plates, and I get the forks, then we set everything on the kitchen table.

Eli places the pan of food in the middle. "Orange juice?"

"Is there still some left?" I ask.

"For one cup."

"You have it then."

"Nah. It's yours if you want it."

I arch a brow, grinning.

"The *juice,*" he emphasizes.

Dammit.

"We'll share it," I say. "Half each."

"I can live with that." He taps his knuckles on the table before going to the fridge. He returns with two glasses and sets them down. Then he leans in, grips my chin, and brings our mouths together.

I moan, loving the taste of him, and wrap my arms around his waist. Pulling him closer, I feel his cock growing hard against my chest, and know I'm getting to him.

Eli grabs my wrists from behind his back and moves them

away.

"I know what you're doing, and it's not gonna work."

"I'm not doing anything. I'm out of clothes and don't know how to do laundry." I bat my lashes innocently, grinning.

"Is that so?" He leans back, folding his arms.

I shrug, nonchalantly. "Yep. So it's naked central until I can find a tutorial online."

Chuckling, he shakes his head. "I just stuff all my clothes into the washer with the detergent. I don't think it's rocket science."

"Most of my clothes are dry clean only."

"You can borrow one of my T-shirts then."

"Seems you're out of them too since you're going without one." I lower my gaze down his body, admiring how delicious he looks. He even has a happy trail going from his belly button to below his sweats. God, I want him so badly.

"Nah. Just felt like giving you breakfast *and* a show." He winks with a shit-eating smirk. He knows exactly what he's doing.

"Well, I can be your dessert if you're still hungry…"

He places a finger under my jaw, then closes the gap between us. His mouth covers mine again, but he retreats too soon. "That's tempting, it really is, but my answer is still no."

I slouch back in my chair, pouting. How the hell didn't this work? I'm fucking naked, for Christ's sake!

"I'm really digging that tattoo, by the way." He waggles his brows, and I quickly cross my arms over my breasts so he stops staring. I got a little butterfly underneath my left boob for my twenty-first birthday, and only my ex, Kendall, and the tattoo artist know about it.

"Too bad you're choosing not to inspect it further," I quip.

"I can see it fine without having sex with you. But the moment I touch you, you'll be on me like white on rice. So…" He holds up his hands. "I'll just admire from afar."

I narrow my eyes. "You're only torturing yourself, you know? I hear blue balls is painful."

"They can be. That's why I'm going to take an extra-long shower this morning."

Grinding my teeth, I growl and turn in my seat. He walks to the other side of the table with a stupid grin on his face. I grab his glass of orange juice and pour it into mine, leaving his empty. Then I look at him over the rim and scowl as he holds back his laughter. I know I'm being childish, but at this point, I don't care. Eli is purposely withholding sex to make a point, but there has to be something that'll make him snap.

And I'm going to figure out what it is.

After my embarrassing naked protest at breakfast, I take my robe and bare ass back to my room and decide if he's not going to do the job, I'll do it myself.

Chanel sits on my bed, watching me. "Don't judge me." I scowl, marching to my nightstand and finding my vibrator.

I turn it on and thank God the batteries aren't dead. I brought it with me since I thought Zane and I would have lots of time to mess around. Instead, I'm single and taking care of myself. I'll get in the tub and have my own fun.

There's a knock on the door, and I smirk, hopeful Eli changed his mind.

"Yes?" I answer.

"Thought I'd bring you a shirt, ya know, in case you needed something to wear." He grins and holds it out for me.

"Thanks, that's *so* thoughtful." I grab it and flash him a pleased grin. "Can you hold this for me?" I hand over the vibrator, and he takes it, holding back his dirty comments. I put on his T-shirt, and it hangs just above my knees. "It even smells like you." I pull up the fabric to my nose and inhale.

He reveals a smug smile. "Guess that'll come in handy when you're using this." He gives the vibrator to me.

"Too bad you don't want to help me."

"I'd be happy to assist you, but I know you wouldn't play by the rules." He takes a step back, crossing his wrists over his body, and covers his crotch.

"Well, then you could watch?" I arch a brow, hoping that'll tempt him enough to break. "That's not against the rules, is it?"

He swallows hard and shakes his head. "No."

Lowering my hands, I use one to pull up the hem of the shirt and the other to turn on the vibrator, then place it over my clit. It starts humming, and I bite my lower lip, enjoying the way it feels.

"Mmm…" I purr, my eyes fluttering closed. "So good."

"Rub it in circles," he orders, his voice gravelly.

I do as he says, forming a fast rhythm. My back arches as I slide it down my slit and feel it vibrate my pussy. It feels so goddamn good, though I wish he'd take control and do it for me.

"Mmm, yes," I hum again, bringing it back to my throbbing clit. I look at Eli and see the fire in his eyes as he tries to restrain himself. Biting my lip, our eyes lock, and I grin.

"I bet you need to come, don't you?"

"Yes, badly." I click a button and increase the speed. "God, I'm so close."

My eyes slam closed, and there's no holding back as my body builds closer to the edge.

Eli takes me off guard when he pushes me deeper into the room and backs me up against the wall. His hand wraps around my throat as he closes his mouth on mine, sliding his tongue in deep and fast. I moan, releasing a satisfying breath as he lowers his other hand and takes the vibrator from my grip.

He lowers it, coating it with my juices, then slides it inside me. I gasp at the intrusion and the delicious way it fills me. Gripping his shoulders, I lean into him to stabilize myself because my knees are close to buckling beneath me.

Eli kisses down my jaw and lands on my neck, sucking hard as he thrusts the vibrator in and out.

"When I'm inside you, you'll be screaming my name, got it? Until then, you come picturing my cock in you."

"Why don't you just fuck me now then?" I challenge. "What are you waiting for?"

"You know exactly why...patience, baby."

The way his tongue rolls the word *baby* has my core tightening, and a burst of heat soars through me. I dig my nails into his skin when he slides the vibrator to my clit, bringing more pleasure between my thighs, and soon, fireworks explode throughout. Everything tightens, and I release a loud moan as another wave of pleasure shoots up my spine. My head falls back as he licks a trail up my neck, then sucks on my ear.

"Fuck, Cami," he growls, turning off the vibrator and tossing it aside. "That was the hottest fucking thing I've ever experienced." He releases a deep groan.

My entire body feels like jelly, but all I want is to climb Eli like a goddamn tree and have his hands all over me.

"It could get *a lot* hotter. You could join me in the bathtub," I offer as he slides his fingers down, cupping my breast.

"*Shit*, that's tempting..." He plucks my lower lip with the pad of his thumb. "I don't trust your wandering hands, though."

"You're the one who can't be trusted." I eye the vibrator. "I was doing just fine by myself when you took over."

"Really? Is that so?"

"Yep," I say confidently. "I have plenty of experience going solo."

He furrows his brows. "That's sad. Mr. Money Bags didn't get you off?"

"Well, truthfully, he couldn't always *find* it."

Eli steps back and glares. "You're joking, right?"

I shake my head. "Stop, this is embarrassing."

"I'm not trying to make you feel bad, Cami. You have nothing to be embarrassed about. His number-one priority as your boyfriend should've been to pleasure and satisfy you. You shouldn't have had to do it yourself if he was doing it right."

"Not all guys think that way," I defend, shrugging. It definitely wouldn't be the first time a man hasn't been able to get me off. It's why I brought it in the first place.

"There's no way you'll be needing it once I've had you, got it?" He winks, placing his hand on my cheek. "Go take your bath, enjoy one more solo session, and then know the next time you're moaning, it'll be because of me."

"Quite confident for a guy who keeps turning me down," I retort. "Join me in the tub and give me a preview of what's to come."

He contemplates it for a moment, then says, "Alright, but on one condition." He closes the space between us. "I wear my shorts, so you can't try anything." Eli flashes a smirk, knowing I would touch him if he was completely naked.

Even though I'm disappointed at his exception, I'm still happy he's agreed to come with me. "Okay, deal."

I cup Eli's neck and lower his mouth to mine, needing to taste him. As I slide my tongue over his, we frantically move toward the bathroom as he lifts his shirt off me, and I bring my hands to his waist.

"You're not wearing boxers," I tell him as I slide my fingers into his sweatpants.

He stops my hand before it can lower to his growing cock. "That's right, shit. Okay, new plan. I watch you take a bath instead."

"That doesn't sound nearly as fun," I whine.

"Oh, it'll be pure torture for me," he says, groaning. "But I like watching you. Been doing it for years."

CHAPTER SIXTEEN

ELIJAH

DAY 12

IT'S BEEN two days since our little game started, and Cami's determined to push me to my limit. One thing's for sure, she's a firecracker and knows how to tease me until my cock nearly breaks off. I've never jacked off so much in my life, but when it comes to her, this isn't anything new. But fuck, she's all I can think about, and it's consuming every part of me. Truthfully, I don't know how much longer I'll be able to stay strong and tell her no. The past forty-eight hours have been pure torture as she's pranced around in lingerie she brought for her asshole ex. Honestly, I should send him a thank-you letter for letting her go because I've been given the opportunity of a lifetime—to be with the woman of my dreams.

I walk into the kitchen, where she's making an espresso. "Good morning."

She glances over her shoulder at my bulge, then back up at me. One look is all it takes from her to have my body springing to life. Just the way she commands me with her sparkling blue eyes is enough to drive me wild, and she knows it.

I move past her, and she presses her back against my chest.

Wrapping my arm around her stomach, I grab her tightly, and she pushes her ass into my already raging hard-on. She gives me an evil laugh but doesn't say anything.

I brush my lips against the shell of her ear, causing her to shudder.

"You're a monster," I whisper.

Quickly, she spins around, then loops her arms behind my neck, and seconds later, I'm lifting her ass onto the countertop. "No, I'm just a woman who knows who she wants and isn't afraid to say it."

"And what do you want?" My eyebrows pop up.

"You," she confirms, and I'll never get tired of hearing it. Our kisses are white-hot as she runs her fingers through my hair, and somehow, I put space between us. "You're trying to break me."

A chuckle escapes her as I adjust myself. "No, I just want you to break *me*. There's a difference, Eli."

"You deserve more than a quick fuck." I grab a mug from the cabinet, and she jumps down from the counter and presses all the buttons for a dark roast coffee.

She groans while I wait. "Your willpower is commendable. I'll make sure to get a trophy made for you."

Now, I'm the one who's laughing. "I want it engraved."

She rolls her eyes. "Guess I'm going to have to go upstairs and have some fun with Prince Harry."

Coffee spews from my mouth as I choke it back up. "Excuse me?" I ask, wiping off my chin.

"The vibrator that got me off when you refused a couple of days ago," she explains with a shrug. "He never denies me and always *comes* through."

I grin at her and then burst into laughter. She continued her torture by taking a bath and playing with herself, knowing I was struggling the entire time and holding back. I was tempted to get in the water with her, but I didn't trust her intentions nor did I trust my self-control. She gave me one helluva show, though.

"What kind of batteries does it take, because you might wear him down."

"Triple A, I think." Immediately, Cami opens different drawers in the kitchen and checks each one. "No. No. No."

Her eyes go wide in a panic, and I shrug. I can tell her where they are kept from when I searched for the smoke detector batteries, but this is way more fun.

"Enjoy him while you can, sweetheart. Because at some point, it'll be useless. And he can't please your clit the same ways I can." I lick my lips, and she watches my mouth, which curls up into a grin. With arms crossed, she shakes her head, and I sip my espresso, smiling over the rim. When Cami huffs, I chuckle.

"Welp, going to give myself the royal treatment." She snickers with her cup of coffee held in one hand.

"Have fun," I say with a grin and wonder if she's really going upstairs to pleasure herself or if she's fucking with me. I never know with her.

Needing some fresh again, I decided to take Bruno for a walk around the property. Well, I walked. He ran around in a full sprint with his tongue hanging out. Though I tried to play with him, he was in a mood today. Anytime I'd throw a toy, he'd run after it, then refuse to give it to me, so it got old pretty quick. He's a bigger tease than Cami.

After an hour, we go inside, and I notice Cami's asleep on the couch. The news is on, and the volume is a whisper. The silk panties and bra she's wearing leave zero room to the imagination. She's giving me everything she's got with her body and smart-ass mouth. While most guys would just fuck her as quickly as possible, I'm not like that, and Cami deserves better. What we have is more than just a physical relationship, and I want her to see that too. Our hormones are raging, and I honestly can't remember the last time a woman's made me feel the way Cami has. She's the first and only.

As I stand with my arms crossed, watching her, she stirs and mutters my name. For a moment, I think she's awake and has noticed me creeping, but then I realize she's asleep, dreaming about me. A smirk touches my lips because she's saying my name with breath as soft as butterfly wings. My willpower is quickly waning, so I force myself to walk away before she catches me and wins this game, after all. I go upstairs and pace around my room, my heart racing as I think about all the ways I'd pleasure her. Remembering the soft moans and pants that escaped her and how she bit her lip as she came have me nearly busting a nut in my boxers.

It quickly becomes more than just want, and I need to relieve myself before I have to deal with blue balls again. I unzip my jeans and push my clothes down and lie on the bed.

I tightly grip my shaft and stroke it a few times, closing my eyes. Most guys use porn to get off, but Cami has given me enough in the past few days that I won't need it for a lifetime. Her name is on my lips, on my tongue, and all I want to do is taste her again and devour her sweet pussy. Fuck, just thinking about her in that bathtub pleasuring herself as she thinks about me has me increasing my pace, but I don't want to come just yet.

A few more pumps and the next thing I know, my bedroom door is being cracked open. Cami sees me, and my first instinct is to put my clothes back on, but she walks in, flashing a devilish smile. Her eyes study my dick, and she sucks in her bottom lip. Goddamn, she's so gorgeous. "Don't stop. I want to watch you, Eli," she whispers, and I brush a finger over my chin, watching her breasts rise and fall.

Cami reaches behind her back and unsnaps her bra, fully revealing her beautiful body. Giving me the best show of my life, she pinches her nipples and moans. I stroke myself so vigorously that I have to force myself to calm down. Slowly, she moves toward me, her perfect tits bouncing as she walks.

"Cami," I let out in a deep gruff.

"Let me ride you, Eli," she taunts and looks at me with pure desire. "I'd love you inside my tight little pussy. God," she purrs, and I can tell she's getting just as worked up as I was when I watched her get off.

"We can't," I whisper, my release growing closer.

She pouts, batting her eyelashes.

"Not yet, baby." My balls tighten, and I squeeze harder, groaning.

"Mmm. That's the sexiest fucking thing I've ever seen," she tells me. "I love watching you, knowing you're thinking about me."

She squeezes her thighs together tightly, and I can just imagine how soaked her little lace panties are right now. The thought of finally sinking deep inside her nearly takes over. After a few minutes of her gaze on me, which is one of the biggest turn-ons, Cami decides she can't handle it anymore. Because she's the type of woman who always gets what she wants, she moves forward and climbs on the bed.

"Let me help you at least," she insists. I remove my hand, and she takes over. She rubs the pad of her thumb across the top, then a second later, her hot mouth is on me, and I don't have the willpower to make her stop. It feels so fucking good that I've lost my ability to speak.

"Cami," I growl. She looks up at me with big blue eyes, humming. "Fuck, your mouth feels so goddamn good," I admit, running my fingers through her hair.

She slides her hand over my shaft as she takes all of me. When my dick touches the back of her throat, she gags but keeps going. Watching her choke on my erection is hot as fuck as her head bobs up and down. I don't know how much longer I'll be able to last as she trails her tongue down to the base, then sucks and licks my balls. She's gentle but also forceful in her own way, letting me know she's in control right now. And fuck, I don't even care. The woman is a savage and doesn't leave an inch untouched as she gives me the royal treatment. Right now, I feel like a fucking king with her mouth all over me.

My eyes roll back, and while I didn't want to cross the line like this, I have no regrets. I let out an animalistic groan as she increases the pace and pressure. Before I explode, she stops with a naughty smirk.

"Good enough?" She looks up at me with a popped eyebrow, casually flicking her tongue against me, making everything overly sensitive.

Leaning closer, I grin, already missing her mouth on me, but I don't tell her that. "Sure. I'll finish," I say, shrugging.

As I lower my hand, Cami laughs and pushes me away, then places her sweet lips back where they belong.

"Not a chance in hell. This cock is mine now, Eli. Remember that." She goes slow, which is fucking agonizing. The orgasm builds in the pit of my stomach as she devours me. Cami is a goddamn fucking pro and deserves a gold medal because she's the best I've ever had. Perhaps it's the fact that my feelings for her are more intense than I've ever had before, but everything is a hundred times better with her.

I fist the comforter as electricity shoots up my spine. She feasts on me, and I can't take it any longer and release inside her. Cami swallows with a satisfying hum, and a huge fucking smile on her face. She licks me clean, devouring every single drop like it's candy.

"You taste so good, Eli," she whispers, not taking her eyes off me. She moans with satisfaction, and I can tell she wants me. All of me. More than what she just had. God, I want to fuck her into next week, next month, next *year*.

"Thank you," I say. She gives me a seductive wink, and I don't know how any man could leave her. My sweet, seductive, sassy Cami is the whole fucking package.

Cami continues up the bed until her mouth presses against mine. "So fucking hot," she tells me, and I can't resist touching her soft skin. My palm goes straight to her pebbled nipple. Her head falls back on her shoulders, and I slide my mouth to her neck until I'm at her ear.

"Let me repay you," I whisper, and she moves away, searching my face with a grin.

"What did you have in mind?"

I love it when she's playful like this.

Rolling her off me, I slip my hand into her panties and move my fingers across her needy clit. Her body instantly reacts, and when I slide inside her pussy, she squeals and arches her back.

"Baby," I whisper as her mouth crashes against mine. "You're so fucking wet," I say between bated breaths.

"Your touch…" she says, trailing off, leaning against the pillows. "It's fucking magical."

Adding another finger inside her tight little cunt, I watch her eyes flutter closed as she sinks into me. "Make me come, Eli. I need it badly."

I love her demanding tone and that she knows exactly what she wants. With all my strength, I rip the panties off her body, and they snap in a second. She lets out a small grunt and then grins as I tuck them under my pillow as a keepsake. My mouth captures her nipple, and I palm the other while thrusting two fingers inside her hot body and rubbing circles with the pad of my thumb against her clit. The way she reacts to my touch has me wanting to come again.

She grinds against me, and I know she needs to come, but I want to put her through the same agony she put me through, so I dramatically slow to a snail's pace. Her chest rises and falls so quickly that it's obvious she's dangling on the edge.

"Eli," she pants, wrapping her hand around my neck. "Eli. *Please.*"

I close the gap between us and kiss her, twirling my tongue with hers. Within just a few minutes of continuing to work her clit precisely the way she loves, her back arches, and every muscle in her body tightens as she sucks in a breath. She moans my name as she relaxes against me, and it's the sweetest fucking sound I've ever heard.

Once I pull away and lie on my back next to her, she rolls over on her side and leans up on an elbow. I can see the pulse in her neck, continuing to race, and I grin at how happy and sated she looks.

"Damn…" She chuckles before her head drops to the pillow. I bow my head down and kiss her forehead.

"Better than Prince Harry?" I quip.

"Oh yeah. He's been fired."

I laugh, cupping her cheek. "That was just the warm-up." I wink.

She laughs and perks up. "So, are you gonna fuck me now?"

"Soon."

With a groan, she playfully smacks my chest, and I capture her wrist, then bring my lips to her knuckles. "Patience."

One side of her lip curls up in disagreement. "You're insufferable."

I gently sweep away pieces of hair that fell into her face. She's even more beautiful when she looks at me with lust in her eyes. It makes it even harder to deny her.

"Now you know what you've been missing out on," I tease.

"Had I known, I would've jumped you in high school."

I snort, shaking my head. "Nah. It's been worth the wait."

Her eyes are sad for a moment, but she quickly smiles. "So what does that mean for us now?"

I lean forward and kiss her, loving how candid we are with each other. "Marriage and babies," I tell her confidently.

Her eyes widen in panic but then quickly soften. "If the sex is as good as your foreplay, I might be the one proposing."

"That's a deal," I say. "One I'd take any day of the week."

CHAPTER SEVENTEEN

CAMERON

DAY 14

TEASING and tempting Eli the past two days has been intense, but I have to give it to him for staying strong. Today, we ate breakfast together then went our separate ways because we're both overwhelmed with school and work. Before I went upstairs, I made an espresso but have a feeling I'll need four more because I'm dragging ass. I have a pile of reading assignments and two papers to write, and Eli has meetings scheduled with clients until dark. Everything has piled up, and now I'm stressing to get it all completed on time.

We make plans to have dinner around seven, so until then, I'll be forcing myself to finish my assignments. Once I'm upstairs, I open my laptop and set it on the desk that faces the window with the best mountain view. I grab a notebook and make a task list, then figure out what will be the easiest way to accomplish it all. After I have some sort of a roadmap, I get started.

I groan when I realize I have to write a three-thousand-word paper on how to drive top-line growth for large companies. It wouldn't be acceptable to tell my professors my father has an entire department to handle all of this. So instead, I pull up my digital marketing book and use some common sense, but it'll take me hours to finish this. Right now, I want to cry into my coffee. Instead, I take a sip and stare outside.

When I close my eyes, I replay the last time Eli and I fooled around. I lean back in my chair and a smile plays on my lips as I remember tasting him. I decide to text Kendall, because the girl needs an update, buts as if she knew I was thinking about her, she texts me first.

Kendall: Sex update, please! I'm living vicariously through you.

Cameron: He's determined to wait! Nothing, and I mean NOTHING has convinced him otherwise.

Kendall: Are you sure he's not gay? You're hot. There's no way he can say no to that ass of yours.

I snort-laugh.

Cameron: I have to hand it to him, though. His willpower is iron tough. I think he just wants it to be natural, not forced in any way, which I get. But still...I'm going crazy!

Kendall: That's respectable. At least you know he's not using you, so that's a plus. Sorry, my friend. Hopefully, Prince Harry can keep you company in the meantime ;) How's the online schoolwork going?

Cameron: If the batteries don't die. LOL! I'm at the point in the semester where I understand why people pay their smarter classmates to do their assignments. I have so many to do. I feel like I'm drowning. Not to mention, I'm a little mentally drained from everything going on, so it's hard to focus on it like before this all happened.

Groaning, I want to bang my head against the desk.

Kendall: Yikes. Sorry. That sucks, but just think, it's almost over, and then you'll have your degree!

Cameron: I know. Send help. And vodka. Oh, and triple A batteries.

Kendall: Haha! Next week, when you're caught up, let's have a video chat happy hour, please. My wine subscription box was delivered, and I'm bored as hell.

Cameron: Deal! Count me in!

I glance at the clock and tell Kendall I'll chat with her later because I need to get back to writing. Every word is painful, but after a grueling three hours, I finish. After a quick bathroom break, I run downstairs and grab some water, and see Eli sitting at the table looking all sexy in a button-up shirt with his hair up wearing headphones. He must be having a meeting with his colleagues because he talks about negotiations for the seller and improving online listings. Damn, he sounds so smart when he talks about sales contracts and contingencies, all which go over my head. Instead of eavesdropping anymore, I make double shots of espresso for both of us. When I deliver it to him, Eli mouths a thank you and shoots me a wink, then goes back to his conference.

As I climb the stairs, my heart races thinking about him. Honestly, he could probably write the second paper I have based on his real-world experience.

When I walk inside my room, I find Chanel lying on my chair. I pick her up and move her to the bed. She bitches with an annoyed meow, then resettles in a different spot. Her attitude makes me chuckle.

For the rest of the afternoon, I sluggishly work through my assignments, and after a while, I need a pick-me-up. I decide to hop in the shower because the hot water typically relaxes me enough to refocus.

After I dry off, I slip on a matching bra and panties set and a slinky sundress that's cute, but comfortable enough to lounge around in. When I go back to my laptop, I write the last five pages and feel so damn accomplished when it's finally done. I suck in a deep breath and glance over the screen. The sunset hangs lazily on the horizon behind the trees and mountains. Soon it will disappear, and darkness will fall. I take a moment to admire and memorize how beautiful it is. It's so different from the city views I'm used to seeing. The only thing that breaks my thoughts is my stomach growling. I check the time and see it's nearly seven. I can't believe I completely lost track of time.

After quickly brushing my fingers through my hair, I leave my room, but when I do, I see a note taped to the outside of my door. Confused, I tear it off and open it.

Cami—it's time to play a game. Follow the clues until you find me. I have a surprise.

I grin so wide my face hurts. Farther down on the paper is the first clue.

If you can't stand the heat, get out of the kitchen.
Preparing gourmet meals will have you bitching.
Open me up and have a look,
Don't worry, baby. You don't have to cook.

A chuckle escapes me, and I feel giddy. This is so unexpected and sweet. I walk downstairs, then go to the fridge and look around. Nothing. Opening the microwave, I find it's empty too. I stop and think a little harder. That's when I see the oven and notice the light is on. Inside is a tray with another slip of paper, and I hurry and unfold it.

There are only three more clues left.
So you must do your very best.
Open me up and climb inside.
I can't wait for you to take me for a ride.

I reread the clue, confused, so I repeat it out loud. The only thing I can think of is my Range Rover. Curious to see if I'm right, I head to the garage. Once I'm there, images of Eli having his asthma attack fill my mind, but I push them away as I open the passenger door. On the seat is a letter, and I snatch it, then go back inside.

Very good. You're so damn smart.
If you allow it, I'll give you my heart.
Screw me in tight, so again you don't fall.
This should be the easiest clue of them all.

"Bastard," I huff with a chuckle and walk upstairs. Somehow, he ran up to the third story while I was in the garage because I took a shower earlier and didn't see anything then. Sneaky and witty all at the same time. The note is on the back of the toilet. I laugh, remembering my ass being on the floor when the seat broke and how he came to my rescue.

I want to hold you in my arms all night.
Even after we argue and fight.
Don't worry. This hunt is almost over.
Sit down, bring some popcorn, and get your closure.

I know exactly where he is. Smoothing down my hair, I take a quick glimpse at myself in the mirror and stack all the clues on my vanity. With a permanent smile on my face, I go to the lower level, walk down a hallway, then open the door to the theater room. He's moved the seats against the walls and set up a small table with chairs to create a romantic dining area. The gigantic screen has a night sky scene playing, and the sounds of summer surround me in the low-lit room. My mouth falls open, and I see him standing with his hands tucked in his suit pockets, grinning.

"You found me," he says as I walk over to him. He hands me some paper flowers with a ribbon tied around them. Taking them, I look around the room and am overcome with emotions and shock.

"Of course I found you," I say, beaming. "How did you get…" I can't even finish my words or thoughts. I'm stunned, wondering how he got all of this together in a few hours, considering he had so much work to complete. Glancing down, I see how much care he put into each stem and petal. It's the most beautiful bouquet anyone has ever given me, and best of all, it'll last forever.

Eli places his fingers under my chin and forces me to look into his emerald green eyes. "It took some planning."

A few tears stream down my cheeks because no man has ever done anything so special for me before. Eli leans in and kisses my tears away. "What's wrong? Everything okay?"

I wrap my arms around his waist. "I'm just overwhelmed with happiness. This is all so perfect and thoughtful. Incredibly sweet. I'm just…I don't deserve all this."

"You do and more. But wait until you see what I cooked." He chuckles, and I notice how good he looks, and damn, I'm ready to undress him with my teeth.

Grabbing my hand, he walks me over to the table and uncovers two large bowls. A plate in the middle is stacked full of homemade-looking crackers, and my stomach is screaming out in protest because it smells so good, and I'm starving.

"Lobster bisque with bread crisps," he says.

"Eli," I whisper. "It smells so good."

Pulling the chair from under the table, he motions for me to sit. We might still be in the cabin but sitting under the fake stars and listening to the sounds of crickets lightly chirp is one of the most romantic dates I've ever had. This is everything I ever dreamed of, more than I expected, and I'm not worthy of this.

He fills two glasses full of wine, and I take a sip, grinning over the rim. I pick up the spoon and taste the bisque. "Yep, pretty sure I just died. This is so good." When did he make this, and how did I not smell it? The man is a pro at being stealthy.

Eli licks his lips. "I'll teach you how to make it one day."

I nearly spew out my wine. "With my current record, we better start with ramen."

"I was worried my clues might be too hard," he says with a chuckle. "I forgot how much shit I remembered over the years."

"The kitchen one got me for a second until I saw the oven light, but honestly it was the most thoughtful thing anyone's ever done for me," I admit, my temperature rising at the intensity that streams between us as he studies me. I'm nervous and unworthy of the man sitting in front of me.

"Well, there's a lot more where that came from, baby."

I chuckle at his playful wink. "I swear I'm living in a Hallmark movie right now." I bite my bottom lip, and he smirks.

"Well, there'll be no fade to black tonight." His voice is velvety smooth, and his confidence is sexy as hell. Is tonight finally the night? Butterflies flutter in my stomach, and my heart pounds at his words.

I down my wine. I'm already feeling it swarm through my body, or maybe it's Eli who's making me feel that way.

Our dinner is delicious. We talk and laugh, and everything between us feels natural and perfect. We finish eating, and I pour the rest of the wine that's left into my glass. He opens another bottle and fills his too.

"I want to dance with you," I tell him.

Eli chuckles and stands. He grabs the remote to the sound system and randomly finds a song. It's an old classic that's played at weddings—Nat King Cole's "Unforgettable." I somewhat stumble getting up, but he's by my side in a second to steady me.

Wrapping my arms around his neck, he pulls me to him, and we slowly move together. All of my exes hated dancing at the events I dragged them to and acted like it was a huge inconvenience. But not with Eli. The song ends, and another begins, and he holds me closer as if I'll slip through his fingers. I lean my head against his chest, and we sway together in harmony.

When I step back and smile, Eli's eyes are locked on me. Seductive and sexy. He dips his head down, and our mouths connect in a feverish kiss, the passion sizzling when our tongues twist. I moan against him and fist his shirt. I need Eli. He groans, and I need him right now, and I don't have to say it because he knows.

We grow greedier, more desperate, and soon, my back presses against the wall as Eli's muscular body leans into me. His touch is light and warm against my skin like a summer breeze.

"Cami, fuck," he growls, standing inches from me as his hand trails up my thighs. Eli lifts my dress, then slides my panties down to my ankles, and I step out of them. I've wanted him since the moment I saw him tonight, and the last hour was grueling as I waited in anticipation. With steady fingers, he rubs my clit, and my knees nearly buckle from how goddamn good it feels. My eyes flutter closed, and I whisper his name like a prayer, knowing it won't be long before he pushes me over the edge.

Eli has my body memorized like his favorite song, and when he gives me not one finger but two, I wrap my arms around his shoulders. His hardness presses into my stomach, and my pussy aches for all of him.

"Come for me, baby," he demands, his voice full of rasp. I hope the wall holds me up as I see stars. Moans escape me as the orgasm rips through my body. Eli wraps an arm around my waist, steadying me because the intensity nearly brings me to my knees. My breasts fall and rise as I pant, licking my lips and smiling up at him.

He places his fingers in his mouth, tasting me, then smirks. "And to think, I'd almost forgotten about dessert."

CHAPTER EIGHTEEN

ELIJAH

CAMI LOOKS up at me with hooded, lust-filled eyes. Our night is just getting started, and I can't wait to give her everything she wants and deserves.

"That was one. How about we go for five?" I ask with a wink.

She raises her eyebrows. "Five? Are you trying to kill me?"

"You just wait, baby," I quip, smacking her ass, then bending over to pick up her panties. She grabs them from me and wraps them around my neck, then pulls me closer. Our mouths crash together in a hot, needy exchange, and when we finally come up for air, I interlock my fingers with hers, leading her out of the theater. Tonight, I'll please her in ways she's never experienced and will prove to her what she's been missing.

When we make it to the staircase, she can't keep her mouth or hands off me, and we nearly fall trying to get to the second floor. The wine doesn't help steady either of us, but I'll be damned if that stops me.

"Fuck, Cami," I say as I lift her and carry her to the third level, claiming her as my prize. She holds onto me, laughing as I take the stairs two at a time. Once we reach her bedroom, I carefully kick open the door, then set her on the floor. Gracefully, she takes a step back and watches as I undo each button of my shirt.

"Mmm, dinner, dessert, and a show? You spoil me," she murmurs with a grin, tilting her head to one side and admiring her view.

My shirt falls to the floor, and I move closer to her. Cami greedily unbuttons my slacks and pushes them down with my boxers, then I toss them aside. She kneels in front of me as she grabs my cock and strokes it in her palm.

I groan. Her grip feels so damn incredible.

She smacks her lips before wrapping them around the tip and sliding her mouth down my cock. I grunt, twisting my fingers in her hair and guiding her up and down my shaft. Her hot breath feels amazing, but if she doesn't slow down, I'm going to embarrass myself and come too quickly.

"Get back up here," I demand.

"I need you so fucking bad," she says breathily. "I'm done waiting."

"That's the understatement of the decade," I say, then lift the thin material of her dress from her small frame. She raises her arms, allowing me to pull it off her. I step back slightly and admire how stunning she is. Cami is a goddamn vision.

Wrapping my arms around her, I undo her bra, and her breasts spill out, giving me the perfect view. I study every part of her, taking a mental snapshot. My fingertips brush across the softness of her collarbone as I dip down and capture her taut nipple in my mouth. Her eyes flutter closed as she arches her back, and I want to ravage her sweet pussy again.

She walks backward, pulling me on top of her as she falls to the mattress. I hover over her as our mouths fuse, our hands all over each other. The sparks fly between us so violently that if I don't slow us down, we might get burned. She's hungry for me, and I've fantasized about this moment so many times, I almost pinch myself to make sure I'm not dreaming. But as Cami peers up at me with her big baby blues, nothing in my entire life has ever felt this real.

"Okay, then. This was fun," I joke, pushing against the bed and pretending to leave.

"Elijah Ross, I swear, you better fuck me like you mean it." She locks her legs around me, pulling me back down.

I laugh, but I won't be *fucking* her. Instead, I'll be worshipping every inch of her, hoping she understands how much she means to me and how hard I'm falling for her.

"On one condition," I say.

She frowns and narrows her eyes at me. "Are you serious?"

"Admit I won," I mock with a smirk, knowing she's gonna be pissed she didn't get her way for once. "I won our bet, and you lost." I bury my nose in the nape of her neck, and she wiggles beneath me, and I pull away, wanting to see her expression.

A sly smile spreads across her plump lips. "There are only winners here, but I guess I'll order you that trophy after all," she concedes, giggling. When I look down at her again, she lifts and gives me a chaste kiss.

I nibble on her ear, and whisper, "You are my trophy. Best prize I've ever had."

"Then claim me as yours already," she purrs.

While she wants me now, I prefer to take my time exploring and cherishing her body. When my fingers brush against her cheek, her pulse quickens. Cami's eyes drift closed, and her breath quickens as I feather kisses along her jawbone, neck, and down to her breasts. I give each one equal attention before sliding down her stomach and burying myself between her legs.

She's a greedy little thing and wants more. Tasting her again is all the motivation I need to devour her as if she's my last meal. I increase my pressure and pace until she yells my name with sweet agony. Her back arches, but I keep going. I slide my palms under her ass cheeks and squeeze as I sink my tongue deeper inside her tight cunt.

"Mmm, Eli. Oh my..." She doesn't finish her thoughts because I place two fingers into her glorious pussy and one in her ass. Her eyes pop open, and she gasps at the intrusion.

"Trust me," I whisper, filling her as I lightly flick and tease her clit with my tongue.

"I do," she says softly, relaxing against me.

"Mmm," I hum when I glance up and see Cami pinching her nipples. I add more pressure as her moans become more guttural.

"Eli," she gasps, and I continue finger fucking her, allowing the orgasm to build until it steals her breath away. It doesn't take long before every muscle in her body tightens, and I want to be the best she's ever had. As I watch her, it's almost as if she's about to be suspended in air, and then the release takes hold.

I kiss her inner thighs as her body seizes, then look up at her.

"Wow. Damn. That was...intense as hell," she says, coming down from her high and looking at me with satisfaction. I kneel between her legs, watching her bite her lip as she cups her breast. My cock is so goddamn hard as I lean in closer and play in her wetness, sliding my tip up and down.

"Eli," she whispers desperately. "I need you inside me."

"Don't you know the magic word is please?" I tease. In a blink, her arms loop around my neck, and she pulls me on top of her.

"*Now*," she demands, slamming her mouth to mine.

"Did you forget who's in control here?" I taunt. Kissing my way back down her body, I then shift back to my knees, spreading her legs wider.

"If I say you are, then will you *please* fuck me?" she says sweetly.

I smirk, then glance down at my bare dick.

I've never not used protection. I know it's going to be mind-blowing because it's with Cami, but to feel her without nothing between us has me eager to fuck her raw like she's begging.

"Good girl." I waggle my brows, amused by how desperate she sounds.

I hover above her, then slowly slide inside inch by inch. There's silence except for the sounds of our shallow breaths as she adjusts to my size and takes all of me. She's so damn tight and warm, and I groan as I lift her hips to rock against me.

Cami grins as she wraps her legs around my waist, and our steady movements create an intense buildup. We escape in each other's eager lips, experiencing intimacy on a higher level than ever before. I nuzzle her neck, smelling her skin and hair, getting caught up in the emotions that swarm through me.

"It's never felt like this before," I admit, my voice a breathless whisper as I rest my forehead against hers.

"Me either. It's so good," she says with desperation in her tone. She has all of me but demands more. "Harder, Eli. I won't break."

Her confidence makes me grin, and I lift one of her thighs, then place it on my shoulder. I slide deeper, then thrust with more power than before. She gasps and drags her nails down my back as her head falls back.

"Yes, just like that. Oh my God," she cries.

"Fuck, I'm not gonna last as long as I want if you keep making those little whimpers," I tell her before crashing my mouth to hers.

"I can't help it." She chuckles softly.

Brushing my fingers over her soft skin, I cup her breast and squeeze. She brings her hands to my head and removes the ponytail, my hair falling down against my face.

"You look so sexy with your hair like this," she says, playing with my strands. "Then again, I love when you pull it up too."

"Yeah, it's a chick magnet," I tease.

"Shut up." She giggles. "No chicks better be touching or even looking at my man."

"Hearing you say that is hot as hell," I admit, lowering until I capture her lip between my teeth.

As we make love, our ragged breaths fill the silent space.

I pick up my pace, pounding faster and causing her glorious tits to bounce. We're needy and moan together, a melodic sound of audible emotions.

"Damn, baby," I groan. "You feel so good. I could stay here all goddamn night."

"Yes, yes, yes," she repeats. As the intensity builds and our releases threaten to take hold, she tugs my hair.

"Come inside me," she urges.

I pant, my heartbeat in my ears. "Cami, that's risky."

"I'm on the pill," she reassures me. "I've…never shared that with anyone before. I want it to be you, Eli."

My mouth goes dry, and I know if I continue pumping into her, I won't pull out fast enough. However, the thought of Cami pregnant with my baby has me wanting to lose all control.

With my arms on each side of her, I hold myself above her petite frame. I move my face closer to hers, twisting my tongue with hers as I ram my cock inside her tight little cunt.

Her pants quicken, and when her body seizes again, she demands I fuck her. Deep in the pit of my stomach, I feel the build. I move upright and pull her thighs toward me, ramming harder like she wants. Cami studies me, and my vision blurs as I spill inside her, releasing deep groans as the orgasm takes over. As I try to inhale, I lean down, and we exchange a searing-hot kiss.

"Wow," she blows out, satisfied, tucking her bottom lip into her mouth.

I give her a wink and then help clean her up, both of us unable to stop touching each other.

Afterward, we lie together and stare up at the ceiling. Eventually, Cami and I move to face each other. I reach over and push her hair behind her ear. I notice her cheeks are rosy red, and her lips are swollen.

"I'm speechless," she finally says, staring like she's scared I'll disappear if she blinks. "And you know how rare that is for me. I feel like we just did this soul-bonding ritual like in those fantasy books."

Laughter escapes me. "You're so fucking cute," I admit, and she leans forward and captures my mouth. I deepen the kiss, and she moans against me.

"It was intense," I admit, trying to make sense of what I'm feeling. I want to tell her how much I love her, how much I've always loved her, but I also don't want to say those words too soon and scare her away. So I keep them to myself, but I think she feels it too.

We make out like ravenous teenagers making up for lost time. When I finally pull away, we're both breathless. "Take a break, because I'm ready for more of you." She glances down at my cock.

"Are you gonna name him too?" I ask, referencing to how she named her vibrator. I place my hands behind my head and grin.

She scrunches her nose, thinking hard. "Maybe. Hmm. Zeus? That sounds like a name for something big and mighty."

A roar of a laugh escapes me. "Oh really? You're too good for my ego."

Wrapping my arm around her, I pull her close to my body, and she lays her head against my chest and listens to my heartbeat. "Do you have any idea how long I've waited to be with you like this?"

"Do you know how long *I've* waited?" she counters.

"A week?" I ask.

"Wrong," she states, peeking up at me. "You're so wrong, and you don't even know."

The words are like music to my ears as she shifts, then straddles me. She grabs my cock that's still hard, then takes every inch of me again, rocking her hips as I grip her waist. Her head falls back on her shoulders, and she takes full control. This is the Cami I love, the one who knows what she wants and takes it without apology.

With her name on my lips, I dig my thumbs into her skin, driving into her. Cami rides me until we're close to the edge, then soon we're spilling over.

"Four," she screams out as we both chase our high. She runs her fingernails down my rib cage and mixes pleasure with pain. Cami paints her mouth across mine while we're still connected, fully satiated.

"One more to go," I tell her with a smug smile.

"I'm numb from the waist down."

"Then you better hold on." Swiftly, I grab her waist and flip her on her back, then rub my fingers over her clit. It's swollen, and I can tell it's sensitive.

"Holy shit," Cami mutters as her eyes roll to the back of her head. It's only another couple of minutes until she's digging her nails in my arm and exploding in relief.

After cleaning up for the second time, I fall asleep with a smile on my face and Cami in my arms.

I've imagined what it would be like being with her, but none of those fantasies even compare to reality.

Not in a million fucking years.

CHAPTER NINETEEN

CAMERON

DAY 15

I WAKE up with sweat covering my forehead, and my body feels like it might be on fire. Eli's legs tangle with mine, and I try to wiggle out of his hold. Drinking too much last night has made me feel like shit. As soon as I sit up, I know something isn't right. It's not the first time I've had stupid amounts of alcohol, but this seems different. I wobble when I place my feet on the floor, and I find some strength to move forward. My chest is tight, and I wonder if I slept weird or if our sexual activities last night did a number on me, but I've never felt this way before. On repeat, I tell myself I'm just hungover. That's all this is.

I walk to the bathroom and slip on a robe when I start shivering and coughing.

"Cami," Eli mumbles from the bed in a sexy morning rasp.

"In here," I respond. My voice sounds different, and it burns when I swallow. "In the bathroom," I say louder, but my throat is scratchy, which isn't typical for me after a night of drinking.

Footsteps lightly sweep across the floor, and he opens the door wearing loose hanging sweatpants and notices me leaning over the sink. When I meet his eyes, they go wide.

"Are you okay?" he asks, concern coating his tone.

I choke down my fear of being sick and push my hair out of my face. "I think I drank too much."

"Do you have a fever?" he asks.

I bring my palm to my forehead and shrug.

"Where's your thermometer? We need to check your temp."

I point at the cabinet between us. He comes closer, grabs it, then hands it to me. I look down at the digital stick in my hand, turn it on, and place it under my tongue. Moments later, it beeps, and when I see the result, I want to cry.

"What does it say?" Eli searches my face, but he knows by my expression that it's not good news.

I create distance as tears build in my eyes. I shake my head, trying to comprehend what this means.

"Cami? What's it say?" he repeats, his voice deep and cautious. He knows something's wrong. We both do.

I look over at him, and when he steps toward me, I hold out my hand to stop him from coming any closer. "It's 101.6. Stay back, please. If I'm sick, you're at a higher risk of hospitalization if you catch it."

Those aren't the words I want to say after the amazing night we shared. Images of his mouth and hands on my body flash through my head, and I replay all the times we kissed. If Eli gets it from me, it could kill him, and I wouldn't be able to live with myself. We've been isolated together for two weeks, which means I've been a carrier since I arrived.

Disregarding my pleas, he takes two steps forward. His voice softens. "No, let me take care of you."

"Please," I beg again. "Being near me is too dangerous with your asthma," I remind him. The episode he had a week ago is still fresh in my mind. It was traumatizing to watch him struggle to breathe.

"You don't know what you have, though. It could be anything. It's flu season, too." He tries to calm me, but it doesn't work. My gut screams that I'm not that lucky, and that this isn't something

I'll get over in a few days. I was around hundreds of people before the shelter in place was ordered. People who were asymptomatic continued going to class because no one knew how bad it was until it was too late.

"A fever this high is enough warning. For your sake, we have to treat it like the worst-case scenario to be on the safe side." I choke back a sob, then turn on the faucet, holding a washcloth under the cool stream. "I'll be okay," I say more to comfort myself than him. Eli stares as I wring out the water.

"If you really have it, then so do I. It's a little too late to think I haven't caught it." He shrugs as if it's no big deal. "We kissed on the second day here and have been around each other every day since then. We'd be foolish to think otherwise."

I relentlessly shake my head in disagreement. "No, that's not one hundred percent true. We don't know, so we have to take every precaution possible."

"I'll text your brother and see if he has any advice so we can be more prepared in the coming days. He might have a few tips and tricks or something, but let me help you, Cami." He's nearly begging, and I'm not sure I'm strong enough to push him away when I just want him to hold me.

"Eli," I whisper. Panic and unease swim through my veins as my chest rattles. The morning after such an amazing night isn't supposed to be like this. I wish we could have breakfast together, spend the rest of the day snuggling, and relive last night. Instead, I have to force him to leave me alone.

He exits the bathroom, and for a second, I think I may have gotten through to him. Moments later, he returns with Tylenol and two bottles of water. He sets them on the nightstand and glances at me. "You can't get dehydrated. Take these and text me if you need anything, okay? Anything at all, even if it's just to keep you company. And if you get any worse, let me know."

I nod, wanting to lie down and cover myself with a pile of blankets. "I will. Thank you."

Once he's out of the room, I grab the thermometer and place it on the bedside table, then take the pills. The sheets are a crumpled mess at the end of the bed from rassling in them last night, and I try to fix them the best I can, but my head is too heavy. I'm scared of what the future holds, more than I've ever been before. I know Eli said he'd text Ryan, but I text him too.

Cameron: I think I have the virus. What should I do?

I don't expect him to answer me anytime soon. Having a conversation with him the past couple of weeks has been difficult. My brother's a goddamn hero, but I selfishly wish he were here with me.

Somehow, even though I'm restless, I fall asleep. My skin sticks to the sheets, but I'm cold, so I stay covered. Fever dreams capture me, and I wake up in a panic with a racing heart. I should let my parents know what's going on, but I also don't want to worry them. My mother gets irrational when it comes to her children. Considering my brother is on the front lines of this war against the illness, she's got enough on her emotional plate to deal with. But if I end up hospitalized, the guilt of not speaking up would consume me. Before I call, I take my temperature again. As I suspected, it hasn't changed.

She answers, and I know she's smiling by how upbeat she is. "Hey, sweetie. Why didn't you FaceTime me?"

I inhale a deep breath, trying to find the strength to speak. "Mom."

"Yes, dear?"

"I have a fever and feel like death. I'm terrified." My voice trembles as I try to swallow down my fear. I don't care that I'm twenty-two and nearly crying. Sometimes, I just want my mom to comfort me and say everything will be okay.

"How high is it?" The concern in her question is clear.

"When I just checked, it was 101," I say with a small cough. "I was fine yesterday, but woke up like this," I explain.

She lets out a fearful sigh. "Can you get tested so you know for sure?"

"They're not testing people like me with no pre-existing conditions who're young and healthy. Only if they have to be admitted. They'll instruct me to stay home, take Tylenol, and if things get worse, call the helpline," I repeat what I read online a few days ago, then take a sip of water.

"Did you call Ryan?" Mom asks, alarmed. "Maybe he can get you one?"

"I texted him, but he's swamped, so I don't know when I'll hear back. He'll say the same, though. I've watched the news, read all the articles, and am aware of what the process is right now." The line is silent for a while. "Hello?"

"Yes, I'm still here. I'm extremely worried about you. If you would've listened, you'd be with me so I can take care of you. I'd call the family doctor to do a house visit, and he'd get you tested."

This isn't the time for her to power play me or use our family's money to get special treatment. I'm not labeled high risk and would feel guilty when thousands of other people are being denied. "No, if I would've stayed home, you'd be sick too. Me being at the cabin is for the best for you and Daddy." I try to ease her mind, but it's no good. She'll lose sleep over this regardless of what I say.

"Promise me if your temp rises or you have trouble breathing, you'll go to the ER. The nearest hospital is only a half an hour away from you."

"Okay, Mom," I concede.

"Cameron," she pushes, not satisfied with my response. "If I need to drive there, I will."

"That's unnecessary. The entire place needs to be disinfected. I'll go if things get worse. Eli is here and will check on me, too," I reassure her, hoping to ease her nerves. We've been FaceTiming or texting every couple of days since I've arrived and when I told her Eli was here too, she had a gleaming look in her eye. She adores him.

"I should be with you," she argues with a huff.

"No, you shouldn't. Please, just stay put," I demand. "Being around me is too dangerous."

She sighs again. "Cameron, I love you. I just want you to be healthy."

"I know, Mom. I love you and Dad too. I should let you go, though, so I can rest," I say calmly, wishing it would rub off on her.

"I'll send your love. Please keep me updated," she orders, and I agree before ending the call and going to the bathroom.

I take a shower, hoping it settles my nerves. As the water runs over my body, I lean against the wall. It's almost too hot, but I breathe in the steam and flower-scented body wash. After a while, I slip on a fluffy robe and wrap a towel around my head.

As I'm walking into the bedroom, I hear a tap on the door. "Cami?"

"Yes?" I ask, going to the edge of the bed.

"I brought you something to eat. It's on a tray on a small table I moved into the hallway," he says.

I blink away tears at his sweet gesture. "Thank you."

"Are you feeling any better?"

I look down at my pruned hands. "Not really, but I just got out of the shower, so I still feel really warm. The steam felt good, though."

"Take two Tylenol every four to six hours," he says on the other side of the door, and I hate that we have to stay so far apart. It's torture after being so close to him.

"I will," I mutter. "I appreciate you cooking. Hopefully, I can get it down."

"If anything, it'll help not to take the meds on an empty stomach and give you some strength."

"Right now, all I want to do is sleep. Maybe I'll wake up better." I snort at my wishful thinking. "Are you okay so far?" I ask.

"Yeah, I feel great besides the fact that I can't be near you. I miss you already. Chanel misses you, too," he adds at the end, and it earns him a slight laugh. She must've snuck out earlier when he left.

"You can send her in," I respond, knowing how often she annoys Bruno.

He chuckles. "Nah, she's fine. The three of us are hanging out. She's spilling all your secrets, though."

Somehow, he has me smiling. Few people can do that so easily.

"Never trust a pussy. Sometimes they're liars." I grin.

On the other side, he snickers. "I'm walking away now so your food doesn't get cold. Text me when you're done, and I'll come and grab the tray."

"Okay, I will. Thanks again," I say and hear his feet shuffle down the hallway with Bruno's big paws trampling behind.

Once he's gone, I go to the hallway, and see my mother's wooden serving tray with a giant bowl of oatmeal, toast with jelly, along with more bottled water and a note.

I lift it, close the door behind me, then climb back into bed. I grab a spoon and dive in. I blow on it and then swallow, enjoying the warmth. It actually feels really good on my throat, and though I have no appetite to continue, I do anyway. Then I open the piece of stationery and smile at Eli's sloppy handwriting.

Can't stop thinking about you :)

I'm swooning.

Completely smitten by this man who's captured my heart.

I wish more than anything we could be together right now and devour each other like we both want.

I take a few more bites then look over at the bottle of Tylenol. Not enough time has passed for another dose, so I force myself to wait before taking more. They haven't kicked in yet, which means I'll have to deal with this fever the best I can.

After I'm finished eating, I place the tray outside, then change into some comfy clothes. I text Eli so he knows I'm done and feel sad when I hear him grab everything. I wish he could come in and wrap his muscular arms around me. Instead of dwelling on that, I turn on the TV, but the news is bleak, and it pushes me into a panic, so I click through the channels to busy my mind.

I don't know for certain what is wrong with me, but it's best to act like I have the virus and take every precaution to keep Eli safe. Thinking about each moment Eli and I have spent together has my heart racing and my head pounding. I'm more frightened about him getting it than I am for possibly having it.

I adjust my pillow and settle on the Hallmark channel. Though it seems impossible, I try to get lost in a movie where illnesses don't exist and all the sex scenes fade to black.

Instead of being cooped up in this room with horrible thoughts floating through my mind, I want to be on the couch with Eli watching stupid shows and playing drinking games by the fireplace. It's become my new normal, and I already miss his company.

In fact, I think I'm falling in love with him. And truthfully, I'm okay with it. He treats me well, calls me out on my shit, and wants the best for me. I've never had a man make love to me and please me in the ways Eli has. We understand each other on a higher level, and over the past few days, I've seen a side of him I never imagined. Elijah Ross is the whole damn package, and I want him in my life forever.

The movie ends, and another begins. This time, it's about a couple who grew up together, lost touch, and are now back in the same town. If I wasn't so out of it, I'd think it was cute and would be more invested in the story. However, I drift in and out of sleep and go from being ice cold to blazing hot. No matter what I do, I can't get comfortable. At some point, I wake up and check my temperature, noticing it dropped some. My phone buzzes on my nightstand, and when I grab it, I see it's my brother. I desperately answer it.

"Just seeing how you are." He sounds exhausted.

"Fever's high. Chills and sweats. I've taken Tylenol every six hours like clockwork, but it doesn't seem to do anything. Drinking water. I'm eating, though I'm not hungry," I explain.

"Seems like you're doing everything you can. I wish there was something more I could say, sis, but there's not. Make sure you try to walk around some. It won't be easy, but it'll keep your lungs functioning. You'll be tired, and your fever will probably stay high for a week, maybe a little longer, but keep an eye on it. If it doesn't go down and your coughing worsens, go to the ER." He recites it as if he's repeated that dozens of times to his patients.

I blow out a frustrated breath, feeling overwhelmed by everything he's said. "I'm going to be okay, right?" I know he can't answer with certainty, but I still want some comfort from him because he's seen different scenarios from those who've tested positive.

"I'm sure you will. If you feel like you can't breathe, try rolling onto your stomach. It's helped some of my patients," he explains. "Stay hydrated. If you're cold, don't cover yourself unless you want your fever to increase."

I laugh, kick off the blanket and pull the sheet over my body. He knows me so well.

"You're your own best advocate with your health. If something isn't right, tell Eli and call your doctor. Most are able to recover from home without major complications, just watch for signs. You know you can text me anytime, too."

"I know."

"How's Eli doing? Keeping his distance from you?" I'm sure Ryan is just as concerned about Eli as I am.

"As far as I know he's okay. Staying away from me but helping from afar." I wait a few moments. "How are you?" I ask.

He lets out a lengthy breath. "Good as I can be. Not sure how much longer my colleagues and I can keep working these back-to-back shifts, but we're short a few doctors because they ended up getting too sick to work. Luckily, we've had teams of medical staff fly in from other states to help."

That's the most I'll get out of him about his well-being and

164

don't push any further because I can only imagine what he's seen or had to do. It's a war zone out there. Ryan has been training to save lives for years, but he wasn't prepared for a pandemic. None of us were.

"Please take care of yourself," I plead. He's my best friend, and I can't imagine losing him.

"You too, Cameron. Call me when your mind wanders and you're in freak-out mode. I'll try to calm you down. Don't forget to take your meds. It might help with your anxiety," he says sincerely. A deep voice speaks to him in the background. "I've gotta go. I'll check on you as soon as I can."

"Sounds good. Thank you," I offer. "Love ya, bro. Take care."

"Love you too."

The call ends, and I sit in silence. Uneasiness and fear build inside me, and the walls seem as if they're closing in.

I'm having a panic attack.

Lying down, I close my eyes and try to steady my breathing, trying to slow my racing heart. I count down from ten, breathe slowly through my nose, and release it through my mouth. It takes several times before I come back to earth and gain control.

My throat's dry, so I take sips of water, but even that's exhausting. Eventually, I fall asleep thinking about Eli. Though I'm not the praying type, I send one up, begging he doesn't get sick. The realization that we were never safe is like a giant slap in the face, and I wish more than anything this wasn't happening.

CHAPTER TWENTY

ELIJAH

DAY 18

THREE DAYS HAVE PASSED since Cameron started running a fever. I've wanted to do nothing but hold her in my arms and tell her everything will be fine, but I can't. All I can do is make her food, leave it in the hallway, and write sweet notes on stationery I found in the kitchen. When I go to her door, I hear her dry cough and that she's gasping for air. I want to burst inside her room and confirm she's okay, but I also understand the severity of the situation. Cami's already warned me, more concerned about my asthma than anything else, and I don't want to upset her further.

Her cough sounded worse this morning, so I called Ryan again. He didn't answer, but I know he will as soon as he can. I keep my phone on me and charged at all times, making sure the sound is up just in case Cami needs anything. She hasn't asked for much help, and I don't know if it's because she's too proud or if I'm doing such an outstanding job of keeping her stocked full of water and food that she doesn't need anything.

Sometimes, I pace in front of her room. Other times, I sit with my back against the door and just talk to her. She responds, but I can tell she's weak and tired. I've never felt so hopeless in my life.

Chanel has rubbed against my legs and jumped on my lap so many times she's learned how to guilt me into giving her double treats and wet food. She sometimes meows outside of Cami's door, which makes her laugh. Last night, she watched the news and learned some tigers in a zoo tested positive, and although there's conflicting evidence confirming that, she won't allow Chanel inside her room anymore to be on the safe side. The cat and I have bonded over being locked out, and I've tried to keep my mind busy by taking Bruno on extra walks as much as possible for fresh air. It's still cool and crisp outside, and I can't wait for spring.

When I'm sitting still is when the fear of what's going on around me settles in. Cami could have the virus. I want to constantly ask how she is, but I also don't want to be annoying.

My mind wanders further, and I can't stop thinking about the night we spent together. I've never experienced chemistry like this with anyone, except her.

Something changed between us, and we haven't been able to explore it further since she got sick. I haven't mentioned us being *together*, and the silence has me doubting everything. In the back of my mind, I'll never be good enough for her or her family's standards. I don't have the social status her parents require, and Cami's always been out of my league. I'm still scraping by financially and hope that eventually changes, but the future is unknown at this point. Even if I got promoted, I don't think her father would approve because I don't have a trust fund to pay for everything.

Just as I'm walking into the kitchen, my phone vibrates in my pocket. Thinking it's Cami, I hurry and answer, but it's Ryan.

"How is she?" he asks. His tone is rushed, and in the background, different medical codes are blared over a loud intercom.

I exhale slowly. "She's coughing nonstop, and I know she's having trouble breathing by the sounds of her wheezing. I check on her every few hours, but I don't feel like I'm doing enough," I tell him. "We FaceTimed a couple times and she looked absolutely miserable."

"All you can do is help her from a distance. Stay away from her, Eli. If Cameron has the virus, she's highly contagious, and I'm worried about what would happen if you got it. Unless her coughing gets worse or she struggles to breathe, they won't admit her with how limited they are on space and equipment. She texts me each time she takes her temp, and her fever seems to be holding steady for now," Ryan explains.

"But it's still high," I say with defeat in my voice.

"It is, but she still won't be admitted unless she's worse than—"

"Worse than what she is now?" My agitation takes over. I'm so frustrated. Not with him, but over the testing situation and how our healthcare system is overwhelmed to the point of nearly collapsing. This situation of uncertainty weighs me down, and I've never been so stressed before.

"I know you're upset. I am too. I'm also concerned about my sister, but the hospitals are complete madhouses. We can't get the supplies we need, and the staff are growing exhausted. Honestly, she's better off staying at the cabin unless her symptoms and condition worsen. She's healthy, young, and is still breathing on her own. Cameron is doing better than a lot of people right now, and she's a fighter."

"You're right, man. I'm sorry for adding more to your plate. I know you're going through hell. I'm not upset with you, just concerned, exhausted, stressed, and anxious—which I'm sure you are too. I hate that Cami isn't well and is all alone in there. I'm worried about you and my family too. Everything feels so damn heavy and uncertain right now, but I'm gonna do whatever I can for her."

"I know you will."

"Don't forget to take care of yourself too."

"I'm trying." I clear my throat, knowing his time is limited, but

I don't want him to be blindsided later. "Before I let you go, I should tell you something."

He chuckles softly. "That you're in love with my sister? Because I've known that for years."

I smirk. "Yeah, but now that she doesn't want to murder me as much anymore, I think I have a real chance with her. I hope at least."

"Well, aren't you glad I offered the cabin now?" he says, amused with himself. "I'm happy for you guys. It's about goddamn time."

"Wait, you knew she'd be here?"

"My mom briefly mentioned Cameron might be going up there, but she wasn't positive. Though she never said anything about Cameron bringing Zane. Honestly, I figured if you both ended up in the same place, you two could finally talk through your issues."

"Sneaky bastard," I quip. "I haven't been able to bring it up to her yet, but no matter what, she'll always be the one for me."

"I better be the best man at your wedding," he taunts.

"Your lack of sleep is making you delusional." I laugh, though the idea of marrying Cami and making her my wife and the mother of our children makes me smile.

"I'll keep checking in on you guys when I can, but I gotta get back." He releases a deep sigh, and I can tell he's broken. Each passing day has become more tragic than the previous.

"No problem. We'll chat soon, or I'll text you."

"Sounds good. Be safe, my friend." Then he ends the call.

I stand in the kitchen with my back against the counter. When I close my eyes, I see flashes of Cami and me together. I replay her lips brushing against mine, and my firm hands on her hips. Right now, I want to kiss the freckles sprinkled across her nose and hold her tight against my chest. Dealing with the unknown while being completely isolated from reality is scary. When we were together, it wasn't so bad, but now that I'm alone, I want nothing more than to be with her.

Though I did a thorough clean of the cabin when she first got sick, I continue to re-sanitize constantly. After I grab some Clorox wipes, which are like gold these days, I wipe down every surface. Whatever I can't use them on, I spray Lysol until the space smells like my mother came over and cleaned from top to bottom.

Grabbing my inhaler and my laptop, I sit on the couch to get some work done. I answer an ungodly number of emails. Though our company's revenue has fallen by thirty percent across the board, some are still reporting to work. Each year around this time, I finalize enough contracts for my commission check to catch me up on bills through the summer. Without that, I'll struggle, even if I have three roommates who help share the bills. I try to push the thoughts away, but it's impossible not to worry. It doesn't take long before I'm surfing the web and reading more articles. I shut the screen, not wanting to see any more, not when Cami is upstairs with a high fever.

Noticing it's now lunchtime, I make some chicken noodle soup and find some saltines for Cami. I grab a few bottles of water and carry it all upstairs.

I placed a small table outside of her room so Bruno doesn't help himself to her food, though I've been keeping him downstairs as much as possible. Setting it down, I tap on the door, then walk away.

She typically waits a few minutes before opening the door to give me time to leave. I go to my room and take a shower. The warm water pounds against my skin and does nothing to soothe the uneasiness I have. The entire world is experiencing loss on such a high level that it seems like a messed-up apocalyptic movie, and I'm trying to process it the best I can.

After I change, I realize I need to do laundry. Cami probably needs clean clothes too, so I text her to leave her hamper in the hallway for me to grab. She doesn't respond, but she's probably sleeping, so I put a load of mine in the washer. Afterward, I busy myself with work for the rest of the afternoon. My stomach growls, and I glance out the window, noticing the sun is setting.

I skipped lunch, so I decide on an early dinner. I make a couple of peanut butter and jelly sandwiches and grab a bag of chips. Bruno sits at my feet while I eat, and Chanel sleeps on the opposite end of the couch. I turn on the TV and get sucked into the news. When I see images of the city with streets that are usually full of people looking like a ghost town, I shut it off. I don't know why I torture myself further by watching it. Standing, I decide to prepare something for Cami to eat and switch over the washer.

When I go back upstairs to grab the tray, I notice what I brought her earlier hasn't been touched. Worry covers me like a warm blanket as I move closer. I stand in the hallway and suck in shallow breaths, trying to hear her on the other side. She's not coughing, and I hope more than anything that she's still breathing. Knowing I shouldn't go in, but not giving two fucks, I crack open the door.

All the lights are off, and the curtains are drawn, making the room pitch black. I see the outline of her body in the bed and notice she's lying on her side. For a second, I stop and listen, and can hear each time she struggles to inhale, but then coughs a few times. My head tells me I should leave, that I need to get out, but my heart protests. Instead of being cautious, I take several steps forward, then crawl into bed next to her. She rustles as I wrap my arm around her blazing hot skin. It might be dangerous, but I just want to comfort her. Forcing her to deal with this alone isn't an option anymore. If she's ever needed me, it's now.

CHAPTER TWENTY-ONE

CAMERON

I'M in and out of sleep. My throat burns, and my ribs hurt from coughing so much. I wish I could close my eyes and the next two weeks would pass by. Yesterday, I emailed my professors and told them I'm sick so they're aware of why I'm behind on my assignments. It should be the least of my worries, but keeping a perfect GPA has been high on my priority list. It's taken years of dedicated studying and late nights doing homework, but none of that matters when the world is in chaos.

This is only the beginning of feeling like shit. Ryan mentioned I'd feel worse before I got better. I've followed his instructions and have walked around some when I feel strong enough. Each time I get the strength to sit up, I check my temperature and track the doses of Tylenol I've taken, so I don't take too much. My mother has called to check on me daily, but I downplay how I am so she won't show up and try to take care of me.

I go from having the chills to my body being on fire several times a day. No matter what I do, I can't get comfortable. I've soaked in the bath, hoping it'll help with the stiffness and body aches, but it hasn't. Though my appetite has vanished, I've forced myself to swallow down food.

Eli has done his best, giving me plenty to eat and drink

throughout the day, so I don't have to leave my room. I'm already going stir-crazy lying in bed, but I can't hang out downstairs with him, which kills me. Though I can't deny how much I miss Eli's company, witty banter, and the way he makes me laugh at the stupidest things. The past two weeks with him, even though they started rocky, ended up being the most memorable moments I've shared with someone. It's because he understands me on a level most don't bother with.

Most guys want me because of who my family is, with hopes to climb the social ladder. That's why I've dated those who are well off because they have nothing to gain from being with me, and they're unimpressed by my fortunes.

Eli doesn't give two shits about my social class and has always been his true self.

As I drift to sleep, I hear a light tap on the door and pick up my phone to see it's a little after noon. I'm not in the mood to eat, but I tell myself I need to at least try. Minutes turn into hours, and I don't move. Eventually, a muscular arm wraps around my stomach, waking me from a deep sleep. I press against him until I realize how close he is.

Turning my head, I panic when I see Eli snuggled against me. Every cell in my body is on high alert because he shouldn't be in here. I try to find my words, but nothing comes. I need to tell him to get the hell out.

"Eli," I say in a hushed tone. "You can't be in my bed."

My words don't faze him as he tightens his arms around me. I have a mini panic attack, knowing what could happen to him if he catches it. If I'm having a hard time breathing, what will it do to him? I've tried my hardest to stay away, but here he is, inches from me.

"Eli," I repeat louder this time, moving his arm off me and creating space between us. Just the quick movement has me breathless, but I stand my ground. "You have to leave. My germs are all over this room."

He gives me a cute smirk and shakes his head. "Nah, I don't think so. I'm staying."

What the hell is he doing? "This isn't up for discussion. You know the rules."

"Cami." He sits up, not taking his eyes off me. "It's okay. Let me hold you through this."

I suck in a deep breath, needing the oxygen and strength. "Please…" I'm nearly in tears as I beg because I don't want to be the reason that something happens to him. The guilt would kill me before the virus could. "This is too risky."

"We had sex three days ago. Before that, we kissed—*a lot*. You undoubtedly had been carrying it this whole time, considering we've been here for over two weeks and haven't been around other people since then. I've come to terms with catching it. It's just a matter of time before the onset of symptoms, so the least you can do is let me comfort you."

Sitting on the edge of the bed, I shake my head. "You don't know that for sure."

"I do. It stays in your system for days, sometimes weeks. You were fine, and now you're not. Do you regret being around me?"

His eyes pierce through me. "Hell no. You're worth it, Cami."

As I open my mouth, instead of words come coughs, the ones that make my entire body protest. I'm having a fit and can't catch my breath as I choke for air. Eli rushes toward me, and I hold up my palm, trying to keep him at arm's length. A second later, he's leaving and returns with his inhaler.

"Inhale a few puffs of this," he instructs, shaking it before handing it to me. "Just inhale and hold it in your lungs. It always helps me with the tightness."

I don't want to use his medicine, but I'm desperate for relief. Listening to him, I do what he says when I stop coughing enough to draw in some air. After I have some, my chest isn't as tight, but I'm shaky. I return the cap and hand it back.

"Keep it," he tells me. "Use it when this happens again."

"I can't do that." I sit and lean against the pillows.

"You need it more than I do." He's stubborn to the bone. "Another option is sitting in the shower with hot water and breathing in the steam. That can help loosen things up."

Once I'm settled, Eli goes to the bathroom and comes back with a cold washcloth.

Leaning over, he rests it on my forehead, and it slightly soothes me. Eli crawls back in bed with me and moves to his side, propping himself on his elbow. I wish he'd be smarter about this and keep his distance. Regardless of not taking a damn test, I have all the common symptoms, and the odds are stacked against him.

"I can tell you're uneasy about me being in here, but even if you demanded I leave, I still wouldn't."

Snapping my eyes shut, I don't want to fight, knowing he'll do what he wants anyway. "So you're okay with me living with guilt if something happens to you? That's not fair."

"I'd never blame you. The choice is mine, and I'm choosing you."

My heart flutters, and I smile. "I don't understand how you can flirt with me when I look like a zombie." It's easy to know how pale I am, along with the bags under my eyes. Every time I go into the bathroom, I avoid the mirror like a vampire.

"You're beautiful," he whispers, grabbing my hand and kissing my knuckles. I pull away.

"It's like you're trying to get sick," I reprimand.

He softly chuckles. "No, I'm not, but I've already accepted it. In the past seventy-two hours, I haven't been able to get you off my mind, Cami. I've wandered around wishing I could be near you. And I can't figure out how you did it."

"Did what?" I ask, meeting his eyes.

"Got into my head and heart so quickly," he admits. "I mean, you're still a major pain in my ass, but it's different now."

We still haven't talked about our night together. I was curious if he'd mention it, or just pretend nothing happened. I've wondered if he considers being with me a mistake, but seeing his expression is proof that he doesn't.

"You're positive I'm what you want?" I ask for confirmation. Though I feel like death, talking about this is keeping my mind off it.

Eli tilts his head. "Are you serious?"

I shrug because I'm jaded to men using me, but his confession has butterflies dancing in my stomach. "Yeah, kinda. Not sure I'm your type and all."

"And what's my type exactly?" he asks with an eyebrow arched.

Honestly, the kind of women Eli likes are beyond me, but most guys find me hard to handle or intimidating. "I dunno, perky boobs, fat lips, brunette, tan and tall." I list out everything I'm not.

He smirks at my obvious lack of confidence.

"I'm thinking about a blonde with freckles, great suckable tits, and the perfect height for fitting under my arm in bed with the best ass in all of Manhattan," he cracks. It's the first time I've laughed in days. Even when I feel like shit, he has a way of helping me escape.

"That's very descriptive. You sure she exists?" I mock.

"Oh, I'm fucking positive." He winks, beaming at me. "And just to throw all your doubts out the window, you're the only woman I want, Cami. I'm confident about that. All those years of teasing each other led us here, and there's nowhere I'd rather be. Must be the fever giving you those crazy thoughts because I thought I've been more than obvious," Eli jokes. He comes closer, pulling me into his arms until my head rests against his chest. His heart pounds as he holds me. Partly due to his confession, the other part because my anxiety spikes at this whole situation. My coughs come in waves, but they're manageable. With him near me, I calm down.

As I drift away to dreamland, my breathing steadies, and Eli shifts, waking me. "You need to eat something. You skipped lunch, and I was getting ready to make you some dinner. What would you like?"

"I'm not hungry, and nothing sounds appealing."

He softly presses his lips to my forehead. I miss his touch and wish I could kiss him. "Eating isn't for enjoyment at the moment. You need to stay nourished and hydrated."

I take shallow breaths, covering my mouth when I cough. "What about some tomato soup?"

He grins and hurries out of bed. "Grilled cheese?"

"No, maybe just a piece of toast." I rest my head on the pillow as he nods.

"I'll be right back. Don't go anywhere." He winks.

I snort and roll my eyes as I pull the sheet up to my chin. Eli walks out, and I'm still smiling. The anxiety I've felt the past few days is slowly fleeting. It's comforting to have Eli nearby, but it doesn't mean I've forgotten the risks and what's at stake—his life.

CHAPTER TWENTY-TWO

ELIJAH

DAY 25

A WEEK AGO, I went against my better judgment and entered Cami's room. I knew I was risking exposure, but I also couldn't forget how close we were just three days prior. Nothing I can do will change what happens. She's been overly cautious, covering her mouth when she coughs and is continually washing her hands. There was a point when she even talked about wearing a mask to keep me from getting sick, but the damage has already been done.

I gave her my inhaler, and she uses it when she can't catch her breath. Each day, I make her three meals, and though she doesn't have an appetite, she eats some of it to appease me. There were a few nights when I was worried as fuck about her because she sounded like she was choking, and all I could do was wait it out. I was so fucking helpless watching her, wishing I could do more but knowing I couldn't.

Each night, I lie next to her until her breathing steadies, and then she finally falls asleep. Her coughing has subsided, and lately, we've slept until the sun wakes us.

This morning, I roll over to see Cami looking at me with a sweet smile.

"I could get used to this," she says in a low voice.

"To what?" I clear my throat.

"Waking up with you in my bed," she admits, and if she wouldn't freak out, I'd kiss her the way I've imagined for the past ten days. Our lips haven't touched once, and she's been adamant about me keeping some distance, though at this moment, we're only inches apart. I watch her chest rise and fall, and I'm tempted but don't. "You hungry?"

She nods. I slide the blankets off and stand, grabbing the thermometer and handing it to her. After she places it in her mouth, we wait for it to beep. She removes it and glances at the reading, then grins.

"No fever," she whispers, turning it around to show me.

"*Finally*." I let out a relieved breath. "You beat it, Cami."

I sit on the edge of the bed and open my arms, and she falls into them.

"What's wrong?" I ask, noticing she's upset.

She lets out a sigh. "I'm just happy and worried all at the same time. I'm feeling a little better, but I'm so goddamn concerned about you."

Gently pushing away, I carefully wipe the tear that spills down her cheek. All I want to do is comfort her. "I've been counting down the days. I might be in the clear."

"It could take longer than that." Her head lowers. "Up to three weeks sometimes."

I lift her chin with my finger, forcing her to look at me, then smile. "I'm thinking positive. And now that you're feeling like a billion bucks, let's get you fed."

"Hardy har har." Cami stands, and I notice how frail she is as she yanks the sheets and blankets off the mattress and holds them in her arms. "I need to disinfect this room."

"Don't overdo it. You've not been fever-free for twenty-four hours yet," I remind her, grabbing the linens. I snicker at the thought of her using the washing machine, and she notices.

"What's so funny?"

I shake my head as I leave her room and head toward the laundry room downstairs. "Nothing. Nothing at all."

I've done laundry a couple of times now, making sure she had clean clothes and changing out of mine twice a day to be on the safe side. One of these days, I'll make her do it for shits and giggles, but she's still not one hundred percent yet, even if she thinks she is.

Cami texts me and lets me know she's going to take a shower. I send her a thumbs-up emoji as I stuff the big fluffy blanket and sheets into the wash. Knowing she's feeling better has me hopeful that if I get sick, I'll be able to recover too. While I hope I'm just asymptomatic, I'm not holding my breath. It's not like I could anyway, my asthma wouldn't allow it, though it hasn't been flaring up as much since I've been here.

After I pour the detergent in and start the cycle, I go to the kitchen and grab a skillet and pull out the ingredients to make breakfast. The cabin still has plenty of food, probably enough to last another two weeks. While I wish we could get back to normal by then, I'm convinced it won't be that soon.

As I'm frying sausage links, Cami appears and looks around. "Wow, it's super clean in here. Feels weird to be down here after all this time."

"You know who my mother is," I remind her. "I learned a thing or two growing up. A person should never go to bed with a sink full of dirty dishes or a filthy floor."

Cami laughs. "You're close with your mom, aren't you?"

I crack the eggs in a bowl and whip them together, sprinkling in cheese, onions, and mushrooms. "Absolutely. One day, I hope to repay her for all the sacrifices she made for Ava and me. I know being a single mother wasn't easy, but she gave us the best she could, and we turned out okay." I look over my shoulder at her and wink.

"You did," she says, and I can't stop grinning. How could a woman like her even think about being with a man like me? "You were always well-mannered, too."

Turning on the burner, I put oil in the pan, swirling it around until it's covered, then dump the ingredients inside. It sizzles and pops. "Well, no, not always," I tell her. "I went to the principal's office quite a lot in high school. Trust me when I say you didn't miss much."

She huffs. "I wish I could've experienced public school. You were lucky to have a normal life. I've dreamed about what it must be like."

I tilt my head. "And there are a billion reasons people would switch places with you."

"It's not all it's cracked up to be, Eli. Money doesn't buy happiness, and it sure as hell can't buy love or normalcy. Sure, there are perks, but being a St. James has done nothing but cause me problems, honestly. Why do you think Ryan went to med school?"

I already know the answer to this question, but I stay silent.

"To make a name for himself, to break out of being more than an heir. I somewhat envy him for choosing a path outside of the family business."

This side of Cami is different, more vulnerable, and I'm sure she doesn't show it to many people. "Well, for what it's worth, I think you've handled things the best you could. And I think you're going to be kick-ass at running a business. You're smart, kind, and compassionate. Even if the media doesn't see it, I do."

"You're sweet to say that."

"I meant every word." I wink. Once everything's done, I put our food on plates, then hand one to her with a fork and napkin. She sits at the bar and slowly eats as I pour some milk into a glass.

"Thanks." She covers her lips and continues around a mouthful, "You spoil me."

"Have to keep you well fed." I sit next to her and eat too.

Her blue eyes meet mine, and she tucks loose strands of hair behind her ear. "I promise I'll repay you for taking care of me."

I laugh and waggle my eyebrows. "I can think of a few ways."

Cami snorts. "*Men*."

"You know it, babe."

Once we're done, I rinse the plates and put them in the dishwasher.

"Oh, I thought we could watch a movie and relax for the rest of the day," I suggest.

Cami grins with a nod, and we enter the living room where Chanel sleeps peacefully. She tries to hold her like a baby, but Chanel is dead set on wiggling free. Eventually, she succeeds and jumps down, prancing away as if Cami inconvenienced her.

"Wow, what a traitor. Chanel doesn't see me for nearly two weeks and acts like she doesn't even know me," Cami says with a shrug just as Bruno runs toward her.

I yell his name and tell him to sit.

"You know it's rude to get in people's personal space. Stop," Cami says as his little tail and butt wiggle. His tongue hangs sloppily out of the side of his mouth.

"This is why dogs are better," I taunt. "When they see you, it's like the very first time. Cats don't give two shits about their humans."

"She misses me in her own way," Cami explains. "She'll come to me when she's ready."

I nod. "Whatever you say."

Cami coughs, then her face contorts.

"You okay?"

"Yeah, my chest and ribs are killing me. But I'm alive, thankfully." She looks at me with sad eyes.

"Hopefully, you'll be good as new soon."

A smirk slides across her lips. "Can we build a fire?"

"By we, you mean *me*, right?" I tease, and she playfully rolls her eyes. "Sure." I glance over at the neatly stacked wood by the fireplace and make a mental note that we'll probably need more in a few weeks. Grabbing some, I place it inside with a quick start log and light it. Once it crackles and pops, and the flames lick upward, Cami smiles. I meet her on the couch where she's already covered with a blanket.

I sit beside her and turn on the TV. Cami snuggles closer and rests her head on my shoulder. There's nothing we could watch that would take my attention off her right now. I've been dreaming of moments like this for weeks.

Eventually, we lie on our sides, spooning as she watches a murder mystery movie. I'm so comfortable, but tired, and end up falling asleep with her wrapped in my arms.

Hours pass, and I'm being woken to Cami repositioning herself. When I sit up and put my feet on the floor, I close my eyes tightly because my head is pounding. I suck in a deep breath, and my chest burns. While I try not to freak out, Cami notices.

The concern in her voice is clear as she asks me if I'm okay.

"I don't feel great," I admit, not wanting to worry her, but not wanting to lie either. I don't know if it's my asthma and a migraine, or the onset of the virus. Immediately, Cami gets up and rushes upstairs, then returns with the thermometer.

"Let's check if you're running a fever," she states, handing it to me. "I disinfected it, I promise," she says as I turn it on and put it in my mouth.

Seconds later, it beeps. When I glance at the reading, Cami leans over to see it.

"Eli." She gasps and shakes her head. "*No*. That's high."

I want to assure her everything will be okay, and that I'll be fine, but we both know what this means. All I can do is take it one day at a time and fight like hell to live if I have it.

"Get plenty of rest, and drink tons of water," she instructs, and I shoot her a look.

"I know, babe. I just took care of you, remember?"

"I'll help you, Eli. Shit, you need Tylenol," she says.

Cami gets up again and comes back with a glass of ice water and Tylenol. I swallow them down. "I kinda wanna go to bed." A wave of exhaustion hits me, and I'm not sure how bad I'll feel later, but so far, it's mostly fatigue and chest tightness.

I glance out the large windows at the beautiful mountaintops and realize the sun hasn't set yet. I've slept for a few hours, but it doesn't seem like enough. I didn't expect to wake up and be symptomatic. Every time Cami and I get some alone time, the universe claps back. But I'll be damned if I'm giving up that easily. As if this year could get any worse, it proves that it can.

I stand and go to the stairs, and Cami follows like my shadow. I go to my room, and when I turn around and look at her, I notice she's holding back tears that will fall any second.

"Come here," I say, opening my arms. "What's wrong?"

"I knew this would happen." She sobs. "I knew you'd catch it from me, and I—"

"Hey. Hey." I put some space between us so I can fully look into her eyes. "Being able to hold you when you were so beat down was worth it. I'd do it a thousand times over. Don't you forget that." I wipe away her tears. "We'll get through this. I have the hottest nurse in New York."

My words make her smile, and I take a mental snapshot of how beautiful she is, even when she's upset. Her heart is so big.

"Now, disinfect everything. I don't want you to catch this again." I suck in air, and it feels like an elephant is sitting on my chest.

"Let me grab your inhaler," she whispers, and I pull her back into my arms, wanting to hang on to her warmth because I know this might be the last time we touch for weeks. "And I'll call Ryan too," she adds.

We break apart, and I walk to the bed. "Seriously, take care of yourself, okay?" I demand. "Promise me you won't overdo it, please. You're still on the mend."

Cami looks at me, wipes away more tears that stain her cheeks, and nods. "I promise, but right now, I'm more concerned about you than myself."

CHAPTER TWENTY-THREE

CAMERON

WHILE I'M NO LONGER RUNNING a fever, I'm still not myself, but it's manageable. I'm not as tired, and even though the dry, unproductive cough lingers, I know I'm on the tail end of this. Thankful is the only way to describe how I feel because it's been devastating for others.

Last night, after Eli went to his room, I grabbed his inhaler. He insisted that I keep it, but I wouldn't feel okay doing that knowing how much he'll need it. It still burns to breathe, but my lungs are stronger than his.

I can't stop blaming myself, and while it's counterproductive, this is my fault. Eli came here to escape his inconsiderate roommates. Who would have thought being here was more dangerous? If I could go back and self-isolate myself for the first two weeks of being here, I would. Then again, we never would've gotten to know each other on a deeper level if I had done that, so I'm torn on how to feel.

After I jump in the shower and dry my hair, I move the small table from outside of my bedroom to his, then I go to the kitchen. Chanel rubs against my legs and meows as I place her favorite chicken and gravy food in her bowl. Taking a step back, I trip over

Bruno, who's right behind me, and catch my fall. I yell at him, and he gives me sad eyes.

"I'm sorry, but you can't stand that close to me."

He takes a few steps back and watches me. "Come on, buddy. I'll feed you the good stuff." He follows me around as I fill his bowl and throw him a few treats, then bring Chanel upstairs to eat. As they chow down, I realize I'm hungry too, a sensation that's new, considering I've not had an appetite. Eli took great care of me, and I'm determined to do the same for him.

Cooking isn't my strong suit, but I'm thankful for the internet because I wouldn't have known how to scramble eggs. I put them on the plate and decide I need to become more self-sufficient. There's no reason I can't teach myself and do more.

A smile touches my lips because I actually made something else without burning down the cabin. I load the tray with everything and some bottles of water, then carry it upstairs. As I'm walking down the hallway, I hear Eli struggling. His coughs are deep, and the wheezing makes my heart drop. Helplessness overtakes me as I frantically knock on his door.

"Eli," I call out. "Are you okay?"

Instead of answering, he continues coughing. I swallow hard, set the tray down on the table, and wait for him to come to the door.

Once he catches his breath, he says my name.

"Eli?" I ask, becoming more concerned with every passing second.

"I'm fine," he finally croaks out.

"I made you breakfast," I proudly say.

"Thanks, baby." He sounds defeated. I'd trade places and experience being miserable all over again if that'd mean he didn't have to. Though I want to go inside his room and be with him, I walk away. As I'm near the bottom step, I hear the door open, then click closed.

Knowing I need to keep myself busy, I disinfected the entire cabin again. After three hours of scrubbing, spraying, and wiping,

I'm finally done and sweating. Though Eli told me to take it easy, I can't stop obsessing about making sure everything's clean. I quickly take another shower, then grab my laptop and try to catch up on the previous two weeks of assignments I missed.

Several professors emailed and asked about my health, along with some of my classmates. It takes a while, but I reply to everyone and explain I'm okay. Afterward, I go through my writing assignments and finish some homework that's due at the end of the week.

I'm so distracted, and it's hard to stay focused. Bruno jumps on the couch and rests his head on my thigh just as Chanel prances by and sits in front of the enormous window. The hours pass, and I try my best to make something for lunch but resort to microwave meals. I'm sure Eli will understand, considering my cooking experience. Dinner's the same. He doesn't complain, though I suspect he's not too hungry anyway.

I text Kendall and update her on everything. The conversation isn't a happy one, and she tries her best to comfort me as she listens to my fears. I'm so thankful to have her in my life through the good, bad, and ugly.

After I eat and get some reading done, I try to fall asleep but struggle with knowing he's suffering. The virus attacked him quicker than it did for me, and I don't know what to do. I text Ryan, hoping he replies and gives me a glimmer of hope, then I force myself to close my eyes.

The next two days are the same routine. I clean, cook, and worry. The worst is still to come, and I'm on high alert, constantly checking to make sure he's still breathing.

On day four, I'm more concerned than I've ever been. The news only magnifies my anxiety.

Just as Ryan enters my mind, my phone rings. I hurry and answer.

"How are you?" he asks, sounding like he got run over by a Mack truck.

"I'm better. Not quite myself, but I'm getting there. I tire fairly quickly and still have somewhat of a cough, but mostly, I'm okay."

"I'm so glad to hear that. How's Eli?"

I pause and release a deep breath, trying to stay positive so my brother doesn't notice how concerned I am.

"He's struggling, and I'm worried he's too stubborn to say he needs anything."

"How do you know?"

"He's gasping and coughing; the kind of deep cough that's buried in your chest. He's using his inhaler, but it's not helping very much. I'm desperate."

"If he's rapidly declining, you should call the hotline and get him to the hospital. I'm not saying that to stress you out more, but to get him help before he progresses too far."

"I will as soon as we hang up," I say, knowing they won't let just anyone walk in and get tested. If I would've called for myself, they would've told me to stay isolated. Will it be the same for Eli, too?

The line is silent for a few seconds. "When this is all over, if I ever complain about working seventy-hour weeks or bitch about being too tired, you have permission to kick my ass," he orders. "Because I'd be happy to only be working that much right now."

"Same, oh my God, same," I agree, feeling bad that he's probably working over a hundred hours right now. "And if I ever complain about not knowing what to order for takeout, kick mine. I didn't realize how good I had it until delivery was no longer an option."

Ryan chuckles and agrees with me. "Did you hear Dad and

Mom donated a few million to a relief fund to help the hospitals in the city get more medical supplies and the proper masks?" Ryan asks. "It's been reported on the news, and people are posting articles about it. I've had so many of my colleagues thank me with tears in their eyes. I'm kinda taken aback since I had nothing to do with it."

"Well, that doesn't surprise me. You're loved and appreciated either way." I smile, hoping he understands how true that is.

"Or rather, our parents love a great PR stunt," he mumbles. "Though I'm grateful and we desperately needed it, they could've made it anonymous and donated without the family name attached to it, you know? But they wanted the recognition, so I got dragged into it. They flashed my picture across the screen a dozen times. You know I don't want that kind of attention," he says. "I'm here doing my job because it's what I'm passionate about."

"I'm sure it wasn't like that, though. They're proud of you," I say. "I am too, Ryan. Though I worry about you."

"I'm *more* worried about you and Eli, and I'm pissed I can't be there for you guys," he says.

"Your patients need you, and I'm better now. I won't let anything happen to your best friend. I care about him a lot."

"I know you do. This weird love-hate thing you two have has been going on for years. I was wondering when you'd both get over it."

I chuckle. "Right? Too bad it took this long to realize it, but honestly, I've never felt this way about a guy before."

"Eli's in love with you," he tells me matter-of-factly. "Please don't break his heart."

Wait, what? I blink hard at his words, my throat dry for a completely different reason now. Ryan blurts that out with ease, as if he has no doubt about it.

"Hurting him is the last thing I'd ever want to do," I say truthfully. "This past month has been a game-changer for me. I'm falling for him, too."

189

"Honestly, it's about goddamn time." He chuckles. "Take care, okay? Keep me updated."

"I'll do my best. I gotta call and check in with Mom, too." I've been texting her because she wants to have full-on conversations, and I was too tired for that.

"Don't forget to call the hotline. See what they say based on his symptoms."

"I will as soon as we hang up," I reassure him. We say our goodbyes, then I look up the number.

Little did I know how much of a disaster it would be.

The phone rings; I'm put on hold, then get disconnected. I'm not a quitter, so I call back, get transferred again, and hung up on after thirty minutes of waiting. Four hours of my time are wasted because I get nowhere, and I'm so goddamn frustrated that I can't contain my aggravation.

I busy myself at the stove and attempt to cook hamburgers. When I remove the meat from the frying pan, it's burnt. Bruno's at my feet, and I pinch off a piece from the patty and fling it to him. He sniffs it, then walks off without eating it.

"Great," I whisper. "The dog won't eat it, and he more than likely eats poop."

I heat a frozen pasta meal, then take it upstairs to Eli.

Not like it's anything new, but I sleep like shit, tossing and turning. Once I wake up and chug coffee, I attempt to cook more eggs. After another successful scramble plate, I deliver them to Eli, then call the hotline again. Determined to get through to someone today, I'm hoping since it's earlier, I won't have as many issues. It takes two hours to speak with someone who's knowledgeable.

She asks me all the basic questions, the same ones people can find online to self-diagnose.

"I'm sure I had it the past two weeks, and now he's caught it. I'm more concerned because he's asthmatic."

"Has his fever risen above 102?" she asks.

I think back to all the times Eli has checked in with me. "No."

"Is he showing signs of improvement?"

"Compared to what?" I ask with a sigh, then continue before she can respond. "Listen, I just want you to be honest with me. What are the odds of him getting a test so we can know if it's the virus, flu, or something else?" I can only imagine how many people she speaks to daily who treat her like shit, so I try to rein in my frustration, but it's so damn hard.

"It looks like they're only testing those who end up admitted and need lifesaving equipment. They aren't testing everyone at this moment…"

"Even for someone who shows all the symptoms and has asthma?" My words come out choked and harsher than I intend.

"I wish I could give you better news. If your friend gets worse, call a local doctor to get a referral first. Otherwise, I'd stay inside and monitor him closely."

The line is silent for a moment, and I thank the woman, then end the call. Tears pour down my cheeks, and I sob into my hands. My hands are tied, and there's nothing more I can do but watch him.

The cabin's clean, the pets are fed, and now I'm lonely. I walk upstairs and knock on Eli's door, wanting his company. I sit on the floor and wait, placing my back against the wood.

"Yes?" he asks. It's not quite lunchtime yet, so I'm sure he's wondering what I want.

I rest my head against the door and look up at the ceiling, trying to find the strength to keep it together. "I miss you," I say.

He chuckles, then coughs before responding. "I miss you, too."

"I hate that you're so close, yet so far away," I admit, thinking back to what Ryan said about his feelings for me. I hear him sit on the floor too. We're back to back with only a few inches of thick wood separating us.

"Me too. What have you been doing today?" He takes several puffs of his inhaler.

"I called the hotline for you to see if we could get a test and…"

"They refused," he finishes. "Amiright?"

"Yes." I grow quiet and close my eyes, wishing this would pass soon.

"I'll be okay, Cami. I'm already on day five and am on the mend."

I smile. "You don't sound like it."

"Oh really? I heard women really like a man with a raspy voice," he tells me. "I've just been practicing to impress you."

I chuckle and shake my head, appreciating the way he's trying to lift my spirits. "I'm worried that if you recover and I get it again, then you could be re-infected. I was reading yesterday about someone who tested positive twice. We'll both just keep passing it to each other, and eventually one of us will get it bad enough to be hospitalized," I say. I know I'm being dramatic, but it's a possibility.

"When I'm better, we'll wipe down every wall, ceiling, and floor, not leaving a spot untouched. As long as we do our due diligence, we'll be okay. I just have to survive the next week," he breathlessly says.

"My cooking isn't the best, so you're probably starving," I mock, wanting to get a rise out of him. It works because he laughs. "Bruno wouldn't even eat my hamburger." I pout.

"To be fair, he's a vegetarian," he states, and I burst out laughing.

"You're such a liar." I shake my head. "It was burnt. He probably thought it was mud."

"I would've eaten it," he says. "I can't taste for shit anyway."

Chuckling, I smile and love that we can still communicate like this. If this is as close as we can be, I'll take it. And when he's better, I'll make it up to him in all the right ways. I miss his touch, his kisses, and the way he looks at me as though I'm his everything. Just the thought of losing him scares me beyond belief.

CHAPTER TWENTY-FOUR

ELIJAH

DAY 35

It's been twelve grueling days of feeling like shit, but when I woke up this morning, I didn't feel like there was a pillow over my face. Though my back aches from coughing so much, I think the hard part is over, as long as I don't relapse or get pneumonia. I roll over in bed and reach for the thermometer. I place it under my tongue and wait, and I'm shocked to see my fever has finally broke. Thank fuck.

There were a few days when I was worried. My inhaler barely provided any relief, and I almost asked Cameron to rush me to the hospital, but I kept holding on, hoping my body would fight it. When I was at my worst, I told my mother I was sick too. She nearly had a heart attack, but I couldn't keep it a secret just in case something terrible happened.

Mom called Ava, who then insisted on coming to the cabin, but I told her it was best if she didn't and that I'd check in as much as I could. I climb out of bed and go to the window that overlooks a meadow. Fog bellows over the dense grass, and in the distance, I can see the mountains. Instead of going back to sleep, I take a hot shower. Though my skin is sensitive to the touch, the water relaxes me and the steam helps my breathing. Once I'm done, I realize I gave Cami all my clothes.

I forgot I asked her if she could do my laundry yesterday. I only packed one suitcase because I didn't know how long I'd be here. At this rate, I should've taken everything I owned, considering I probably won't be returning home for at least another month. Probably longer, though. Not that I'm complaining because that means more uninterrupted time with Cami.

For the first time in ten days, I leave my bedroom and walk down the hallway with a towel wrapped around my waist. I carefully take the stairs, and when I get to the bottom step, Bruno comes rushing toward me.

"Hey, boy." I smile wide as he tries to jump on me, and I tell him to sit, then pet his head. It's barely past six in the morning, so everything is quiet.

When I walk into the washroom, my clothes are in the dryer. A grin touches my lips because she actually figured it out, not that I completely doubted her. Okay, maybe just a little. I put all of my items into a spare basket and put on a pair of joggers and my favorite Yankees T-shirt. Just as I turn around, I nearly run into Cami.

"Oh my God!" she yelps, covering her mouth with her hands. "I thought you were a burglar."

I chuckle. "Who broke in to steal my underwear?"

"I came downstairs to make some coffee so I could start doing schoolwork, and I heard noises."

I look down at her hand and notice she's tightly grasping a skillet.

"And what's that for?" I point at it and grin.

"To kill you!" She swings it in the air, putting all of her weight into it. Bruno runs to her and thinks it's time to play.

I hold the basket under one arm and laugh. "Not sure if that would do the job, babe. You should stick with statues. At least they're heavy as hell."

Her eyes meet mine, then she gazes down my body and back up. A blush hits her cheek, and I smirk. "Are you feeling better?" she asks, swallowing hard.

I nod. "Much. Not fully, but I'm on the rebound. No fever."

"Thank God," she whispers, her shoulders relaxing. Cami drops the pan, then wraps her arms around me. Dropping the basket, I hold her close, smelling the sweetness of the shampoo in her hair, and never want to let her go. "I've been so worried."

"I know. Me too," I admit. "I got lucky. Didn't hurt having you take care of me." I smirk.

"It's easy to take things for granted when you suddenly realize you may never be able to again," she says, then pulls away. "I had tons of time to think about that between my fever-induced nightmares. The fear of not living is what scared me the most. But the realization that tomorrow isn't promised was empowering in a way."

I grin and pick up my basket of clean clothes. "I can relate. I thought about all the things I wanted to do and never have, along with adding to my bucket list. I've never been in a situation like this before, and I never want to be again." I cough, and suck in as much air as I can, but I end up dropping the basket, and Cami moves toward me.

"I'm fine." I gasp, trying to catch my breath. This has rapidly become my new normal for the past week and a half. While I bend over because I don't have much strength, I know it's best to stand straight to open my airway. Quickly, fatigue takes over, and I have a full-blown asthma attack.

"What can I get you?" Cami asks, panicking. I can't even catch my breath long enough to say two syllables, but she figures it out on her own. She rushes away, running as fast as she can out of the room. I feel like someone is squeezing the air out of me as the pressure of a million pounds sits on my chest. Though she's only gone for a moment, it seems like an eternity.

She hands me my inhaler, and I put the plastic up to my mouth and push down, allowing the medicine to fill my lungs. I take three more pumps, needing it to work faster than it is. Eventually, it does, but my heart is galloping at full speed, and my hand is unsteady from the medication hitting my bloodstream. Cami watches me intently with fear written all over her face.

"I'm okay," I tell her. "My asthma attacks are a million times worse right now. Go wash your hands," I remind her, knowing she touched something that came from my room.

She quickly does, and I pick up the basket, then follow her into the kitchen as she scrubs her hands under the hot water. I'm exhausted all over again, and my body aches, but I'm determined to have a little time with her today.

"You're going to make me worry to death or give me gray hair."

"You'd be sexy with some gray." I chuckle and notice how spotless everything is. "You know what would be great right now?"

Blinking up at me, she grins. "Coffee?"

"Yep. The caffeine helps with my asthma."

"Really?" She tilts her head. "That's good to know."

"Yep, I learned that in college. My doctor suggested it when I didn't have a rescue inhaler at work one time. He said coffee acts as a bronchodilator and in a pinch can help with attacks. It's a reason I drink several cups in the morning."

She nods. "Strong ass double shot of espresso coming right up," she sing-songs, using the fancy machine that auto grinds the beans. As it drips, she places a can of Lysol in my basket. "When you go up there, spray everything down, then take your linens off the bed and put them in the washer. We have some cleaning to do. I want the virus out of the cabin *forever*. We'll know we're in the clear in a couple of weeks if we're both healthy and then should just live here for eternity."

"I could definitely get on board with that plan." I'm dying to kiss her, but don't. It's too soon.

Bruno moseys into the kitchen, goes to his bowl, and barks

three times. Cami looks at me with a proud smile. "I taught him to do that when he's hungry."

I nearly snort because he's been commanding me like that since he was a puppy, but it's sweet that they've been bonding, so I don't want to burst her bubble. "Nice. Maybe I should stay in my room, and you can teach him how not to get in people's personal space."

She pets his head, then grabs some food and pours it in his dish. "We made a deal. I think by the time we return to the real world, Bruno will have his act together."

"He's his own boss. But hey, you're cuter than me, so it's possible he'll listen." I shoot her a wink, then go upstairs. I take a few puffs from my inhaler and set my clothes on top of the dresser. Though I feel weak, I pull off all the sheets and blankets, and put them in a big pile before spraying as much Lysol as I can handle in the room. Considering the smallest tasks exhaust me, I sit down for a short break.

Grabbing the linens, I carry them downstairs, stuff them in the wash, and start it before going to the kitchen and lathering my hands with soap. It's weird how it's become an obsessive part of my everyday life—wash, clean, sanitize. I didn't think much about it before all of this happened, but now I can't do it enough.

Cami stands at the stove, and I admire the booty shorts she's wearing that show off her perfect ass cheeks. She's making scrambled eggs, something she recently learned how to do when I first got sick and even whipped up some pancake mix. After a second, she catches me staring and turns and grins. "Coffee's ready."

I can't stop staring as the early morning sun reflects through the window and casts a glow over her skin. Damn, she's just so gorgeous, and she's going to be mine. A small smile plays on my lips as I walk toward her, and she hands me the mug. I thank her, then grab some creamer before taking a sip. "Whoa," I say, tasting the hint of chocolate. "This is different. What kind is it?"

"Some ridiculously expensive kind Daddy enjoys," she says. "You like it?"

I nearly down half of it in two gulps. "It's incredible."

"Apparently…" She lingers, then chuckles. "It comes from cat poop."

"What?" I nearly choke, looking at her with wide eyes, hoping she's joking. "Are you serious?"

She acts like it's no big deal. "Yeah, Kopi Luwak. Some luxurious bean. I don't know. Sounds odd, but glad you like it, though."

"Rich people are so fucking weird," I murmur, and she laughs.

Cami places the eggs on two plates, covers them, then goes to a cabinet. "We have enough to last us through an apocalypse." Cami waves her hand down a shelf, and she's not lying. It's full of golden coffee bags. I lean against the counter, admiring how sexy she is. "Great. Guess we're drinking cat shit coffee for the rest of our quarantine."

She turns around and notices my gawking, then laughs. "What? Do I have food in my teeth?"

"Nope, just thinking how fucking beautiful you are and how it was torture being away from you," I say, setting my mug down. Reaching for her, I pull her into my arms, tempted to close the gap between us. Our mouths are inches apart, and all I want to do is kiss her. I've missed her so damn much, but I also don't want to re-infect her. She should have some immunity built up, considering she survived it, but there are still a lot of unknowns about this particular virus. As I'm about to pull away, she stands on her tiptoes and moves in. Taking the lead, she parts her lips and presses them against mine. I should push her away, but now that I'm tasting her, I lose all my willpower. We exchange a searing-hot kiss, and we nearly melt into one another. I can't help but grab her ass as she moans into my mouth.

"Eli," she whispers.

"Mmm," I say, plucking her bottom lip between my teeth when she pulls away.

"Our eggs are getting cold," she says dreamily, then goes in for another.

"Not the words I want to hear right now." I groan, adjusting myself.

Her hands twist in my hair, and the only thing that stops us from going any further is the fire alarm blaring through the cabin.

Her eyes go wide. "Fuck, fuck, fuck!"

I notice the burner is on with a skillet on top, and it's smoking. Immediately, I turn it off and let out a hearty laugh.

"Right when I thought I was becoming a chef." She groans. "At least I took the eggs out before walking away."

"This is true," I reassure her with a wink, opening the windows and fanning a towel to try to clear the smoke. "Nice save."

Once the alarm is off, and our ears are safe, Cami grabs another pan and pours the pancake mix inside. "I thought I'd try my hand at pancakes since the video I watched on TikTok made it look easy."

"You shouldn't make them so big. They might not cook all the way through and will be difficult to flip," I explain because I learned the hard way when I was thirteen. It always seems like a good idea, but it's not.

She turns and throws me a smart-ass look. "I've got this."

"Pretty confident for someone who nearly caught the cabin on fire," I tease.

She wrinkles her nose and snarls.

I lean against the counter and watch her. Because she's so stubborn and wants to prove her point, she grabs the handle with both hands and proceeds to flip it as though she's a celebrity chef. Only she puts too much strength into it and the cake flies in the air, then falls dough side down on the floor with a splat. Seconds later, Bruno rushes into the kitchen and gobbles it up, not caring how hot it is.

Cami frowns, then shrugs. "Good boy." She leans down and pets his head. "He's a champ at cleaning messes."

I nearly fall down laughing. "I wonder how many *messes* he's eaten in the past two weeks."

"It's our little secret." She looks at him. "Right, Bruno?"

He stares up at her, his little tail wiggling as he begs for more. "Bruno," I warn, and he turns and trots away once he realizes he's not getting it. I try not to feed him too many table scraps because it's not healthy for him.

"Let me help," I tell Cami, and she reluctantly moves over. I scoop the batter, then pour it into three perfect circles. They're palm size and don't take too long to cook before I flip them over.

She playfully scoffs. "Okay, now you're showing off."

"Pancakes were one of my favorite things to make when I was old enough to stay home alone. I remember cooking so many one time that I was nearly sick from eating them. I had a stomachache for days."

A giggle escapes her. "I can only imagine. We never ate stuff like that growing up. I would've probably killed someone for a stack of pancakes at thirteen. And now, I go between eating like a rabbit and gobbling up all the processed shit because of how strict my mother was."

"She *was* weird about sugar," I confirm, remembering the weird shit she'd try to feed me when I was playing with Ryan. It always tasted like cardboard.

She nods. "Apparently, it goes straight to your hips. So every Valentine's Day, Easter, and Halloween, I buy ten bags of candy. You'd probably throw up if I told you how much of it I eat. Then I go back to refusing carbs for a few months. It's a vicious, stupid cycle."

"Your secrets are safe with me." I make a few more pancakes and give her a stack of four, then she grabs some fancy ass maple syrup from the cabinet.

"Well, now I know the way straight to your heart. Bread, sugar, and sweets."

She nods, takes a bite, and moans loudly. "And your cock," she adds.

"That too." I chuckle. "And what's his name?"

She eyes me with a smirk. "Zeus. How could I forget?"

"Damn, I've really missed you," I admit again, imagining our night together.

"Me too." She grins with a mouthful. "I've missed having real food. It's so much better when you cook," she says.

I snicker. "Probably because it's actually edible."

"That is most definitely why."

I meet her eyes as I take my own plate to the table. There are unspoken words and stolen glances as we eat, both wanting to be all over each other but knowing we can't just yet.

We clean the kitchen once we're finished, but it takes a while since I get out of breath quickly.

For lunch, we pop a pizza in the oven and eat on the couch while we watch some new docuseries about a religious cult in Texas on Netflix. We lie around the rest of the afternoon, holding each other close, and I squeeze her just a little tighter while we watch the news.

Though it's been over a month since I left my apartment, I don't want this to end. I could get used to this. Cami's become such an integral part of my days that when this is all over, and we go back to our everyday lives, I'll probably be lost.

Eventually, she changes the channel, and we try to tune into something more comedic to take our mind off what's happening in the world. Though I have a lot of work to catch up on, one more day off won't hurt. We spend the rest of the night together, taking every advantage of this time as we can.

CHAPTER TWENTY-FIVE

CAMERON

DAY 41

It's been a week since Eli's fever broke, and I'm so damn relieved. We've taken extra precautions around the house and have cleaned it top to bottom several times. I've never been this germ cautious, but I find myself washing my hands regularly.

As I look inside the freezer, I see there's only one package of chicken left. We're out of eggs, bread, juice, and other stuff. When Eli enters the kitchen, he wraps his arms around my waist and kisses the nape of my neck. My eyes flutter closed, and I lean into him as he mentions making a run to the store. I turn around and watch him as he pulls his wet hair up into a bun.

"I was thinking the same thing, but just the thought of it makes me anxious as hell."

"I know, me too, but we need stuff." He leans down and slides a kiss across my mouth, and then it intensifies to something more possessive.

"Mmm," I hum, inhaling the scent of his freshly showered skin. He slips his tongue between my lips, deepening our connection.

By the time we break apart, I'm breathless, and a cocky smile plays on his lips. As my breasts rise and fall, he glances over at the clock. "I should probably get going if I want to find the good stuff before it's all gone."

"Should I come with you?" I ask. I've lived in shorts and T-shirts for the past few weeks, but I'd change into something warmer.

He shakes his head. "You'd have to sit in the car and wait. Most stores are only allowing one person per household inside at a time," he explains.

"Well, I don't mind. I've got my phone to keep me occupied and—"

Leaning forward, he kisses me again, making me forget what I was saying. "You're too sweet, and I'll never get enough of you, but you should stay here and hold down the fort." His mouth crashes against mine, and heat rushes through my body. I try to hide my smile, but he notices.

"What?"

"Just realizing how much of a flirt you are, trying to distract me with your delicious mouth." A blush hits my cheeks as my internal body temperature rises. I can't stop thinking about him being inside me again. We've been taking it slow while we both try to recover because Eli still has difficulty breathing.

He pops an eyebrow. "You're the only cock tease in this room."

I scoff. "Seriously? You're the guilty one."

"Babe," he says. Moving closer, he traces the shell of my ear with his mouth. "I've been thinking about the way you taste for weeks and would have you for breakfast every morning if you'd allow it."

"Damn," I say breathlessly. "I'll be your breakfast every day starting tomorrow. Also, I'm pretty sure I just had an orgasm."

He tucks loose strands of hair behind my ear, and I look up at him as he smirks.

"That's all it took?" He chuckles.

"Tease!" I push against his chest, then start running when he charges for me.

"Take it back," he playfully warns as he chases me around the kitchen.

Once he catches me, he tickles me until I nearly piss myself laughing.

I keep protesting and shaking my head until his lips capture mine again. "I don't want you to go," I admit, wrapping my arms around his neck. "Don't leave me."

"Trust me, I don't want to, but we're out of shit. I'll try to get enough to last us a few more weeks at least. Make a list of things we need, and I'll do my best to grab it all. Remember, the sooner I leave, the quicker I'll return." He winks.

"Think you can pick up some toilet paper?" I ask, half-joking, knowing it's nearly impossible right now. Pretty sure it's selling for several hundred dollars a roll on the black market.

I would've never imagined a time when toilet paper would be such a hot commodity, but everyone started hoarding it the moment people started panicking. Now it's like finding the golden ticket in a Willy Wonka chocolate bar.

"I'll see if I can find some," he says. "If not, I'll teach you how to do the pee and shake."

"Gross!" I laugh.

I grab a sheet of paper from my notebook and begin to make a grocery list. Eli randomly adds stuff to it too.

"I want to make you a fancy dinner. What are you in the mood for?" he asks.

"You. On a plate. Naked." As if he needed the reminder.

Eli takes off his shirt and stands in the kitchen. "Don't tempt me, sweetheart. I'll dick you down right now." He growls, causing me to snort.

"Uhh," I say. "Did you just say *dick me down*? Is that what all the players say these days?" Laughing, I lower my gaze down his body and admire every solid inch of him.

He shrugs, putting his shirt back on. "Apparently. Heard it from one of my roommates who's addicted to Bumble and Tinder."

I giggle. "Mm-hmm, sure. How about you surprise me? I don't want to give you a meal choice because what if it's impossible to find the ingredients? I've heard some things are tough to come by. You might not find half of what's on this list." I glance down at it. Who knew in today's world there'd be struggles to get common everyday items?

"You're right. I kinda forgot about that. I haven't been out in so long, I'm not sure what to expect. I'm a little nervous being around people."

I meet his eyes. "We could place a pickup order instead? I'm not sure when we could schedule it, but it's an option if you don't want to go out."

"No, it's okay. We need these things now unless you want to eat shitty microwave dinners for the next three weeks. You brought enough, but seriously, they're kinda gross, and the chicken tastes weird after a while." He gives me a look, and I snort.

"Remember the story about my mother? She would have a heart attack if she knew how much processed food I was eating here." I chuckle.

Eli tilts his head at me. "You're such a rebel."

I finish adding things to the list, then hand it to him. "I was able to order a few masks before I came here. Do you want to take one?"

"Yeah, that'd be good," Eli tells me, and I nod. I head up to my room to grab one while he grabs his keys.

When I return, he chuckles as he reads over the list. "Cadbury eggs. Mini Snickers bars. Reese's cups. You're not joking, are you?" He arches a brow.

"Hell no," I retort, handing him the mask. "If so, buy out the store. There's no dieting in quarantine. I've decided."

He lets out a hearty laugh. "You are something else, Cami."

"A hot mess and a handful? You're welcome." I glance over at the clock and then back at Eli. "Better get going. Maybe it won't be so busy this morning, but they're on restricted hours."

"You're right," he says. Taking a few steps forward to close the space between us, he kisses me until I'm breathless, but I still want more.

When we break apart, I squeeze my arms around him tighter. "Please be careful out there."

"I will. Don't worry, I'm not fighting vampires or zombies," he teases. "I grabbed my tiny bottle of hand sanitizer. Got a mask. And as soon as I get home, I'll put everything up, sanitize the hell out of it, then strip down naked and take a shower."

"Ooh, stripping. That sounds fun. Dicking me down later on that list too?"

"Only if you're a good girl," he throws back before tucking the small bottle back in his pocket and then folding the list and putting it in the other.

I kiss him goodbye one final time. Before he walks away, I grab a handful of his ass. "Hurry back."

"If you keep that up, I might not leave."

"Get out of here." I playfully point toward the door. "And watch out for zombies."

He shakes his head and throws me a wink. I watch as he leaves and frowns, immediately missing him.

While he's gone, I pull out all the cleaning supplies and rubber gloves so we can safely unload the groceries when he returns. I'd come across a video online demonstrating the proper way to disinfect items, and I'll watch it again before he returns.

After I have the counter ready for when Eli is back, my phone rings, and I'm giddy when I see it's Ryan. I haven't been able to get him off my mind, and it's been a while since we've chatted. When I answer the phone, I'm a little too excited.

"Ryan!"

He chuckles but sounds defeated. "Hey, sis. Doing okay, still?"

"Yep, pretty much back to my old self," I say happily.

"Ahh, so back to being a major pain in the ass," he retorts.

I scoff. "That's no way to talk to your favorite sister. How are you holding up?"

"I'm making it. I wanted to check in with you. How's Eli?"

"He's better. Not coughing nearly as much. He left not too long ago to get groceries. We were running out."

He lets out a breath. "Good. I'm so relieved and happy to hear that. Hopefully, he's being careful out there."

"He is. I was really scared there for a few days. It was horrible, but he pulled through," I say.

"Yeah, me too. I've been thinking about you two nonstop. Also, have you been watching the news?"

"I haven't in a few days. It's been depressing and wasn't good for my anxiety. The stories throw me in a panic, so I've been trying to busy my mind with other things." I'm happy I can quickly turn it all off but sad that Ryan can't.

"Good. Don't. We're low on ventilators, and things are a shitshow. The governor has been begging other states to send some. Companies are supposed to be making them, but they can't keep up with the demand. They set up tents in Central Park, Cameron. There's a military ship coming to help treat those who need medical help since the hospitals are at capacity. It's like living in the twilight zone," he says, his voice flat.

"Oh no," I whisper, ignoring his orders and going into the living room. I sit down on the couch and turn on the news, and he's right. I put it on mute, but I see the images of the tents and the boat. My mouth falls open in shock. I've never seen anything like this in my life. "Ryan, please be—"

"I'm extra careful," he interrupts before I can finish. "Thanks to all the donations swarming in, we have more PPE coming in, but it's still not enough. I spoke to Mom and Dad yesterday, and she said they're donating another few million to the relief funds, but I begged her not to make it a publicity stunt again."

"Good," I say, knowing how much he hates that. "I read about a lot of celebrities and other companies pitching in, so that's good news. Hopefully, Mom and Dad are staying home, though."

"They say they're locked in the house. But…" He pauses for a moment. "Staff is still coming in and out, which is ridiculous.

I've told them for weeks to stop doing that, but they're stubborn."

"I don't think they could survive without the help, though. Mom hasn't cooked since before you were born." I laugh, trying to lighten the mood, but he doesn't take the bait.

"You're right, but still. Let Eli know I called to check on him, okay?"

"I will. I love you so much," I tell him.

"I love you too, sis. I'll call you soon. Take care. Wash your damn hands. And stay inside," he repeats his orders like always.

I chuckle at his strict doctor tone. "Yes, I will. Bye." I hang up, staring at the TV in shock. Chanel prances up and crawls on my lap, purring. I pet and scratch under her chin, then seconds later, Bruno comes barreling in. He doesn't realize his size and believes he's still a puppy, so he jumps on the couch, then lays his head on my lap. Chanel turns around and hisses at him, batting at his nose. He looks so offended, and I laugh at his adorable reaction. As soon as I do, she jumps down.

"Aww, Chanel, sweetie. Come back by Mama," I coo. She glances at me as Bruno nearly crawls on top of me, looking at me with sweet, begging eyes.

"Now you've pissed her off," I tell him, and he licks my face.

"No, stop," I protest, but he doesn't listen. I eventually stand to get him off me, though it barely works. If my parents saw this big ass dog on their leather couch, I'm sure they'd shit a brick, which makes me snicker.

As I go to the kitchen and rummage through the fridge, I get a text from Kendall, and I can't stop grinning. I told her when I got sick, and I updated her when I could, but then Eli got sick, and my full attention was on him. However, I haven't had a chance to fill her in on any recent events. She went to her parents after self-quarantining in her penthouse for two weeks since she was at NYU before the lockdown. Now she's convinced it was the worst mistake of her life.

Kendall: So…this is my weekly health check-in.

I grin and immediately start typing up a reply.

Cameron: I'm great. How are you?

Kendall: Living my best life. I haven't washed my hair in two weeks, and my wardrobe consists of no bra, leggings, and witty T-shirts that drive my mother crazy. Also, wine. Lots of it.

I snort. Kendall then explains how annoyed she is that her mother keeps inviting people over to their house to socialize. I sympathize with her, and then she abruptly changes the subject.

Kendall: So, how's the Eli situation?

Cameron: He's doing good.

My heart races when I read his name. While I haven't told a soul about us having sex yet, I feel as if I'm obligated to spill it all to my bestie. I wanted to wait to see how it all plays out, but deep down, I know how happy he makes me. I swallow down my nervousness and try to find some courage. I type a few messages, wondering how to break the news that this is so much more than a physical attraction. Before I hit send, I delete it, then type it again. I'm nervous.

Cameron: I'm falling in love with him, Kendall.

I can see her typing, then the next thing I get is an emoji with heart eyes followed by nearly twenty exclamation points.

Kendall: I KNEW IT! I wish I would've bet you on it.

Cameron: Ha! Yep, you would've won.

Kendall: I mean, he is hot as hell, so I don't blame you.

Cameron: Yes, he is, but he's soooo much more. Sweet, considerate, and spoils me. Tells me how beautiful I am on the inside and out, and kisses me like tomorrow will never come. As cheesy as it sounds, it feels like we're living in a fairy tale being isolated out here just the two of us.

Kendall: Oh. My. God. I'm so fucking jealous. I wish I were stuck with a man right about now. I'd never leave the bedroom.

I giggle at her message, but this is a big deal for me. I've never felt this way about anyone before. Never. Kendall knows that too.

Kendall: Wait, did you have sex already? You never filled me in because you were so sick. HOW COULD YOU KEEP THAT FROM ME?

My cheeks heat instantly. I guess there's no going back on this conversation now. She sends another message before I have the chance to reply.

Kendall: OMG, you did. And you need to give me every dirty detail right fucking now.

Cameron: Imagine the best sex of your life and multiply it by a thousand. There you go.

Kendall: So, he's better than Prince Harry?

Cameron: Oh, hell yes. I can't even explain the things he

does with his mouth. And his tongue. I swear, it has superpowers.

Kendall: Lord, I think I just came on the spot. Does he have a brother?

She has me drowning in giddiness. Though Kendall's being silly, I know she's had a crush on Ryan since we were teens, but I don't rag on her today. There's plenty of time for that later.

Cameron: No, but I do ;) Eli only has a sister. You could bat for the other team if you wanna live out one of your college fantasies?

Kendall: I love the D too much. NOT Ryan's though. But truthfully, I'm happy for you. Zane was a bag of shit, and I always knew you could do better. Can't wait to start the next rumor that he cries after he orgasms.

Cameron: So, you said something so it would get back to Zane about me and Eli. Haha! I knew it!

Kendall: What are best friends for? Shit, my mother is calling. I need to answer this before she has a meltdown.

After we say our goodbyes, I'm floating on cloud nine. I go upstairs and jump in the shower, so I'm clean and ready by the time Eli returns. As I'm towel drying my hair, I see him pull into the driveway. I hurry and get dressed, then rush downstairs. Unlocking the door, I charge toward him, but he quickly stops me.

"Cami, wait." He holds out his hand. "I need to take off all these clothes first, but then…" He lifts an eyebrow, then pops the trunk, and I pull out a few bags.

"And then?" I laugh with my hands full. "You better not be talking the talk unless you plan to walk the walk…or fuck me into tomorrow," I say over my shoulder and head inside, setting everything down on the left side of the counter, ready to explain what we need to do before we unload it all.

I wait another second and notice he's not behind me and go outside, talking shit about how I'll do it all on my own if he's gonna be a slow poke. But when my feet hit the driveway, I immediately stop. My smile fades, and my heart drops into my stomach.

Eli turns and looks at me with his arms in the air as two men point guns directly at him. One sees me and is startled. Rapidly, he turns his weapon on me. I hold my hands up as my adrenaline spikes.

"Go inside," Eli says calmly.

"Fuck that!" one man shouts. "She's staying where I can see her. Don't fucking move," he demands, his beady eyes trailing over my body. I'm more frightened than when I was in bed with a deadly virus. I tremble, unnerved by how fidgety they are.

"What do you need?" I ask. All I want is for them to go, to take whatever, then leave us alone.

The other guy speaks and looks maniacal like he hasn't slept in days. Dark circles are under his eyes, and his hair is a greasy mess on top of his head. "You bought the last of the items I need for my pregnant wife and three kids. And the only other option is to pay double in the next city over, which I can't afford."

"I can give you plenty of money," I speak up, wanting to dissolve the situation and for them to disappear.

"You can have everything in my car. All of it. Anything that'll help your family," Eli offers.

His partner looks at me. "Come here," he demands, motioning with the gun for me to move closer. I don't dare defy him and do what he says. I stop when I'm standing next to Eli, both of our arms still in the air.

"I want your wallet, cell phone, and keys," he demands, and Eli gives him what he wants. The guy turns to me. "Your phone too."

I swallow, pulling it from my back pocket and handing it over. They turn and whisper to each other, and Eli glances at me. "Everything will be okay. Stay calm. They'll take everything and leave, and we can figure out what to do. We'll be fine. I promise."

Eli is always giving positive reinforcements, but I'm so damn scared that I don't know if I can believe him this time. Panic rolls in like a storm, and my breath feels like it's stuck in my chest. Seconds later, Eli has a coughing fit, and he needs his inhaler, but there's nothing I can do.

"What the fuck? Are you sick?" one of them asks, alarmed, then coming back over to us.

"No, he has asthma," I explain. "He needs his medicine."

Their eyes are wild like they're tweaked out as they dart back and forth between us, and I wish I could read their minds.

"You both need to turn around and get on your fucking knees," he orders.

Eli wheezes, and I turn around to help him but slip on the gravel. He reaches to catch me, and then the gun goes off. The shot is so close, my ears immediately ring. It all happens in slow motion, and I see Eli collapse to the ground, and he's bleeding. There's movement and yelling behind us. When I glance over, I see one man jump into Eli's rental, and he peels out of the driveway with the other guy behind him in a truck. Looking back at Eli, I start panicking as the realization hits me.

"Eli," I whisper, seeing the dark pool of blood, and I try to put pressure on his shoulder. I'm frantic as tears stream down my face. I'm not sure what I can do, considering we don't have our phones.

He's moaning out in pain as he reaches up with his other hand, but I warn him not to touch it. The sound of his agony is something I'll never forget for the rest of my life. There's so much blood. "Please don't die on me. *Please*. Elijah," I emphasize his full name, hoping to capture his attention enough to hear me.

I take off my T-shirt and place it over the wound, putting all of my body weight on him. Thankfully, his asthma attack wasn't severe, and he's breathing okay, but I'm still scared. "Hold this the best you can. We need to get you to the hospital."

Eli groans, and I dart inside the house and grab the keys to my Range Rover. "Fuck, fuck, fuck."

I reverse out of the garage, drive as close to him as I can, then get out and rush back to him. With all the strength I have, I somehow get him to his feet, but he's so fucking weak. I get him in the passenger seat, then buckle him in. My hands shake as I shut the door and run around to the driver's side. As I place my hands on the steering wheel, I notice his blood on my hands and arms.

"Eli." I put the SUV in drive, then speed down the long driveway that leads to the main road. He's fading quickly as he groans, and I try to keep him focused on my voice by talking to him. "Please, stay awake. Don't close your eyes."

I reach over and add as much pressure as I can to his shoulder while I keep one hand on the steering wheel. I tell him how much I love him, how much I've always loved him, but I'm not sure he hears me.

"Please, baby, please stay with me," I beg.

The nearest hospital is almost thirty minutes away, and he's losing so much blood. Tears spill down my face, and I know I need to stop and focus because I have to get us there safely, but at this rate, I'm scared we'll never make it.

This can't be the way I lose him. It can't be.

CHAPTER TWENTY-SIX

ELIJAH

DAY 45

I WAKE UP GASPING, open my eyes, and notice I'm in a stark white room. Machines beep around me, and there's an IV in my right hand. Pain shoots through my shoulder, and I wince as I look around. My left arm is in a sling, and my muscles feel stiff from lying here for only God knows how long. What the fuck happened? Where is everyone? What day is it? I have more questions than answers, and it frustrates the hell out of me.

I press the call button on the remote that's haphazardly looped around the hospital bed. A woman answers and asks what I need, but my throat is so dry I can barely get out any words. "Nurse."

"I'll send someone in."

Leaning back, I struggle to get comfortable. Twenty minutes pass, and eventually, someone enters.

"Oh, you're awake," she tells me.

"Where am I?" I ask gruffly. There are so many thoughts zooming through my mind, but I try to focus. I have a feeling I'm drowsy because of the pain medicine they're pumping in me, but I also feel out of it and exhausted.

"You're at Margaretville Memorial. I'm Patricia, and I've been your nurse since you arrived four days ago," she explains. "The doctor should be in soon." She's wearing full protective gear from head to toe, and her kind eyes are all I can see, but they remind me of my mother's.

Wait. My eyes go wide. "Four days?" I ask, clearing my throat.

"Yes. It's nice to see you awake," she says sweetly.

Patricia moves to the computer, looking at the monitors around me. She types as she asks me questions about how I'm feeling and what I would rate my pain level.

The door gently opens, and a male doctor enters, wearing the same protective gear as Patricia. "Hello, Elijah. I'm Dr. Jenner," he tells me.

"Hello," I say. "Nice to meet you."

He steps toward me, checking the monitors. From what I can see on the screens, my blood pressure and heart rate all look normal.

"I was just about to tell him," Patricia interjects, then smiles at me.

Dr. Jenner nods, then continues, "Your surgery went well. Being shot in the shoulder isn't an easy wound to manage, but you're lucky. A little farther over, and you might've not been so fortunate."

"You've been *very* lucky," Patricia emphasizes. "No spiked fevers, no infections, and all your stats have been stable the past twenty-four hours."

I blink. Surgery? Then I glance at my left shoulder again and realize it's all bandaged in the sling.

"Gunshot…" I mutter as flashes of that day begin to surface, and then I remember the two men who followed me to the cabin from the grocery store.

"I was able to stop the bleeding, and with some physical therapy, you'll be as good as new in a few months," Dr. Jenner explains.

"That's a relief," I breathe out.

"Patricia will get you on their schedule, so you can meet with someone for a consultation before you go," he explains.

"Thank you," I tell him.

Dr. Jenner nods and gives Patricia further instructions before he excuses himself.

"The medicine has had you in and out since the surgery, but we started to wean you off this morning to see how you'd react."

"I feel like I could sleep for another four days," I say with a grunt.

She grins. "Getting shot and having surgery will do that to you. We'll continue to give you pain meds until you're discharged. We just have to keep an eye on your stats for another couple of days to make sure you don't have any complications arise."

Another two days? I groan at the thought. She begins talking about how PT will teach me some at-home exercises to do since the facilities are closed. But I don't give two shits about that right now. The only thing on my mind right now is Cami. Sweet Cami. Is she okay?

With the little strength I have, I reposition myself in the bed and sit taller. The nurse adjusts my pillow when she notices me struggling. "Where's the woman who brought me here?"

"You came from the ER, then the ICU, so I'm not sure. Unfortunately, the hospital isn't allowing any visitors. No one's allowed to visit."

Well, that fucking sucks. I bet she's been going crazy not being able to see me because I know I am already.

"Though, someone has been calling at least once a day asking about you but since she's unable to prove she's family, we couldn't give her any information due to HIPAA."

That has to be Cami. "Did she leave a phone number?" I ask, and she shakes her head.

I vaguely remember giving the man my wallet, phone, and keys. I think he took Cami's too. Without my cell, I don't have anyone's number memorized except my mother's, and the last thing I want to do is alarm her, considering how nervous she was when I told her I was sick. I'd call Ava, but she recently changed her number, and I don't remember it. Basically, I have no choice but to lay here and wait for Cami to call.

I move a bit and wince. The pain shoots through my body and is like nothing I've ever experienced before. Leaning back, I tuck my lips into my mouth and hold in all the obscenities I want to scream.

Patricia looks at me and notices I'm uncomfortable. "You aren't due for another dose of meds, I'm sorry."

"It's okay," I tell her, though this fucking sucks.

"Do you have any other questions?" Patricia asks when she steps away from the computer.

"No, I don't think so." I let out a sigh, hating that I'm in here with no communication with the outside world. "Thank you," I add before she leaves.

"Hit your call button if you need anything."

"Oh, could I get some water?" I quickly ask, feeling thirsty regardless of being pumped with fluids.

"Sure thing," she replies with a smile.

She leaves, and I find the remote, then turn on the TV.

Moments later, she returns with a full cup of water and another with some ice chips. Setting them on the tray, she moves it closer to me. I thank her, and then I'm left alone, just me and the constant beeping. I take a sip of water, and the cold soothes my dry mouth. I can only use my right arm, which is annoying, but I know things could've been worse so I'm counting my blessings.

As I watch the screen, my eyes grow heavy, and I end up falling asleep. All I can think about is Cami and what she's doing. I hope she's okay and those men didn't go back to the house while she was there. I wish I could remember more, but the last memory I have is Cami tripping and me catching her. Then it goes black.

Two more days go by, and the hours pass in a blur. I go between sleep and watching the news, which doesn't help my nerves, but I can't seem to stop.

Breakfast is delivered, and I raise my bed to an inclined position. Once I'm settled, the phone rings. I try to answer it as quickly as I can, hopeful it's Cami, but when I do, a man speaks.

"Hello, this is Deputy Pomfrey. I'm looking for Elijah Ross."

"This is," I tell him.

"Oh, good. I've called a few times but haven't been able to get through. There was a police report made involving you, and I'd like to take your statement so we can move forward with an investigation."

Inhaling deeply, I try to recall exactly what happened. "Okay."

"Just start at the beginning, if you don't mind. Whatever you can remember," he says.

"Alright, well. I went to the grocery store, and as I was leaving, I noticed a truck followed me home. I didn't realize they had pulled behind me in the driveway until two men jumped out and held me and my…" I abruptly pause. What are we right now? Before I get too caught up in my thoughts, I clear my throat and call her what she is. "My girlfriend at gunpoint. Took my wallet, phone, and keys. They told us to get on the ground, and when I did, I started having an asthma attack. That's when she came to me, and the gun went off. I don't remember much after that," I explain, and it hurts to relive it all over again. It's all I've thought about for the past forty-eight hours, but repeating it aloud causes my anxiety to surface. I still can't believe this happened amongst everything else.

"According to Cameron's statement, one of them took off in your rental car while the other drove the other vehicle. We found yours totaled a few miles from the cabin. They ran it into a grouping of trees close and emptied it out before abandoning it."

"Great. Glad I got insurance on it," I say, shaking my head. Those two fucking idiots had to be completely tweaked out of their minds.

"Can you give me a description of them?" he asks.

"One said he had a pregnant wife and three kids. Both tall, around six feet with scruffy facial hair. Crazy eyes. They were driving a blue truck. Chevrolet. It was an older model, maybe mid-nineties." I think harder. "And the bumper had a dent in it like it'd been in a previous accident." It's coming back to me in pieces. I remembered seeing the truck in my rearview mirror as I pulled out of the parking lot, but little did I know they were following to rob and fucking shoot me.

"Any other details or information you can think of?" the officer asks.

"No, I don't think so. That's about it," I tell him.

"Great. If you remember anything else, I left my number with the nurse. I'll call you if we find them."

"It might be a while before I get a replacement phone, but I'll give you my number anyway," I tell him, then give it to him.

After the conversation is over, I set the phone down and get resettled in bed. Moments later, the door opens, and Dr. Jenner walks in.

"How are you feeling today?" he asks.

"Better. Still in pain, but mostly okay."

"Good to hear. Your stats are looking great, PT said the mobility in your shoulder was already improving, which is fantastic. I'll put in the order for your release papers so you can be discharged this afternoon."

For the first time since I got here, I smile wide. "Great. That's the best news I've heard all day."

"Figured you'd be happy to hear that," Dr. Jenner says, then explains he'll be prescribing me pain meds and some other antibiotics to take home. I thank him once again before he leaves.

When Patricia enters, she looks exhausted, and I tease her, asking if she ran a few marathons today.

"Feels like it," she says with a light chuckle. "I hear you're getting discharged today. I bet you're ready to go home." Though I can't see her mouth, I can tell she's smiling by how her eyes crinkle at the edges.

I nod. "I definitely am." I miss Cami like fucking crazy. We still haven't talked, and I'm eager as hell to get back to her. "Quick question. Are there any pharmacies close by?"

"There's one in Roxbury, but it might take them a while to fill it. They're doing curbside, I believe."

"Okay, uh. Hmm..." I grab the hospital gown I'm wearing. "What about my clothes?"

"I believe they were thrown out. My guess is they had to cut you out of your shirt, and you were probably covered in blood," she explains. "I can check if we have anything that's been left behind that might be your size. Or you can always leave in the gown."

I let out a huff. "Great. Is there a taxi that can take me around? My family isn't close."

She tilts her head. "Sure, I can call one of them."

"Thank you. You're an angel, Patricia," I say, grinning. She really has been nothing but amazing since I woke up.

Lunch gets delivered as I wait, but it literally looks like something Cami made on a bad day, which isn't saying much. I chuckle at the thought but can't force myself to eat it. Patricia enters with a pair of jogging pants and an oversized T-shirt along with a stack of papers in her hands.

"They're my son's and have been in my trunk for a while now. Might be a little big, but much better than that gown with the open back." She snickers.

"Thank you so much. I'd kiss you if I could."

She laughs. "You're welcome. You remind me of my son, so it's the least I can do."

"You're the best. Seriously," I tell her.

"I have your discharge papers finally. I'll need you to sign in a few places, then you can be on your way. I called a cab for you, and they'll be here soon. I'm leaving a mask for you to wear while you're out. Be careful with your sling while you change. Let me know if you need help." Patricia shoots me a wink, then leaves. It takes me a minute to figure out how to do it one-handed, and she's right, they're large, but I'd take this any day of the week over that itchy gown that lets my ass hang out.

While slipping on my shoes, the only items of mine that were left, I notice blood splattered across the top.

I slip the mask over my face, and when I walk out of my room, it feels weird to finally be going home.

When I pass the nurses' station, I wave goodbye and thank Patricia once again, then make my way to the elevator and go to the lower level.

Once I'm out of the main entrance, I'm shocked to see the nearly empty parking lot. Guess that's what happens when visitors aren't allowed, and only emergency surgeries are being done. My anxiety spikes as I sit on a bench and impatiently wait for my ride. All I want to do is talk to Cami and hold her. My dark thoughts appear as the fear of what the future holds consumes me. Is she upset with me? Does she regret the time we had together? Why hasn't she reached out? Everything feels so wrong without her, and I don't know if she's still at the house or what's going on. If anything, I just hope she's safe.

Cami's the only person on my mind, and I can't stop thinking about her or us. I'm madly in love with her, and I don't know how much longer I can go on without her knowing. I almost lost the opportunity to tell her, and I don't want to wait any longer. When I see her, I'll make sure she knows how much she means to me.

The taxi takes forever, and all I want is to return to the cabin to see Cami and our pets, but I need my prescriptions. I also need my laptop, so I can order another phone and check in with my boss. After that, I'll need to decide what my next steps are. Going back to my apartment is out of the question, but if Cami is no longer at the cabin, I'm not sure I want to stay without her.

Too many thoughts are happening at once, and I suck in a deep breath, but it's shallow. I need to calm down before my blood pressure rises, but I hate the insecurities flooding through me and not knowing what I'll be walking into when I return.

After an hour of waiting, the cab finally pulls up, and I grab my papers and get inside. I ask him to take me to Roxbury and will have to find the pharmacy when we get there since I can't look it up myself. He talks to me while he drives, but my focus is elsewhere.

Cami.

CHAPTER TWENTY-SEVEN

CAMERON

ONE WEEK AGO

After I rushed Eli to the emergency room, they told me I couldn't stay due to their lockdown restrictions, but I could call for an update. I was completely frustrated and angry over everything that had happened, and then not being able to stay with him made it worse.

As I drive back home, tears streak my cheeks, and I'm hysterical by the time I pull up to the road that leads to the cabin. Stains of Eli's blood are on the seat, a reminder that he's fighting for his life right now without anyone there to support him. I pull into the driveway and replay what happened just hours ago as I stare at the spot where they shot him.

When I get out of the SUV, I see the pool of dark liquid on the ground and force myself to look away before I have a panic attack. I can't stop glancing over my shoulder to make sure no one is around. My paranoia is in overdrive as I walk toward the front door and input my code on the keypad to unlock the door. As soon as I enter, Bruno barks and sniffs me. Chanel is lazily lying on top of the couch and doesn't even lift her head to greet me.

"Bruno, down," I tell him. I'm still only in my sports bra and covered in blood. I need to wash up and change. The house feels so empty without him and the fear I have over losing him consumes me while I shower. I can't stop crying as the hot water covers my skin, and I watch the red water pool to the bottom.

Once I'm in clean clothes and throw up my hair, I go to the sofa and lie there bawling for the better part of the night, hoping Eli will be okay. By the time we arrived at the hospital, he was pale and fading in and out of consciousness. Everything happened so fast that my head is still spinning.

This is the second time in a month that I've worried about losing him. My heart can't handle much more as I sob into a pillow. At some point, my tears dry up, and my stomach growls in protest because I haven't eaten in hours. I go to the kitchen and throw together a peanut butter and jelly sandwich on the last few slices of bread we have left. The groceries I brought in earlier are still on the counter, and thankfully, it's nothing but produce and boxed items; otherwise, I'd have to toss it from sitting out for so long.

I call the hospital with the satellite phone my parents had installed through our internet for emergencies, and right now, I could kiss them for it. When they told me they were getting one installed, I explained how ridiculous the whole idea was because we have cell phones. It's my saving grace, though I can't remember anyone's numbers other than Ryan, Kendall, and my parents'.

I need an update on Eli before I drive myself crazy with worst-case scenarios, and after I'm routed to several nurses' stations, I find out he's out of emergency surgery and in the ICU. Since I'm not his spouse or related to him, they tell me they can't give me much information, but that I can try calling back once he's in recovery

I'm so unsettled that I don't even notice I'm pacing until I hang up the phone. The next person I call is Ryan. He answers the phone immediately, and as soon as I hear his voice, I burst out into tears.

"Cami, what's wrong?" He's on full alert, and I hate to throw this on him on top of everything else, but I have no choice.

"Eli got shot," I choke out as I cry.

"What?" He's nearly yelling on the other line. "Did I hear you correctly?"

"Yes. Two men followed him back to the cabin after he went to the grocery store and held us at gunpoint for our groceries. After they took our phones, one of them shot Eli in the shoulder, then they took off in his rental. There was so much blood, Ryan. By the time I got him to the hospital, he was barely conscious."

He's speechless.

"I'm worried they'll come back for me. I don't know if I should try to get back into the city or if I should wait for him to be released." Assuming he makes it out alive.

"I know this might not be what you want to hear but do not come to the city. You're safer there, trust me. As long as the security system is on, and the doors and windows are locked, no one will be able to break in. That place is like a fortress. I can't believe this happened. Dammit, Cami. You're gonna give me gray hair."

"I know. It was the last thing we expected, and then it happened so fast. I don't want to call Mom and Dad because they'll demand I come home or hire a whole SWAT team to guard the cabin. And if I tell Kendall, she'll drive out here even if I tell her not to. You're the only logical person I can talk to."

He chuckles. "I'm the only logical person you *know*. Period. Point blank."

I crack a slight smile. "I need to call the cops and make a report. Let them know what happened."

"Okay, keep me updated with everything. Send me a text if I don't answer. I'm checking my phone as much as I can," he tells me.

We say our goodbyes and end the call. I grab my laptop and report my cell phone as stolen and order a replacement. I pay extra for overnight shipping, so I'll hopefully get it tomorrow.

After that's taken care of, I look up the number to the local police department and tell them what happened. I give them all the details I can remember, though it all feels like a blur as I run through it.

Recounting the events aloud has my hand trembling, and I feel the uneasiness in my body. The officer tells me they'll need to speak to Eli, and I tell him where he currently is, but honestly, I'm not sure how much Eli will even remember. Once he knows the full story, he states they'll look into it immediately. I don't care about the groceries or the items we lost, but they deserve to pay for shooting Eli. As soon as that thought crosses my mind, my chest tightens, and I feel a panic attack surfacing.

Though I have breathing exercises, they don't always work, and right now, they're not. I'll wait fifteen more minutes, and if the panic attack doesn't subside, I'll take one of my anxiety pills. Knowing how hard it'll be to get them refilled, I've used them sparingly. Time passes, and I grow more edgy. I rummage through my bag and find my meds, deciding it's time to take one.

It takes nearly an hour for the clouds to fade, and while my head isn't fully clear, I feel more in control of my emotions. After everything I've been through with us getting sick and then this, I was spiraling.

I stretch out on the couch, and Chanel jumps up and sits next to me, then starts purring. She makes me smile. Moments later, Bruno jumps up by my feet and tries to crawl on me too, but I quickly scold him, and he leans his head on my thigh instead.

"You are such a big puppy," I tell him. "But we gotta have a little chat."

He looks up at me with his big dark brown eyes and blinks.

"You're gonna have to be a watchdog while your dad is getting fixed up." My words choke because I really hope Eli is doing okay. "Like, if I say *attack*, you need to rip someone's head off, okay?"

Chanel settles in and lies down. Bruno continues to stare at me as if he's waiting for a treat.

"Got it? Bite someone's leg off or something. You're a big bad Doberman, so you better act like it if someone breaks in. Be ferocious and scary," I tell him with a firm nod. He readjusts his position, then leans his weight against me. I look up at the ceiling and suck in a deep breath.

I tell myself he's going to be okay.

He has to be because I'm in love with him, and I didn't even get to tell him.

The days have been grueling since Eli was shot. It's been some of the hardest days of my life knowing he's been up at the hospital alone, and I have no way to speak to him.

The guilt of it all eats at me, and I feel like it's my fault. If I wouldn't have turned and fell, he wouldn't have tried to catch me, and the two idiots who were holding us at gunpoint wouldn't have been startled. Each day, I've beaten myself up for putting Eli in that situation. This is the second time I've put his life in danger, and it's really fucking with my head. It feels like me being in his life is all wrong even though having him in mine is what I need.

I've called the hospital every day since he was admitted, but they're swamped, so I'm continually transferred from the operator to the nurses' station or even hung up on. Eventually, I'll get connected to Eli's room, but then he won't answer because he's passed out, then I start the process all over again to get an update on him. They won't tell me anything specific, just that he's alive.

Once my new phone arrived, I was able to keep Ryan in the loop and also FaceTime Kendall. She happily told me I looked like shit but still poured an enormous glass of wine and drank with me as I cried. It was therapeutic and helped pass the time since I don't know when Eli will be back.

Bruno has stayed at my heels, refusing to leave my side and even started sleeping in bed with me, but honestly, he's a bigger scaredy-cat than Chanel. The big doofus is growing on me, even if he takes up half of the mattress and snores like a human.

When I climb out of bed, my stomach growls more than usual, and I realize I have to stop eating cereal for every meal. When I walk downstairs, there's a chill in the air, and I glance next to the fireplace where there is only one log left. Another cold front is supposed to move through, which means I'll need more wood. Sucking in a deep breath, I walk to the kitchen and decide to make pancakes, and smile as I recall the last time I tried when Eli was home. Of course, he showed me up.

I mix the batter, heat the skillet, then pour them in the same size he did. I carefully put the spatula under them one by one and flip them over. My mouth waters as I see the perfect golden brown pancake. I wait a few more minutes for the other side to cook, then slide them onto a plate, spread butter on top, and pour syrup.

I sit at the bar with my coffee and eat, satisfied that I didn't burn them or the cabin down. I watch a handful of YouTube videos that explain the steps of how to chop wood. I know we have an ax, but honestly, I don't know if I can even swing it over my head, but I'll try.

After I finish my food, I change into jeans and boots, and just to amuse myself, I grab a plaid button-up shirt. When I walk outside, Bruno follows, being my protector. Bruno runs as fast as he can to the pond, and when he goes to jump in, I yell at him at the top of my lungs, but he doesn't listen and sloshes through it, jumping around.

"Oh for fuck's sake," I mutter under my breath. "You're going to stink like shit!" I yell. His tongue hangs out of his mouth as he runs around the property, dirty and happy as can be. Bruno sprints toward me, and I squeal, quickly moving away so he can't jump on me. The damage is done, so I don't even scold him for it anymore.

I find the ax in a stump and manage to wiggle it free, then grip it in my hand. I take a few practice swings, putting all of my strength into it. As Bruno plays, I grab a wheelbarrow and wheel it to the stack of wood on the side of the shed, and struggle to lift the pieces in. I wasn't built to carry heavy shit, but I'm trying regardless. Once I have enough, I move to the cutting area and dump them on the ground. Grabbing a log, I place it down on the chopping stump but lose my grip and break a goddamn nail.

"Are you kidding me?" I groan, shaking my head. They're long overdue for a manicure anyway, but still, that hurt like a bitch.

I try again and adjust the piece of wood. Grabbing the ax, I lift it over my head, putting all of my strength and body weight into it, and then the sharp blade crashes down and slices the log in two. I drop the ax, and my mouth falls open in shock. Soon, I'm jumping up and down with victory, then laugh my ass off. If my mother could see me doing this, she'd probably faint with shock, then ask me if I've lost my damn mind.

I repeat the steps, doing precisely as I did before until I have an entire wheelbarrow full of logs. As I'm rolling it toward the patio door, Bruno barks, and my internal alarm goes off. Immediately, I turn around, searching the surrounding areas and see him chasing after a rabbit. Placing my hand over my heart, I try to calm myself, then continue forward.

"Bruno!" I shout. That dog needs a Xanax.

I make it to the patio door, then slide it open. I carry each piece inside one by one, and neatly stack it next to the fireplace. My arms and body are so sore, and I don't think I've ever done this much physical work in my entire life. Knowing Bruno needs a bath, I go to the kitchen and grab the Dawn dish soap. If it's good enough for the ducks during oil spills, it'll be good enough for stinky dogs. I go back outside and put the wheelbarrow up and wrangle Bruno to the back patio, then grab the water hose.

He jumps all over me, leaving muddy paw prints on my clothes, and scratches me with his nails. Bruno nearly knocks me over when he gets excited like this. I try to use my best Eli manly voice and tell him to heel, but he doesn't listen, so I resort to begging him instead of yelling. Eventually, he sits, and I run water over him and soap him up real good. Once he's clean, he tries to run off, but I grab him by his collar, and he shakes himself all over me.

"You're a little shit sometimes, Bruno," I tell him, but I'm laughing about it because he's so happy. "And now I need a shower too."

I open the door, and he runs inside, hyper as can be. He chases Chanel around the living room until she's had enough and runs upstairs. Water is all over the floor as he continues shaking and air-drying. With an annoyed groan, I clean up the mess, then try to towel dry him off. I'm filthy, and my back is already aching. Tonight, I'll try to make myself dinner that doesn't include a microwave while downing a bottle of wine. I'm going to need all the luck in the world to actually make something edible.

Eli's been in the hospital for a week, and I still haven't spoken to him. I think he'd be proud of how I've taken care of myself for seven days. Even I'm kinda shocked, considering I couldn't boil water before arriving here. I've chopped wood, learned to open wine with a corkscrew, and even baked homemade lasagna. Next up is learning how to change my oil and build a house with my bare hands. I laugh at the thought, but honestly, Eli is to thank for this. If he hadn't made fun of me and challenged me to do things on my own, I probably would've eaten TV dinners and ramen for a month.

Today, I slept in because I've stayed up late doing home improvement tasks after my homework assignments, trying to keep my mind busy. I hung photos that have been in a closet for years. I cleaned the cabin, did more laundry, rearranged the living room furniture, and even dusted the top of the kitchen cabinets. At some point, I won't have anything else to do but worry and waste away.

Calling the hospital is one of my everyday habits now. I'm transferred to the nurses' station, who then tells me Eli was released nearly two hours ago and left in a cab. I wish I'd known so I could've at least picked him up instead. My heart races in a semi-panic because the cabin is only thirty minutes away, and he's not here. Did he not plan to come back here? Is he mad? Does he blame me for what happened? I hate not knowing what he's thinking and hate even more that I couldn't speak to him.

While I nervously wait, I make my second espresso of the day. Another hour passes, and there's still no Eli. I know he doesn't have his phone and probably doesn't remember my number, so I text Ryan and see if he's heard from him. I don't get a response, which only annoys me even more.

I'm nervous as hell and filled with worry. He wouldn't go home without seeing me or taking Bruno, would he? Did he go to his mom's? I'm literally driving myself crazy not being able to talk to him.

My stomach growls, reminding me I skipped dinner. I pull out the macaroni I made last night and reheat it, noticing Bruno is on my heels. I feed him a few noodles and tell him to keep it our little secret.

After I eat, I sit on the couch and turn on the news, knowing it's not what I need but still wanting to know what's going on in the city. It's been almost a week since I turned it on. Before I lose myself in the scene unfolding at the hospital where my brother works, the front door opens. Bruno lets out a roar of a bark, and I jump up, my eyes wide as I spin around to see what's going on.

Eli's eyes meet mine; his hair is a shaggy mess and his arm is in a sling, but he's smiling when he sees me. My hands cover my mouth in shock as my eyes water. I rush to him, and he immediately wraps his good arm around me and presses a soft kiss against my lips. Uncontrollable tears stream down my face, and when he puts space between us, he rubs the pad of his thumb over my cheeks and wipes them away.

"I didn't think you'd come back," I whisper, swallowing down the emotions that have been bubbling inside me for a week.

He searches my face and shakes his head as he tucks loose strands behind my ear. "Why wouldn't I come back, Cami? You're all I've been thinking about. I've been going insane without you."

His words cause goose bumps to trail up my arms, and my cheeks heat. "When I called this afternoon, the nurse said you were discharged hours ago, and I thought you didn't want to be here anymore..." My insecure thoughts linger, and a small smile plays on his lips.

"I waited over an hour for a cab to pick me up. Then he drove me to Roxbury to drop off my prescriptions, then after another hour of waiting for them to be filled, I remembered I didn't have my wallet. After figuring out that mess, he got lost on his way here, but I didn't realize it at first, or it wouldn't have taken so long." He blows out a breath and shakes his head. "It's been a weird fucking day."

I feel so bad for him and wish I'd been able to help. "How did you pay for it all?" I ask.

"I gave him a handie," he jokes, and I roll my eyes. "The pharmacy is gonna charge it to the hospital, and they'll add it to my bill. The cab driver is gonna mail an invoice."

"I was so worried," I tell him. "They couldn't tell me anything about you except that you were alive, and every time I tried to call, it took forever to get through, and then you'd be sleeping. I can't believe you're here right now." Happy tears stream down my face, and I want nothing more than to hold him. I carefully wrap my arms around his neck. "I've missed you so much."

"Those words are like music to my ears, baby." He tightens his arm around me. "I've missed you too. So fucking much." He pulls back slightly until our gaze meets. "You're the only thing that kept me sane in there," he admits.

I paint my lips across his, claiming him as *mine*.

Bruno wiggles between us, clearly annoyed he's not getting any attention. "Hey, buddy." Eli kneels and pets him as Bruno slobbers all over his face.

"He missed you," I say. "And he sucks as a guard dog. He's a bigger baby than me."

Eli laughs, then grabs my hand and leads me to the couch. I look at the clothes he's wearing. "Where did you get those from?"

He looks down at the oversized T-shirt. "The nice nurse who took care of me gave me her son's extra clothes since mine were ruined. I need to write her a thank-you letter and send it with the biggest bouquet," he tells me. "She was a godsend in the midst of all the chaos."

"Hmm...is that who's been keeping you busy? Flirting with your nurse?" I tease, popping a brow.

He leans over and plucks my bottom lips between his teeth. "Nah. I'm much more into bossy blondes who can't cook," he mocks, and I want to smack him, but I lean over and press my mouth to his again. I can't get enough of him.

"I've been dreaming about that for days," he admits, cupping my face.

"Me too," I say as a blush creeps up my cheeks. "I thought I lost you."

"Never," he says. "I'm not going anywhere, baby."

Relief washes over me as my pulse increases. I know I can't live another day without telling him how I feel. "Good. I'm not sure my heart could survive without you."

"Cami," he whispers, his eyes searching my face. "I only thought about you while I was there. What you were doing, how you were feeding yourself," he says with a chuckle. "I was worried how this was affecting you."

"You were worried about me?" I roll my eyes with a smirk. "I kept thinking the worst. Eli…I—"

He sweeps his lips against mine. "I love you, Cami. I don't think I'd be able to live another day without telling you how much you mean to me."

I choke up, tears falling because he somehow stole my breath and the words I was going to say. "I love you too."

Our mouths crash together, and as we become greedy for one another, Eli winces in pain. "Sorry," I say. "What do you need? More pain meds?"

Eli smiles. "As long as you're with me, I've got everything I need."

CHAPTER TWENTY-EIGHT

ELIJAH

DAY 69

Iт's вееn a month since the accident that landed me in the hospital for a week. So much has changed in that amount of time, and though my shoulder isn't fully recovered, every day I feel stronger. I video conference my physical therapist twice a week, and I do daily exercises to keep up the mobility. It often leaves me breathless and needing my inhaler. I was so used to working out but have had to take it easy.

Cami's been extremely helpful with everything, doing way more than she needs to. I can do things one-handed, but she insists. She reminds me to keep up with my PT and doesn't let me get lazy with it.

After a couple of days back, I noticed the things she did around the house and considering how much she struggled before, she's really putting in the effort to be more independent. She's definitely changed, and without a doubt, she's changed me too.

I get tired a lot faster than before, which frustrates me. Sometimes, I wish I had my old life back, the one I had before the pandemic and before getting shot, but then I remember that life didn't include Cami. I wouldn't change having her for the world. If having her means all the other bullshit had to happen, I'll happily accept it.

New York is still in lockdown with shelter in place orders. I'm kinda shocked it's lasted over two months, but then again, it makes sense with the current data. It reminds me to hold Cami that much tighter each night because I know how lucky and fortunate we are. We can help flatten the curve by doing our part and staying here as long as it takes. People like Ryan and all the essential workers are the true heroes during this crisis, so until there's a safe way to reopen the state, we'll isolate together.

After spending so much time with each other, I notice the littlest things about her. Like when she laughs really hard, her nose crinkles and sometimes she snorts, which I find cute as hell. She likes to sleep on her side, and sometimes snores like a Mack truck. When she's obviously tired, but I'm not, she'll try to stay awake to be with me longer. When she thinks I'm not watching her, she'll steal glances at me, and then I'll catch her, which makes her laugh. Cami is my rock, and I'm grateful everyday for our second chance.

I still can't believe she's fallen for me as hard as I have for her, and now I can't live without her. Hell, I've nearly died twice since coming here, but she's been the light at the end of the tunnel.

We FaceTimed my mom and told her the pleasant news that we were officially dating. My mother cried with joy, then asked us when we were getting married. I just shrugged and laughed. But honestly, I'd marry Cami in a heartbeat even though I still don't feel like I'm good enough for her.

Next, we called my sister, Ava. Cami was nervous as hell about it, but it was time they talk through their differences so there's no hostility. Their conversation lasted well over an hour, and by the end, both were laughing at my expense as they took turns telling stories about me and talking shit. Though, I don't even care because I'm just happy the air has been cleared between them.

We haven't told her parents about us yet. I've been too

nervous, knowing her father would never approve of the poor kid being with his princess daughter, but Cami has assured me she couldn't give two fucks what her parents think. When the time's right, we'll tell them, but not yet. I like the bubble we're in right now and don't want anyone's outside opinions to burst it.

After another physical therapy session, Cami and I go for a walk outside. Spring is finally coming, and the weather has been much nicer. Eventually, I'd love to cook using the outdoor kitchen and watch the sunset with Cami while we eat. Though I can't buy her expensive things—but even if I could, they don't impress her —I can make memories with her in ways that count.

A few days ago, we drove to Roxbury and got more food for the next month. She went a couple of weeks ago, but only got the necessities, and now we need more to stay stocked up. We went together this time so we could double team and get out of the store faster. As we drove home, she continuously looked behind us to see if anyone was following us. I know what happened still affects her, but I'm doing my best to reassure her we're safe. The two guys who did it were finally caught, so I can breathe a little easier knowing they didn't get away with it, but we still stay alert.

Once we're back home, we unload and sanitize the groceries before putting them away, washing our hands in between a dozen times. It's become such a part of our lives that we don't even think twice about it.

We haven't been intimate in weeks. Even though she's given me all the hints, I know she hasn't wanted to rush me with my shoulder recovering, but it's doing much better now. We've been taking things slow, but right now, she's looking at me with a fire in her eyes.

"I think we should change out of our clothes and take a shower," I tell her, brushing my lips against her ear. Her head falls back, and she lets out a ragged breath as I drag my teeth against her skin.

"Yes," she says breathlessly. "Absolutely, yes."

I smirk as I take her hand and lead her to the master bathroom.

Slowly, I peel off her leggings and shirt, allowing my fingertips to brush against her soft skin, and each time I touch her, her breasts rise and fall with shallow breaths. Cami watches me intently with a smile playing on her lips.

Walking toward the shower, I turn on the water and wait for it to get hot.

"You're so goddamn beautiful," I tell her, and she blushes.

"You're just saying that," she throws back, and I hate it when she downplays my compliments. "I've been in sweats with messy hair for days."

"Just how I like you," I tease, sprinkling kisses on her shoulders.

She reaches forward and helps take off my sling. I've still been wearing it daily but not for too much longer.

Cami lifts my shirt and pulls it over my head. She runs her fingers down my abs until her fingers are unbuttoning my jeans. Quickly, she slides them down my legs, along with my boxers. She stands confidently in a sexy as hell matching bra and panty set, and I take in the view before I remove them. Leaning down, I capture her taut nipple in my mouth. She arches her back and moans while running her fingers through my hair, then tugs. I release an animalistic growl, then scrape my teeth along her sensitive flesh, adding just enough pressure to drive her wild.

I move to the other, licking and sucking. She pants as I lick a trail up to her mouth and lower my hand to her pussy.

"Fuck, Cami. You're so tight," I murmur, feeling her wetness on my fingers.

Before I lose myself in her, I grab her hand and lead us into the shower. Once we're inside, she stands under the stream of water, letting it cascade down her body. She tilts her head back and gets her hair wet. I watch in awe at the gorgeous woman in front of me, waiting for me to pleasure her in all the right ways.

Stepping closer, I bring my hand down and begin stroking my thumb against her clit. Cami moans and nearly crumples under my touch. She's so damn sensitive, and seeing her like this has my dick growing harder. At this rate, I won't last five minutes inside her, but I want to go all night. She bites her bottom lip, causing me to let out a throaty moan as she writhes.

"Eli," she whispers. "I want you so badly."

"Me too, baby," I admit. "I don't want to rush, but damn, I don't know how much longer I can wait to taste you. It's been too long."

Water spills over her chest, and as I trail kisses down her body, it soaks my hair and falls into my eyes. I brush it back and lift a brow when I catch her gawking. Flashing her a quick wink, I kneel in front of her and settle between her legs, running my nose along her sensitive bud. I love the way she tastes and the soft moans that escape her as I flick my tongue against her clit.

"Eli, Eli," she whimpers, fisting my hair as I worship her body with my mouth. Cami's back arches as I wage war against her pussy, and I know she's close by the way her body shakes. As she sinks into me, I pull away with a smirk. I love how quickly she loses herself with me and how willing she is to please me in return. In the bedroom, Cami is a fucking goddess, and I plan to worship her body for the rest of our lives.

Her eyes pop open in protest. "Nooooo!"

I shrug with a laugh. "What?"

"I swear, I will bring Prince Harry in here and let him finish the job," she threatens, and I chuckle at her eagerness.

Her perky breasts rise and fall as I ease my fingers up her legs and bring my mouth back between her thighs. She's so damn wet that all I can do is smile as I taste her sweetness. She shudders under my touch as I insert one finger and then another, twirling my tongue against her clit.

"I'm so close. Don't stop," she pleads on a whisper, and while I want to tease her, my baby deserves this release. I slow my pace, allowing the orgasm to fully build before she completely unravels. Moments later, she's trembling and groaning as she loses herself. I pull away, kissing her inner thighs before standing.

She looks at me with hooded eyes, begging for a kiss. Our

mouths fuse and our tongues twist under the hot stream. The emotions overwhelm me because I still can't believe this woman is mine. The way I feel about her is unfathomable. I'm never letting her fucking go.

"I can taste myself on your lips," she tells me, and I chuckle.

"And you're so goddamn delicious I'd eat you for every meal." I slyly smile as my erection presses into her stomach.

"Should we get you cleaned up?" I muse.

"No, you should fuck me."

I chuckle, reaching for her body wash.

I lather it on a loofah between my hands. "I'll make it worth your while, don't worry."

Cami narrows her eyes and pretends to sulk.

Gently, I wash her shoulders, chest, arms, and legs. Then I spin her around and scrub her back and down her ass. I wrap my good arm around her waist and lower my hand between her legs.

"You smell so good," I murmur in her ear, teasing my tongue along her neck. I thrust a finger inside her, and she tightens against me. "God, you drive me fucking wild."

Cami turns, places her palms on my cheek, and forces me to look into her bright blue eyes. "Quit being a gentleman and *fuck* me," she demands.

I pop an eyebrow, loving her eagerness. "That's what you really want?"

"Be careful with your arm, but I won't break, Eli," she says as a devious grin spreads across her face.

Cami quickly rinses before turning off the shower and stepping out. She hands me a towel, and I swiftly dry myself. While she wraps hers around her body, I charge forward, and she squeals as I chase her into her bedroom. She falls onto the mattress with a laugh as I hover over her.

"Hope you're ready for what you asked for," I taunt as she moves to the middle. My cock throbs between us, and I can't wait any longer. Grabbing her thighs, I pull her body closer and settle between her legs. Stroking my shaft a few times, I slowly ease into her, and she gasps before I pull out. I've always loved teasing her, but it's even more fun when we're naked. Then I slide back in, thrusting deeper.

"Harder," she pants, but instead, I pull out, grab her ankles, and drag her to the edge as I stand. "Oh my God," she squeals.

"Flip," I demand. She licks her lips before she gets on all fours.

With a firm hand, I smack her ass, and the sound echoes through the room. She purrs, which is a complete turn-on. I dig my fingers into her hips as I guide myself inside, fucking her hard and deep. Our skin slaps together and mingles with our moans. My dick is so goddamn hard it feels like it might break off as she arches her ass against me, screaming my name and fisting the comforter.

"Yes, yes, yes! Oh my God, *yes*," she cries out. "Eli…" Her breathlessness, combined with how her muscles tense, tells me everything I need to know. Wrapping my arm around her waist, I pull her up until her back is to my chest. I slow my pace, cup her jaw, then bring our mouths together.

Her body shakes, and she comes, moaning my name. My movements are slow and calculated, and soon, I'm losing myself too. We collapse on the bed and crawl to the middle where I hold her in my arms. Emotions pour through me, and when I look at Cami, she's flashing a satisfied smile. Cupping her cheeks, I fuse our mouths back together, unable to stop kissing her.

"Pretty sure I need another shower," she says when we break apart. "I'm a sweaty mess."

"Me too. I think we should conserve water," I tell her, and she nods, then follows me to the bathroom. I turn on the water and allow her to step in, taking in every inch of her gorgeous curves. I'm so fucking lucky.

I squirt shampoo in my palm and gently massage her scalp. She closes her eyes, and a small smile plays on her lips.

"Have I told you how much I love you today?" I ask her, grabbing her body wash and paying extra attention to her breasts, then moving down to her sensitive areas.

"Actions sometimes speak louder than words," she mutters, and I chuckle.

"I love you," I whisper against the shell of her ear as the warm water falls over our bodies. "I'll love you till the day I die."

She smiles so sweet as she plucks her lip. "I love you too, Eli."

I reach around and grab a handful of her ass until she squeals. She washes me, and then we make out until our skin prunes. We wrap fluffy towels around our bodies and go back to the bedroom.

She lifts an eyebrow as she gazes her eyes down my body. "Ready for round two?"

Genuine laughter escapes me as I move closer to her. "I'll never tell you no. My cock is yours. Prince Harry 2.0."

Cami nearly doubles over, then takes me in her hand before kneeling in front of me as she sucks me long and hard.

We make love for the rest of the afternoon, only taking breaks for food and quick naps. I hold her and make sure she knows how much she means to me, and how in love with her I am. What we have is more real than anything I've ever experienced, and I wasn't lying when I told her I'd love her until the day I die. Honestly, I can't imagine a day without her in my life; that's how quickly she's burrowed into my heart and soul.

Cameron St. James is my everything, and I'll spend forever proving that to her.

CHAPTER TWENTY-NINE

CAMERON

DAY 90

WE'VE OFFICIALLY BEEN in the cabin for three months, but it hasn't been what I expected at all when I first decided to come here. When Eli first arrived, I was convinced it'd be hell sharing this space with him. Little did I know, I'd fall stupidly in love with him and end up never wanting to leave this place or his side.

A week ago, I got the news that my graduation ceremony was canceled, and I feel cheated as hell. I understand why, but for the past four years, I imagined walking across that stage and getting my diploma. I've been excited to give my valedictorian speech since I knew I was in the running. Though I won't be giving it in front of everyone, I still plan to record myself so they can hear it. Getting this honor was hard work, and I don't want to miss the opportunity to speak to my peers one more time. I know I'm not the only one who's missing out on events such as this right now, and even though I understand this is our new reality, it's still hard to cope with.

Eli notices my mood is off and wraps his arm around my waist as I make coffee.

"What's wrong?" he asks. Anytime he's around, my whole demeanor changes.

"Just thinking about graduation, that's all," I tell him, turning around and wrapping my arms around his neck as he dips down and presses his mouth against mine.

"Babe." He smiles, lifting my chin. "You should be so fucking proud of all that you accomplished, especially since you finished your last semester online and during a pandemic when you were sick. You are at the top of your class at one of the most difficult universities in the country. No one or nothing can ever take that away from you. Ever."

I smile and nod. "You're right. I don't want to seem like a brat. I'm just disappointed."

"You're not a brat for that. For other things, absolutely, but for that, nah," he tells me with a wink, and I playfully smack him. I love how grounded he keeps me. It's nice to have a boyfriend who isn't an elitist.

"Hungry?" he asks.

"I'm always hungry," I throw back. "For your Prince Harry."

"I thought you named him Zeus?" He arches a curious brow.

I giggle. "Not when it gets me off better than the vibrator. Then it deserves the royal name."

He laughs and goes to the fridge and pulls out ingredients for breakfast. "You're a sex fiend, but that's why I love you."

"That's not the only reason," I argue. My stomach growls just as the espresso finishes brewing. I fill two mugs, then hand him one. After I add cream to mine, I lean against the counter and admire how sexy Eli is. I can't stop staring at his bare chest and how his sweats hang low on his hips, showing that V that goes to the happiest place on earth, but I'm not referring to Disney World. Though what he does sure is fucking magical.

He catches me gawking and lifts an eyebrow, and I swear if he wasn't almost finished cooking, I'd fuck him until tomorrow. "Yes?"

I clear my throat, not even sorry he caught me. "Stop looking sexy, and I'd stop staring."

"My bad." He smirks.

"So..." I speak up to get my mind out of the gutter. "I'm going to FaceTime Mommy Dearest today."

He laughs. "Yeah?"

"I still can't believe how giddy she is about us being together," I say. I think back to a couple of weeks ago when I finally told my parents. They were so supportive that if I wasn't already living in the twilight zone, I definitely would be now. Daddy always stressed to marry a wealthy man with status who could contribute to the family name. My mom, on the other hand, always told me to marry for love. She didn't and later regretted it. It's obvious they're not *in love* and would be happier apart.

"Your mom has always loved me. Seriously, I was more worried about your dad than her."

"Really? I was worried he'd give you one of those fatherly 'you break my daughter's heart, and I'll break your neck' speeches. Or worse, they'd make you join the country club." I look down his body again. "But there's just no way you'd properly fit in," I say with laughter.

He chuckles, shaking his head. "Oh really? Don't think I can pull off a thousand dollar polo and slacks and order the servers around while I brag about my mistress?"

I roll my eyes at his mockery. "You're hilarious. Keep that up, and they'll forbid us from being together. Then again, if they would've disapproved, we'd be married right now."

"Hot damn!" he shouts ecstatically. "That's too bad because I'd marry you in a heartbeat."

He turns off the stove, slides our food onto plates, and we move to the bar. I'm sitting so close to him as we eat that I'm practically on his lap. "Did you mean it?"

"Mean what?" he asks around a mouthful.

"That you'd marry me in a heartbeat."

Eli finishes chewing, then turns and grabs my hand. We're

nearly facing each other in the barstools. "Without a doubt, Cami. I've seen you nearly every day for the past ninety days, and while I hate the state of the world, I'm grateful to spend this uninterrupted time with you. I honestly don't remember what life was like without you in it, and I don't want to. You're my everything, baby. I mean it, but I do worry sometimes that I'm not good enough for you."

My eyes go wide, and I pull back slightly at his confession. "Not good enough for me? Don't be ridiculous. You're more than enough."

He shrugs shyly. "I know the *type* of guys you've dated. The money, well-known name, extravagant dates. But all I can offer you is my love."

I tilt my head and flash him a small smile. "You are definitely *not* the kind of guys I've dated in the past, and I'm grateful for that. I've never felt this way about anyone before, which isn't something I'm used to. It's different with you. Most men just want to use me to get to my parents. Status and materials don't matter to you, and when it comes to who I want, it doesn't matter to me either. You've loved me in ways I've never been loved before. It can't be faked or bought, and I hope you know that because I don't want to lose you."

"Lose me? You'll need to put a restraining order on me to leave you alone," he says with a chuckle.

I sigh, hoping he's right. "When all of this is over, and we go back to the real world, things will change. I know that, and I'm trying to prepare myself for it. Some people don't want to be in the spotlight, and I don't want the added attention to ruin what we have. It scares the shit out of me, Eli. You're the best thing that's ever happened to me, and I'm scared of losing you and everything we've built. I keep telling myself it's all too good to be true, and I don't know what I did to deserve you." I can feel my emotions bubbling, but I need him to know what's burning inside me.

"Cami," Eli whispers my name. "I've known you for a long

time. I've been best friends with your brother since we were kids. I understand what you and your family go through, and I'll be there by your side, no matter what happens. I promise you with everything I am. It'll take much more than some paparazzi and gossip stories to ruin what we have. And if we go out of town, I could always hide you in the trunk of a car when we leave for the weekends just like Taylor Swift does."

I snort and laugh. "Yeah, I heard that rumor too. She was wheeled out in a suitcase and loaded in the back of a car to avoid the photographers. It's clever actually, and I wish I would've thought of it. Kendall suggested it one time, too."

"Of course she did." He shakes his head and picks up his fork. "I've waited this long, and I'm not giving up being with you for anything or anyone. Love you, baby."

"Love you more. You're mine forever, Eli."

"Forever and ever," he echoes. "I promise."

I let out a relaxed breath, and we finish eating. After we're done, I go into the living room to call my mom while Eli cleans up the kitchen. She answers, and I can tell she's in a pleasant mood by her wide grin.

"Cameron! So happy you called. Eleanor was just putting on some morning tea for me, and your father is outside playing golf on the mini green he had installed a few weeks ago," she says. She's well put together with her hair perfectly done, pearl earrings, and a diamond necklace. I wouldn't be surprised if she's wearing pantyhose as well because my mother dresses up like she's hosting a tea party every day. She's weirder than those who quarantine in jeans.

Eleanor is one of the maids who helps around the house, and it worries me that my mother has still allowed her workers to come and go. They could easily afford to pay her time off.

She clears her throat, bringing the attention back to her. "I was thinking about you this morning. I miss you dearly, sweetie. I wish you'd come home and see your father and me soon."

"Mom, I know. I miss you too, but I have no desire to set foot in the city right now. I talk to Ryan as much as I can, and it doesn't sound like things will let up soon."

"Honey, we're past the curve. That hunky governor said things are better. I'm sure life will get back to normal soon."

I roll my eyes, but she doesn't notice. He never said that. The fact that our political views don't always align can be frustrating, but I learned a long time ago to keep my mouth shut to avoid a family feud. "It won't, Mom. It may take years."

"We'll see," she says in her typical patronizing tone. I watch as she reaches for her tea that's being served on fine china. She even holds out her pinky when she sips, and I almost laugh, but hold back. "So, how's Eli? Where is he?"

I snort. "I swear you have a crush on him, Mother."

As if he was summoned, Eli comes from the kitchen and leans over the back of the couch. "Hey, Mama C! You're looking so gorgeous today," he says in an overly flirty voice.

I turn and shake my head at him. "Why, thank you, Eli. How have you been feeling?"

He takes the phone from my hand, laughing, and chats with my mom. I swear she loves talking to him more than me. I even hear her giggle, and the way he charms her has me chuckling. Popping up off the couch, I walk toward him, and he has the camera turned around facing Bruno, showing Mom how big and well-mannered he is. I shake my head. "He doesn't know how to listen," I whisper-hiss.

As soon as I do, Bruno jumps up on me. He's so heavy he nearly knocks me over, then he starts licking me to death. "Aw, sweetie. I wish you treated Coco like that. You never were much of a dog person."

Bruno is relentless, and once I push him down, I lean over and pet his head. I motion for Eli to give me the cell so we can end this conversation.

"Okay, well, I'll give the phone back to Cami. Chat soon. Bye!"

Eli flashes a cheesy grin, then hands it over to me with a cocky smirk.

"He's such a nice young man. So charming and handsome. I love what he does with his hair. Perfect for you, dear," Mom gushes, and I swear I catch her blushing.

"I'm so glad you approve," I deadpan, and Eli does a little dance on the other side of the screen, completely distracting me. His fingers play on the edge of his jogging pants, and he slides them down just a tad lower, and my cheeks burn. I don't even know what my mom is saying because I stopped paying attention.

"Don't you agree, Cameron?"

I try to ignore him the best I can. "I'm sorry, what was that?" I ask, clearing my throat.

"I was saying how disappointed and upset I am that I won't get to see my little girl walk across the stage to receive her diploma," she repeats. "After all the money we spent for you to go there," she mumbles, and I suck in a long breath, reminding myself not to engage.

Nodding, I give her a forced smile. "I know. Me too."

"Well, hopefully it'll make graduate school that much sweeter for you," she says.

"Yes. It'll be extra special when I finally walk across the stage." In two more years.

Thankfully, Mom changes the subject and chats about Ryan and praises all the good work he's been doing. Then she mentions the hefty donations they gave in his name, but I don't tell her what he told me about not wanting people to know. She voices her concerns but, in the same breath, downplays the situation, which is one reason I get so frustrated speaking with her. I love my mother, but sometimes, she pushes my buttons, even if she's not trying. For decades, she's been living in her own little elite world where money can buy anything and problems don't exist, so during a pandemic is no different. Instead of going back and forth with her, I ignore it and discuss the weather and Chanel.

"I'm just waiting for things to get back to normal. I knew it was dire when fashion week was canceled," she brings it up again. I swallow down a groan. My head is about to explode if I don't get away from this conversation. "When do you think you'll come back?"

"I'm not exactly sure. Eli's still working remotely, and I think we might stay through the summer and just see how it goes before we decide." Things change every day so if I give my mother a timeframe, she'll expect me to abide by it, but if I leave it open, then she can't hold me accountable.

"Summer? That's nearly four months from now," she exclaims as I sit back down on the couch. "Surely, you can come back before then."

All I do is shake my head. "I want to, Mom, I really do. But I don't know what the future holds, so we're just taking it day by day. No telling what's going to happen in a few days, nevertheless, a few months." While some parts of the country have loosened their restrictions, the hospitals are still overflowing, and there's still no cure or vaccine. I may be in limbo with my penthouse and graduate school, but as long as Eli is with me through it all, I don't care. We'll figure it out together.

"I worry about you," she says.

"We'll be fine and can FaceTime as much as you want," I remind her.

"Cameron, you know I'm not very good with technology."

"Well, luckily, you'll have plenty of time to figure it out. But anyway, I'll let you go. I'll chat tomorrow if you want," I say quickly, wanting off the line.

After taking another sip of tea, she grins. "Okay, sweetie. I love you. Chat soon." She blows two kisses, then I end the call.

If I was home, I know she'd wrap me in a big hug and press a kiss on each of my cheeks. I let out a lengthy sigh and lean my head back on the couch, then close my eyes. When I open them, Eli is standing above me, and I jump.

"Jesus, you scared me."

His lips tilt up. "We should go for a hike today."

"Seriously?" I ask, furrowing my brows. I haven't hiked since Ryan and I were kids. "Do I look like someone who hikes?"

He licks his lips and chuckles with a shrug. "I noticed there were some trails cut out. They might be slightly overgrown, but I'd love to go check them out. Take Bruno with us and let him wander around the property for a few hours."

"Alright, I'm down, but you can't make fun of me if I trip and fall or something." Because it's a high probability.

"I can make that deal." He leans over and places his lips on mine. Wrapping my arms around the back of his neck, I smile against his mouth.

"Go get dressed," he tells me, and I notice he's already changed. When I get up, he takes the opportunity to smack my ass before I run upstairs.

I dress comfortably in one of my tennis skirts because it's so beautiful out today, then tie my running shoes nice and tight. As soon as my foot hits the bottom stair, he's grinning ear to ear, reaches his hand out, and I meet him. "You're wearing a skirt to hike, huh? Why am I even surprised?"

I roll my eyes at his little dig. "It's a thing. Google it."

He shrugs. "If you say so. I mean, I'm not complaining about the view at all."

"That's what I thought." I wink. "Now, let's get some fresh air. I'm shocked we haven't gotten cabin fever yet."

"You and me both," he retorts.

Bruno follows us, and as soon as he can get around us, he's off in a full sprint going straight to the pond. Eli laughs, and I groan, knowing that means he'll need a bath when we return. We take a trail that leads to some woods, and Eli and I walk in silence, holding hands. The wind rustles through the dense forest, and it brings me back to being kids and playing out here with Ryan. We never had a "normal" childhood, and the only time I felt like a kid was when we came to the cabin. I didn't have to put on fancy dresses or sit up straight or do any of the things my parents wanted me to do to impress their friends and the media. Out here, I got to get dirty, play outside, and be a kid.

We continue walking farther down the path, and the sunshine peeks between the trees. A smile plays on my lips as Eli squeezes my hand, then kisses my knuckles.

"I love you," I tell him. "Thank you."

"Love you too. And for what?"

"For the escape. I needed it," I say truthfully.

Eli stops walking and turns to me. The space between us disappears, and I'm getting lost in his mouth and touch. His large hand slips under my shirt, and he palms my breast. I'm panting, and all I want is him. I take several steps forward, guiding him until his back rests against a gigantic tree. We're breathless already as I untie his shorts, then fall to my knees and take him in my mouth. I look up in his eyes, and when he runs his fingers through my hair, I stroke his shaft as I suck harder. Eli breathes out deep grunts as I increase my pace until I'm nearly choking on his cock.

I slow my pace, then suck and lick his tip as I stroke him.

"Cami, fuck," he groans, and his legs begin to tremble. "Baby," he whispers, fisting my hair tighter around his fingers. I know he's close because his cock jerks in my grip, but I don't stop. After a few more moments, he tenses then releases in my mouth. I swallow it all down, not wanting to waste a drop, then stand with a smile as I lick my lips.

"Baby," he murmurs, then cups the back of my neck and fuses our mouths. I love that he doesn't even care I just had my lips on his cock and kisses me anyway. "Your turn."

I look around. "What do you mean?"

He arches a brow and lifts my skirt. "I feel like you had this planned all along," he slyly says, sliding my panties down to my knees.

I shrug. "Maybe." I'm so fucking wet from pleasuring him that it won't take much to get me off.

"Goddamn," he says as his fingers twirl on my clit, then he

pushes one inside my pussy. I nearly lose my balance at how good it feels. "You're fucking drenched, baby. So smooth and tight, too."

"Always," I tell him. "You turn me on so much."

A boyish grin plays on his lips as he continues, then thrusts another finger inside. They're so big I nearly gasp as he pounds into me. Seconds later, he pushes my panties all the way down. I step out of them, and then he slides them in his pocket. It's no mystery I'm running out of underwear, considering he's always stealing them. Then he gets on his knees and loops one of my legs over his shoulder. I hang onto him as he leans in and devours every inch of me like I'm his favorite meal. He moves between finger fucking me and twirling his tongue on my clit, and I'm so thankful for this tree because I'm not sure how much longer I can hold my weight.

"Your pussy tastes so fucking good," he says. I moan out his name as the midmorning sunshine reflects through the trees. "You have such a tight little cunt."

"I love it when you talk dirty," I say between pants, and I don't know how much longer I'll last.

"Yes, baby. Come for me. Let me taste all of you," he continues, and when the orgasm builds, I nearly see stars as it rips through me. My voice echoes as my body loses complete control. Eli doesn't stop until I've fully come down from space.

"Wow…" I say, trying to catch my breath.

"You need my inhaler?" he teases, pulling it from his pocket as he stands, and my skirt falls back into place. I squeeze my thighs tightly together, not sure how I'll make it back to the cabin. I don't even think I'm on planet earth right now as my heart rapidly pounds.

"That was intense," I finally say, and a smirk slides across his lips, which is so damn adorable. I love that look on him, and it makes me crave him all over again.

"I had to return the favor." He leans forward and kisses me just as Bruno rushes up at a full sprint.

I laugh. "Do not jump on me." I point at him, and he actually sits. My mouth falls open. "Oh my God, he listened."

Eli wraps his arm around my shoulders as we walk back, enjoying the spring air and cool forest breeze. Bruno runs around, digging in the brush, and pees every thirty seconds. Watching him has me giggling because he's so excited to be outside. I've never seen a dog so damn happy all the time. We take our time walking to the cabin, and I make him promise we'll do this more often, especially since the weather has turned warm.

Bruno is filthy, so before we go inside, we rinse him off with the hose, and immediately after, he shakes, getting me completely soaked. Eli knew it was coming and was smart enough to step away, and he cracks up at my face.

"Every single time!" I shout with a groan. "Bruno, you're a jerk." He comes up to me and licks my hand, and I almost feel bad for raising my voice.

"You should go upstairs and hop in the tub," he tells me when we walk into the house. "Relax a bit. I'll bring a glass of wine up for you."

I look up at him in awe because that sounds amazing right now. "Why do you spoil me so much?" I ask, then kiss him.

"Because you're hot." He winks, then goes to the kitchen.

After I head upstairs, I take off my clothes and run the water, then add some bubble bath. When it's half full, I get in and immediately sigh in relief. Like clockwork, Eli comes in with a glass of wine.

"You're a saint. Thank you." I grab it and smile. I'm so relaxed already. Eli sits on the edge of the tub with a grin.

"Want to get in with me?" I ask, waggling my brows.

"I'll take a rain check. I need to get some work done this afternoon," he says sweetly. "But tempting." He stands, adjusting his groin. "*Extremely* tempting."

Eli tells me he'll be back later, then leaves. I sip my wine and stare out the big window. I nearly drink the entire glass, and when I get out, my eyes are heavy with exhaustion. I text Eli and tell him I'm going to take a nap, not wanting to bother him while he's working. He responds with how much he loves me and to sleep well.

By the time I wake up, I can tell it's late afternoon. I pick up my phone and see I slept for nearly five hours. When I walk downstairs, I smell something delicious and see Eli's busy at the stove.

"Babe," I say, and he nearly jumps. "Sorry, didn't mean to startle you." I walk closer. "Whatcha making?"

"I know how upset you were about graduation, so I thought I'd make you a special dinner to celebrate."

My face lights up. "Wow, seriously?" I glance over and see the table's set with one of Mom's lace cloths. The crystal wine glasses and fancy china from the cabinet are set out on it. I look back at him in shock. He wraps a hand around my waist and pulls me close. "I can't believe you did this."

"Of course, baby. Nothing but the best for you." He kisses my forehead. "I made lobster, sautéed spinach, and gratin potatoes. And your mother sent a bottle of Dom Pérignon Rose Gold."

"She sent a fifty thousand dollar bottle of champagne?" I gasp.

His eyes widen as if he hadn't realized the value, though neither of us should really be surprised at my mom's gesture. Everything about her is over the top. "She insisted. Only the best for her *princess*."

I grin and roll my eyes at the way he emphasizes the word. Then my smile spreads wider when I realize he's wearing a suit and tie, looking sexy as hell. Taking a step back, I study how good he looks and know I'm the luckiest woman in the world. He treats me like a fucking queen and makes me extremely happy, but this is beyond incredible.

"You didn't have to go through all this trouble, baby," I say, looking at the spread of food and how hard he's worked while I napped.

"Yes, I did. I wanted to make it special for you as best as I could."

I wrap my arms around his neck and crash my mouth on his. The kiss deepens when he slides his tongue inside, and now I'm tempted to skip dinner and have him instead.

"You already have," I tell him, pulling away slightly. "More than you'll ever know."

EPILOGUE
ELIJAH

IT'S BEEN eighteen months since Cami graduated, and things have been crazy ever since, but there hasn't been a dull moment since we both arrived in Roxbury. She's my everything and being able to wake up next to her every morning has been the highlight of my life. Growing up, I never imagined I'd be good enough for her, and each day, she proves to me I'm more than enough.

The cabin holds a special place in our hearts now that we ended up staying there for eight months. We returned to the city last October when the state lifted the lockdown orders, but certain things were still restricted. No large gatherings over fifty people, limited business hours, and social distancing was encouraged. All schools and universities continued with online learning programs for their students. It felt a bit safer to return to the city, especially after Ryan said they were no longer struggling to get what they needed for their patients. The curve was flattening, and things were slowly going back to some kind of normal.

Cami was determined to buy a new penthouse, one that we could decorate and make a home together, but it had to have a view. Of course she paid for it, and I contributed by negotiating a great deal on an incredible sky rise. Working in real estate helped us find a place that we now call our own. We make love with the blinds open, allowing the skyglow of the city to light the rooms without worrying that anyone can see us.

Four months ago, I planned a weekend getaway at the cabin for her birthday with just the two of us. I surprised her with flowers, balloons, and a chocolate cake I made from scratch. And of course, we brought Bruno and Chanel. After we had a candlelight dinner and she blew out her candles, I got down on one knee and popped the question after telling her how much she meant to me. I was more nervous about asking her than I'd been about anything else in my life. When she said yes and cried, I picked her up and carried her upstairs, and we made love until the morning. It was the best day of my life.

We made the announcement to our family and friends a couple of days later after we went home. Everyone was so damn happy and supportive and were ready to add the big day to their calendars. However, until the lockdown was completely lifted, we weren't able to set a date. Though, two months ago, a vaccination was finally approved for mass distribution, and we immediately started planning every detail.

Sometimes when I wake up in the mornings, I don't know how this is my life, or how someone as sweet and funny as Cami is going to be my wife. Now in less than three weeks, it'll be official, and we'll be married the first weekend of December. A winter wonderland wedding is everything Cami's ever wanted, and I'll do whatever it takes to make sure it's perfect for her.

I glance over my checklist of things that still need to be done while Cami is at school. Since everything is now open, she was able to finish her last semester of graduate school on campus. Better yet, she'll finally get to walk across the stage and receive her diploma. Knowing there's quite a lot to do, I decide to call her best friend and maid of honor. I was going to ask my sister since she wants to be involved too, but I know she's busy with work through Christmas.

"Hi, Kendall," I greet her when she answers.

"Hey! How's it going, groom-to-be?" she asks in her typical

bouncy voice. The girl has so much energy that sometimes she exhausts the piss out of me.

"Just getting some final touches together before the big day," I tell her with a smile.

"Of course. Give me all the tasks."

"So, since Cami wants to spend two weeks at the cabin to relive old times, I want to make sure it's completely stocked and ready. Any way you can pick up enough food and things to last us that long?"

She snorts. "Is Ryan gonna help me? I might need some strong muscles."

I shake my head. "I think I can arrange that," I murmur, knowing I'll have to coax my best friend into taking off work, and even though he's more than willing to do whatever we need, I feel guilty for asking. He's not been the same since the pandemic started. He's the strongest person I know, but it broke him.

"Then absolutely," she says matter-of-factly. "Food for two weeks. Enough booze to have you drunk 24/7 and a case of lube. Got it."

I can't even hold back the laughter, and I'm sure as hell not going to argue with her. "Whatever you say, Kendall. You know what Cami likes."

"Oh, then I can't forget chocolate, sparkling water, and shitty microwave meals."

I think back to when we were quarantined in the cabin together and all the unhealthy processed shit she brought to eat. Kendall knows her as well as I do.

"Extra wood, too," I tell her, knowing that'll be Ryan's job. "Maybe some holiday decorations." We'll return five days before Christmas Eve, so it'll be nice to have the tree and stuff up while we're there.

"I've got this, Eli. I was basically born for this task."

I chuckle. "Alright, great."

"I think I can make it happen this weekend. Check with Ryan and see if he's down, then we can carpool up there on Saturday."

"Will do," I say, and we end the call. I was ready to give Cami a glamorous, over-the-top, super-expensive honeymoon, but she didn't want our first moments as husband and wife to be captured by the paparazzi. She knew if we went anywhere public, they'd undoubtedly find us, and our privacy would be gone.

Moments later, Cami walks through the door with a smile on her face.

"Hey, baby." She pulls me into her arms and presses her lips against mine.

"How was class?" I ask as we settle on the couch. Cami reaches over and lights the fireplace with a push of a button, then kicks off her shoes.

"Great. Getting a little stressful with exams coming up, but then it'll be the wedding, and we'll officially be married! Then I'll graduate, and we can finally start our forever without interruptions." She leans her head back on the couch and looks at me with a smile.

"We're almost there, babe. Everything's gonna work out," I tell her encouragingly.

"You're right. I'm just getting antsy now that it's all coming up."

I grab her hand and kiss her knuckles. "So, um. I called Kendall," I say, and she immediately perks up.

"For what?"

"Well, since we're staying at the cabin after the ceremony, I asked if she could go up and stock it for us beforehand and get it all nice and ready. That way, you don't have to worry about it since you're studying for finals."

"What'd she say?"

"She wants me to see if Ryan will join her. Give him the hard tasks."

A big smile fills Cami's face, and she nods. "Mm-hmm. I bet she did."

It's no secret that Kendall has the hots for Ryan because of the comments she's made. But Cami's convinced her brother has a major crush on her best friend even though he denies it and acts like he can't stand her. Honestly, he's never mentioned anything to me before, so I don't want him to think I'm playing matchmaker because I'm not. That is Cami's area of expertise, not mine.

"I'll call him and make sure he joins her," she says with a chuckle. "You know, so they can get fully *acquainted*." She lifts her hand to give me a high five. "Come on, don't leave me hanging."

I scoff. "I don't know why we're high-fiving. Leave me out of this."

"Because you found the perfect way to hook up my brother. He's in love with her, Eli. I swear he is, but he's just too damn stubborn to admit it."

I let out a groan. "Great, he's going to think I'm in on this."

"No, no. I'll call him and pull the little sister card. He will not deny me during my special time. Don't worry about it." Cami stands, grabs her phone from her backpack, then starts texting Ryan. I can't see what she's typing, but she's got an evil grin on her face, and I know that means she got her way.

"He'll join her on Saturday." Cami snorts. "This is too easy. Like feeding candy to a baby."

"You are so wrong," I say. "So, *so* wrong."

She shrugs. "They need to just bang it out, fall in love, and get married so she can be my sister already. I've got it all planned out, and now you've helped."

The weekend quickly comes, and on Sunday, I'm waking to a phone call from Ryan.

"Dude, I think we're stranded here," he says.

I sit up in bed and look outside to see everything is coated in white. Last night when Cami and I were watching the news, an arctic blast was mentioned, but I didn't think anything of it. Upstate probably got it even worse than the city.

"There's no alternative ways out?" I ask, knowing there's only a single highway that leads to and from the cabin.

"No, the main road is snowed over. It's so bad they won't be able to get the plows out for a few days, and apparently, the news said they expect more snow to come. I had to take a few emergency vacation days from work. We got twenty inches so far, and it's still coming down. The wind is brutal, so it's just fucking blowing everywhere. Even if the roads were open, I wouldn't be able to see shit."

"Holy fuck. Man, I'm sorry. I didn't think it'd be that bad." I brush a hand through my hair, pushing it back off my face.

Cami rolls over and looks at me. She sits up and grabs her phone, noticing it's six in the morning and then gives me an annoyed look that we're up this early on the weekend. I mouth her brother's name, and she perks up.

"If you need anything, let me know, okay? I'll try my best to help you out."

Ryan lets out a huff. "Thanks. I just wanted to let you two know so you don't get worried about us. Hopefully, we don't lose power. With my luck, an ice storm would make its way here too."

"God, let's hope not. Well, I appreciate the update. Take care of yourself and Kendall," I tell him.

"Yeah, she's a fucking trip." He groans, and I hold back my laughter.

"Good luck," I say before we end the call.

Cami looks at me as I lower my phone. "So!"

"There's a huge blizzard in Roxbury, and they're stranded at the cabin until the snow lets up. Apparently, it's worse up there, so it might for a while, depending on when the roads clear," I tell her.

"Yes!" She claps her hands. "I knew it."

"Knew what?" I ask, tilting my head and watching her excitement.

"That the cabin is lucky and helps people fall in love." She comes closer and wraps her arms around me.

"You think so, huh?" I ask as we exchange a heated kiss.

"I know so," she says matter-of-factly. "Look at us. How else do you explain what happened?"

I smirk at her happiness. She does have a point.

CAMERON
6 MONTHS LATER

Eli and I have been married for six months, and it's been pure bliss. I can't imagine my life without him, and every day, I'm thankful for what we've been through to get where we are today. He's my best friend, biggest supporter, the voice of reason, and the love of my life. I honestly don't remember how I survived without him. While the circumstances that brought us together were awful, we were able to find love in the midst of it.

Our wedding ceremony was beautiful, and while my parents wanted it to be an elitist event, I refused and planned it my way instead. We got married in front of close friends and family only. I made them all promise not to leak any of the wedding details to the media because the last thing we need to deal with is the paparazzi following us all day. I got so spoiled living in the country that when I returned to the city, it was a wake-up call for Eli and me. But just as he promised, none of it affected our relationship. If anything, it brought us closer. Honestly, I love seeing the printed pictures of us together because it's proof to everyone that he's mine. It also doesn't hurt that my exes saw too. Eli doesn't care for the attention and has even come up with creative ways for us to escape without being seen. I have yet to sneak out in a suitcase, though. The thought makes me giggle because who knows, maybe someday I actually will.

I roll over and see the early morning light peeking through the windows, but the side of the bed is empty. Reaching over, I feel the sheets, and they're cold, which means Eli must be up working. He got promoted in his company and now works mostly from home unless he's doing showings or meeting with clients over drinks. He's worked so hard for it, and I'm so incredibly proud of him.

After I go through my morning routine, I put on a fluffy robe and walk into the kitchen where Eli is sitting with his laptop. I study him, admiring how handsome he is with the scruff on his chin before he notices me. As soon as his eyes meet mine, he stops typing, and stands to kiss me good morning.

"Coffee?" he asks with a cheesy grin, pouring me a mug and adding a splash of creamer until it's the color I like. I take it, then sit at the barstool next to him at the island.

He glances over at me. "Hungry?"

"You should just automatically know the answer to that by now. I will never turn down a meal. Especially from you," I tell him.

"Breakfast coming up," he says, pulling food from the fridge. He chops veggies and throws them in the skillet, and when they're sautéed, he cracks a few eggs on top with cheese. After he plates it and grabs two forks, he brings them over, and I immediately take a bite.

"You didn't drink your coffee..." He looks at the mug that I haven't touched, then glances back at me.

I swallow and tuck my bottom lip into my mouth. I can't hold my secret in much longer, especially when it comes to not drinking caffeine. It'll be the most suspicious thing about me.

"No. I think I'm going to have to stop drinking it for a while," I say casually, taking another bite of food with a knowing smirking.

His face contorts. "Why? Are you hopping on some weird no-caffeine trend?"

I laugh because I live off coffee and fashion. "No, just

pregnant," I say it so nonchalantly with a shrug, I wonder if he'll comprehend it or not.

Eli takes a bite, then hurries, and swallows it down. His eyes go wide as a smile sweeps across his perfect lips. "Wait, what did you say?"

"We're having a baby."

He stands so fast the barstool falls over, and I laugh at his excitement. I get up as he wraps his arms around me.

"Wow, babe. This is the best news I've ever heard," he says, and when I pull away, I see tears of joy waiting to spill over, which makes me an emotional mess. I start crying too, and then we're laughing and hugging and kissing.

"You'll be an amazing dad, you know." I wipe my cheeks. Considering he never knew his dad, I know he'll give our baby everything he or she needs along with tons of love.

"I hope so. Either way, I know the kid will be loved unconditionally, and if your parents have any say, completely spoiled rotten." He grins.

"Very true."

"Have you told your parents yet? When did you find out?" he asks.

"No, no one. Just you. When you were at the office yesterday, I felt a little weird and realized I was over a month late, so I got a few tests. Each of them were positive. I was shocked, but then was so exhausted and fell asleep before I could tell you."

He's grinning from ear to ear. "We're going to be parents." Eli kneels in front of me, then lifts my shirt and kisses my stomach.

"I can't wait to see you barefoot and pregnant." He winks up at me, and I burst out laughing at the very thing I mocked him for.

"Elijah Ross, we are not having ten babies, though, so get that thought out of your head," I say firmly.

He winks. "We'll see."

Groaning, I shake my head at his stupidly cute smile. "And to think just last year, it was only the two of us," I say, running my fingers through his hair.

Looking up at me with bright blue eyes, he chews on his bottom lip. "And now we're starting a family. Maybe it'll be twins." He waggles his brows.

I snort. "Maybe."

Eli stands, wraps me in his arms, and slides his lips gently across mine. Even after all this time, my heart gallops when he touches or kisses me. It always feels like the first time with him.

"I love you, Eli," I tell him.

"I love you too, Cami. So fucking much. You've made me the happiest person alive."

I shake my head and laugh. "Impossible because I'm the happiest person alive, and it's all because of you."

Curious about what happened with Ryan and Kendall being stuck in the cabin for two weeks? Find out next in *The Best of Us*

AVAILABLE NOW

Read Ryan & Kendall's story in *The Best of Us*

What happens when the biggest blizzard of the year hits and you're trapped in a cabin with your best friend's brother? You take every opportunity to spend time together and make him fall in love with you.

The Best of Us is a best friend's brother, opposites attract, and snowed-in together standalone romance.

ABOUT THE AUTHOR

Brooke Cumberland and Lyra Parish are a duo of romance authors who teamed up under the *USA Today* pseudonym, Kennedy Fox. They share a love of Hallmark movies, overpriced coffee, and making TikToks. When they aren't bonding over romantic comedies, they like to brainstorm new book ideas. One day in 2016, they decided to collaborate under a pseudonym and have some fun creating new characters that'll make you blush and your heart melt. Happily ever afters guaranteed!

CONNECT WITH US

Find us on our website:
kennedyfoxbooks.com

Subscribe to our newsletter:
kennedyfoxbooks.com/newsletter

f facebook.com/kennedyfoxbooks

𝕏 twitter.com/kennedyfoxbooks

⊙ instagram.com/kennedyfoxbooks

a amazon.com/author/kennedyfoxbooks

g goodreads.com/kennedyfox

BB bookbub.com/authors/kennedy-fox

BOOKS BY KENNEDY FOX

DUET SERIES (BEST READ IN ORDER)

CHECKMATE DUET SERIES

ROOMMATE DUET SERIES

LAWTON RIDGE DUET SERIES

INTERCONNECTED STAND-ALONES

MAKE ME SERIES

BISHOP BROTHERS SERIES

CIRCLE B RANCH SERIES

LOVE IN ISOLATION SERIES

Find the entire Kennedy Fox reading order at
Kennedyfoxbooks.com / reading-order

Find all of our current freebies at
Kennedyfoxbooks.com / freeromance

Printed in Great Britain
by Amazon